About the Author

Catherine Ferguson burst onto the writing scene at the age of nine, anonymously penning a weekly magazine for her five-year-old brother (mysteriously titled the 'Willy' comic) and fooling him completely by posting it through the letterbox every Thursday.

Catherine's continuing love of writing saw her study English at Dundee University and spend her twenties writing for various teenage magazines including *Jackie* and *Blue Jeans* and meeting pop stars. She worked as Fiction Editor at *Patches* magazine (little sister to *Jackie*) before getting serious and becoming a sub-editor on the Dundee *Courier & Advertiser*.

This is her eighth novel. She lives with her son in Northumberland.

Second Chances
at the Log Fire Cabin

Catherine Ferguson

Published by AVON
A division of HarperCollins*Publishers* Ltd
1 London Bridge Street
London SE1 9GF

www.harpercollins.co.uk

A Paperback Original 2018

3

Copyright © Catherine Ferguson 2018

Catherine Ferguson asserts the moral right to
be identified as the author of this work.

A catalogue copy of this book is available from the British Library.

ISBN: 978-0-00-830249-8

Typeset in Birka by Palimpsest Book Production Limited,
Falkirk, Stirlingshire

Printed and bound in UK by CPI Group (UK) Ltd, Croydon CR0 4YY

MIX
Paper from
responsible sources
FSC® C007454

To Dave, for all your brilliant support

Chapter 1

It's the most perfect Christmas tree I've ever seen.

I gaze at it from my perch on the sofa. We went a bit mad with the tinsel and it's definitely leaning a bit towards the left – but wrapped in my happy festive glow, I swear I've never seen anything so beautiful.

The soft glow of the fairy lights blended with the evocative aroma of pine forest is having a thoroughly intoxicating effect on my mood. As is the warmly spiced mulled wine we drank while we decorated the tree.

Jackson surprised me with the mulled wine. When I opened the door, he was standing there, a big smile on his handsome face, holding up one of those special gift packs that include the red wine and the cinnamon sticks and cloves.

'Ooh, lovely,' I lied.

'Only the best for my best girl!' he said, pushing the gift pack towards me. He cupped my face in his hands and gently kissed me on the tip of my nose – a tender gesture that makes my heart skip a beat every time he does it. Then he led the way into the living room. Glancing in the mirror above the fireplace, he ran a hand over his on-trend haircut with the tapered sides and volume on top, which I always think makes him look like a sexy honey-blond version of Elvis. Jackson is very proud of his hair. (Mine, by comparison, is blonde and fine, and completely resists any attempts I make to tame it.)

Jackson sank onto the sofa, legs splayed out, and ran his eyes over me admiringly. 'You look gorgeous tonight, Roxy Gallagher.' There was a sexy gleam in his blue eyes. 'Come here.'

Heart beating fast, I walked over to him, feeling ridiculously nervous. The house was empty. My flat-mate and best friend, Flo, was out with her fiancé, Fergus. I hoped Jackson didn't think . . .

But no, I'd had The Conversation with him only the week before.

He was quite surprised when I told him I believed in taking things really slowly but it didn't seem to put him off. If anything, he seemed tantalised by the idea of deferred gratification in the bedroom. I wondered if the novelty value had something to do with it. Because, let's face it, there wouldn't be many women who'd hold back for long if a tall, blond Greek-god-like man looked deep into their eyes and said, 'Let's go to bed. I'm going to make your wildest dreams come true.'

Jackson says these cute, rather old-fashioned things all the time, with a perfectly serious face. If anyone else came out with them, I'd probably cackle in appreciation because I'd know they were joking. But Jackson will look at me with his mesmerising blue eyes and I'll just melt and think: it's the feeling *behind* the words.

We've only been together a couple of months, but after all the trauma of the past – including having my heart well and truly stamped on by Billy, my first love – I'm finally starting to feel happy.

I leaned down to kiss Jackson and he grabbed my waist. Then he frowned and glanced in the region of my left boob. I followed his eye and he carefully pulled away a stray thread from the top buttonhole of my silky shirt.

'Better,' he remarked, before pulling me down on top of him and proceeding to kiss me very thoroughly. When I felt his hands tugging at my shirt and creeping underneath, I broke away, smiling coyly at him.

He sat back, folded his arms and studied me with a slightly perplexed grin.

'Roxy?' he said, and my heart lurched at the look in his eye.

'Yes?' I sounded a little breathless.

'Mulled wine?'

'Sorry?'

He pointed at the presentation box that was lying on the floor.

'Oh. Yes.' Smiling, I picked it up and took it through to the kitchen, then proceeded to unpack it with a grimace. As I stirred the ingredients on the hob, I heard the TV go on, blaring with some football match.

I'm actually not that keen on mulled wine. I remember telling Jackson this but I suppose he must have forgotten, and he looked so pleased with himself when he presented me with the package that I couldn't bear to spoil his fun.

In the end, I managed to throw down almost a whole glass of the revolting stuff while we decorated the tree, hiding my impulse to gag fairly well, before depositing the rest in an ornamental jug on a nearby side table.

And now, lounging back happily on the sofa, gazing at the newly decorated tree, while Jackson makes a business call in the kitchen, I'm feeling like the luckiest girl in the world.

If I'm honest, the reason I'm feeling so blissed out and warm on this freezing late November night has less to do with the real tree (my first ever) or the effect of the mulled wine – and rather more to do with the fact that I think I might be in love.

In fact, I'm sure I am.

I've never met anyone like Jackson. He's so gorgeous, brilliant and charming, and he could basically have any woman he wanted. But, for some weird reason, he seems to want to be with me. Plain, ordinary Roxy Gallagher.

I said exactly this to Flo earlier, before she went out with Fergus, and she gave me a severe look and said, 'Stop it, Roxy. *Jackson's* the lucky one, having *you* in his life.'

I laughed and said I was only joking.

And I was. Sort of . . .

We'd planned dinner out but Jackson keeps asking if I mind if we watch a bit more of the football. Until, eventually, I suggest I just make food here then he can settle down to watch the rest of the match.

'You're so good to me, Roxy.' On my way out, he grabs my wrist and bestows on me one of his raffish, whiter-than-white smiles – the kind that makes me feel so incredibly special.

I smile back and head for the kitchen, and he calls something after me that sounds like, 'I really love your melting green eyes.'

My heart cantering along happily at such a romantic comment, I pop my head back round the door, but he's deeply engrossed in a free kick.

Suddenly aware I'm there, he says, 'Oh yeah, I said I really loved those melted cheese pies? The ones we had last time. Don't suppose you could . . .?'

'Ah.' I nod, smiling, feeling slightly silly for having

5

heard what I wanted to hear. 'Yes, I think there's some in the freezer.'

He holds out a thumb without prising his eyes from the action on the screen.

In the kitchen, I manage to find some more pies at the bottom of the freezer and pop them into the oven. Then I pinch a can of sweetcorn from Flo's cupboard and make a mental note to replace it next day when I go food shopping. Jackson likes plain, unadventurous food, which I find quite surprising in a man with such sophisticated tastes in everything else. I think he would live quite happily on chicken and chips, given the chance – and he can't stand anything spicy.

We met two months ago, back in September. Flo had taken me to the pub one night, soon after I was made redundant from my factory job, to cheer me up. We'd already had a few cocktails by the time we walked into The Red Lion and I saw Jackson for the first time. He was standing at the bar with what looked like a group of work colleagues, all dressed in suits. Our eyes met and I smiled, emboldened by the alcohol, and he raised his glass at me.

Flo had made me get dressed up, so I was wearing my favourite pale blue tea dress and heels, and when Jackson came over to talk to us, I was glad she'd been so bossy.

I was a bit tongue-tied and awkward, but Jackson

was charming and seemed to find me attractive anyway, which boosted my flagging confidence no end. He took me out for dinner the next night and we've been seeing each other a couple of times a week ever since.

At thirty-two, Jackson Cooper is a very successful businessman, having built up a large property management company in the time since he left university. I tell myself he deserves an evening relaxing in front of the football. He works so incredibly hard.

An evening in will probably be better for me, too, really. I'm out of work at the moment and money is really tight.

Flo has been so good to me since I lost my job at the factory back in late September. The redundancy package was okay, mainly because I started there when I was twenty-three, which meant I had seven years of service under my belt. But the money is draining away and I'm starting to get worried, having applied for dozens of jobs, so far with no luck at all – not even an interview. Flo has insisted on halving my rent until I get back into work, but I hate being a burden like this. It's just not fair on Flo. Worry has been affecting my sleep lately and I'm forever nodding off on the sofa in the evenings.

We eat in front of the TV on trays, and after I've cleared away, I join Jackson on the sofa and snuggle into him, closing my eyes and letting my mind drift with the background noise of the football commentator. I can't keep taking advantage of Flo's generosity. I need to find a job. I know she doesn't see it that way, but, the problem is, I do and I feel bad.

I'd started my working life far later than my school-mates.

I was twenty-three before I found the confidence to finally push past the trauma that happened on my nineteenth birthday. But because I'd missed the chance to train for a career, I'd fallen into the first job I was offered – packing biscuits at a local factory. It wasn't exactly challenging but it was so good to finally have a job and feel 'normal' for the first time in years that I stayed there and somehow the years passed by . . .

Recently, though, I'd started to wonder if I was brave enough to begin something new. An opening was coming up at head office for an admin assistant and my line manager had said she would fully support me if I applied. But then I was made redundant, and after that, my dreams of striking out in a new direction were put on hold.

There's a loud roar from the TV. Someone must have scored. I snuggle more comfortably into Jackson's side.

If I don't find work soon, I might have to move back in with Mum and Dad. As much as I love them, the idea of returning to the little backwater town on the south coast, where I grew up, and sleeping in my old single bed is not an appealing thought. I'd be miles from all my friends in Surrey.

And miles from Jackson . . .

A log shifts in the grate and makes me start. I stare into the flames, lulled by the seasonal cheer of the blaze and the thought that it will soon be Christmas. Whatever happens on the jobs front, I'll still be spending the festive season with Jackson. It will be our very first Christmas together!

It's so snug in the room, I feel myself starting to drift off . . .

I can't breathe. I feel like I'm choking.

My heart is thundering as panic flares inside me. The hands of a faceless stranger are squeezing my throat and pressing on my face, blocking my airways. Slowly suffocating me.

I'm desperate to escape from the room but the door is locked. Pulling on the handle, I try to call out for help, but no sound emerges. Grasping to pull the obstruction away from my face, I find to my horror that there's nothing there. The so-called hands choking me are invisible.

I'm going to die . . .

Someone is calling my name. At first it sounds far away in the distance but it's getting closer.

'Roxy? Wake up. You're having a nightmare.'

I open my eyes and Jackson's face is right there, frowning. I take in a huge gulp of air and start coughing, as if the action will clear the blockage in my nose and throat. I'm still trying to shake off the last remnants of the horrifying dream.

'What on earth happened?' asks Jackson when I've calmed down a bit.

I swallow and turn away from his scrutiny. 'It was nothing.'

'Christ, that must have been some nightmare.' Jackson looks appalled. 'Look, you're still shaking.' He takes hold of my hand. 'Can I do anything? You're not going to be sick, are you?' He recoils slightly, in alarm.

I shake my head, wanting to put his mind at rest. Jackson's not great with people throwing up. Or any kind of mess, really.

'Don't worry, I'll be fine in a moment,' I manage to croak. 'I just need to do some deep breathing.'

'Do these nightmares happen often, then?'

I try to shrug it off. 'I've had a few.'

To be honest, I thought these terrifying dreams would start to fade over the years, but if anything, they seem to be happening with greater frequency. And they're just as scary as they were at the beginning.

But I don't want Jackson to know any of this.

'Roxy, you're white as a ghost. Are you sure you don't need to – erm – go to the bathroom?'

I shake my head.

'Have you any idea what's *causing* these bad dreams?'

I stare at him. If ever there was a time to tell him everything, it's now. But I'm not prepared to risk losing Jackson, the way I lost Billy. So, instead of telling him the truth, I take a deep breath and say the first thing that comes into my head. 'It's money. I'm stone broke and I'm going to have to move out of here and go back to live with my parents.' I give a rueful smile. 'Nightmare.'

He blinks. 'Oh. Right,' he says, as if that hadn't been what he was expecting. 'Where do your parents live?'

'On the south coast? Worthing?' His question throws me for a moment. I can't believe he's forgotten. We've had a few chats about where we grew up and I can remember all the details of his childhood. I can even name the school he went to.

He frowns. 'That's a long way from here.'

I nod gloomily.

'So move in with me,' he says with a shrug.

There's a brief silence as I stare at him, completely befuddled. Did he just say: *So move in with me*?

My heart starts to thump. I must have misheard him, surely.

He chuckles. 'Well? Say something, Roxy.'

I sit up straight so I can properly read his expression and he's smiling down at me with this cute, slightly vulnerable look on his face. He might even be blushing, although it could be the Christmas tree lights casting a rosy glow.

Oh my God, he actually means it! He wants me to move in with him!

My mind is racing at this quite surreal turn of events. It's all so sudden. But I'm crazy about Jackson, no doubt about that, so . . .

'I'd love to.' I gulp. 'Move in with you.'

And in the blink of an eye, I go from the aftermath of a painful recurring nightmare to dancing a Highland fling in my head with happiness . . .

Chapter 2

'You do realise you'll be on the telly, Roxy.' Flo grins excitedly at me in the mirror above my dressing table.

It's a week later – the first day of December – and I'm getting ready to go out with Jackson.

I laugh. 'I hardly think so, Flo. It's not as if we're actual contestants on the show. We'll just be part of the audience.'

'But still,' she insists. 'You should wear that beautiful pale green dress Jackson bought you, just in case the camera lands on you. The colour will look fab with your long blonde hair.'

'It's sleeveless, though.' I haven't been able to wear it since he gave it to me last month, for that very reason.

'So wear it with that little cream shrug.' She says this matter-of-factly as if it's no big deal.

I get back to applying mascara, which is proving a challenge because my hand is trembling so much.

The truth is, it's not the TV show that's making me jumpy. It's the thought that, tomorrow, I'll be moving in with Jackson. It's only natural to be nervous about something like that, I suppose – it's a bit like pre-wedding nerves. It's a big commitment, after all.

And actually, the more I think about it, the more certain I feel that living with Jackson is absolutely the right thing to do . . .

At ten o'clock tomorrow, a van will arrive to transport all my belongings to his gorgeous house in a gated community twenty miles from here, in the heart of the Surrey countryside.

Flo seems more excited about the cutting-edge design of his house than anything, although since she's really into architecture, I suppose that's understandable.

But to be honest, I'd live in a caravan as long as I was with Jackson.

And I think he feels the same, judging by what he said to me the other day before he flew off to Spain.

He was heading abroad to negotiate a property deal. I drove him to the airport, parked at the drop-off point and asked him if he'd miss me while he was away – and his reply was so lovely, I find myself still thinking about it days later.

He unbuckled his seat belt and turned to look deep into my eyes. 'Roxy,' he murmured, 'just the thought of spending even a couple of days without you is unbearable. What's the bee supposed to do without the honey?' He shrugged with a wistful smile, looking so cute and vulnerable that tears sprung to my eyes.

When I told Mum I was moving in with Jackson, she burst out, 'And about time, too!' She didn't mean it was time I moved in with *Jackson* – we'd only been together a couple of months – but that it was time I finally let a man get close to me.

Now that it's actually happening, I can't help feeling nervous. But I'm really excited, thinking about our future together.

'How on earth did Jackson get tickets for this TV show?' Flo asks now, looking green with envy.

'Oh, you know Jackson.' I can't help saying it with a touch of pride. 'He's got contacts everywhere.'

It's true. He's always networking, dashing off to some event or other to 'press the flesh'. Flo once joked that he'd attend the opening of an envelope if it meant widening his business circle, and there's more than a grain of truth in what she said. But I think it just shows how much drive Jackson has to succeed. He's got an entrepreneurial mind with a keen eye for a new business opportunity. He puts it down to growing up in a single-parent household with his mum, Maureen, who was utterly devoted to him but had very little money. She held down three jobs, cleaning and working as a wait-ress, to keep their heads above water.

Last year, Jackson bought Maureen a modern three-bedroom house in a lovely area of Guildford. It makes me feel warm inside just to think of it.

I finish my make-up and spin round on the stool to face Flo. 'Do I look all right?'

'You look fab.'

I frown. 'Are you sure?'

She shakes her head. 'I wish you'd believe in yourself more, Roxy. Honestly, you look fantastic. And once you've got that dress on, Jackson will think he's the luckiest man alive, I promise you.'

She crosses her hands over her heart and smiles goofily at me. 'By this time tomorrow you'll have moved in with him. Are you excited?'

'Of course I am.'

I spin back round to face the mirror, catching the trace of anxiety on my face. I *am* excited. Of course I am. It's just that, living together, I'll have no more excuses not to let my barriers down . . .

Jackson is picking me up in ten minutes. He flew back from Spain only this afternoon. The plane was late landing and I texted him to say I'd be just as happy with a quiet night in. But I knew he'd still want to go to the show tonight. That's one of the things I love about him. His incredible energy. He routinely works late into the night then has to be up for a seven o'clock breakfast meeting. It's the kind of schedule that would kill most people, but for Jackson, business is like a labour of love. His enthusiasm for what he does carries him through.

The doorbell rings and Flo dashes to the front door, returning – after some giggling in the hallway – with Fergus. They're so loved-up, it can be pretty gruesome at times, to be honest.

But I'm really happy for her.

She's a shining example that relationships *can* work out perfectly. She and Fergus had known each other for only three months when *she* proposed to *him* – and he said yes right away. Which I knew he would because they're both absolutely smitten and totally right for each other. Everyone can see that. As I joked in my speech at their engagement party last month, no one else would have them, what with their mutual passions for battle re-enactments and liver and onions.

I'm in awe of Flo's ability to wear her heart on her sleeve.

Five minutes later, the doorbell signals Jackson's arrival and I grab my winter coat and bag, and totter to the door in the pale green dress, cream shrug and shoes that are much too high to actually walk in. Because I stand at five foot eleven, I've tended to stick mainly to flat shoes, so it's a bit like learning to walk all over again. Jackson bought these beauties for me – nude skyscrapers with their distinctive red sole – to go with the dress. He believes a woman can never have too much glamorous footwear. He's six foot four, which means I'm as tall as he is when I'm wearing the shoes.

'Have fun,' calls Flo. She catches me up in the hallway. 'And just relax, hun. The fact that Jackson's asked you to move in with him means he thinks you're pretty special, okay? So stop acting as if you think he's doing you a favour!'

I grin. 'Yes, boss. Trouble is, *no one* can be as happy as you and Fergus. It's just not possible. I mean, that proposal on the battlefield as he lay wounded will go down in history as the most romantic ever. Especially the bit where the fake blood spurted all over your face.'

She gives me a look. She's used to me glossing over awkward moments with humour.

'You know what I mean, Roxy. Stop holding back because you think you're not good enough or something.' She shrugs. 'If I'd held back from proposing to Fergus, I wouldn't be planning my wedding now, would I? And feeling the happiest I've ever been in my life.'

I laugh. 'Er, you're not suggesting I propose to Jackson, are you?'

'No, of course not.' She grins. 'That's just idiot me, rushing headlong in. You have to be true to yourself. And that just wouldn't be you.'

'I'll stick to being boringly *un*-spontaneous, then, shall I?'

Before going to the TV studios, we head to an elegant bar Jackson knows for cocktails.

Although it's only the first week in December, Christmas has arrived in style on the high street. The shops, bars and restaurants glimmer with fairy lights and a huge Christmas tree takes pride of place in the town square.

My mood soars. I love Christmas. I love the lights and the glitter. I love going for frosty walks and coming home to hot chocolate by a roaring fire. I love everything about it, really. And, this year, it's going to be even more special than usual.

I smile up at Jackson, loving the feel of his warm hand wrapped around mine. Tonight is going to be a good night!

In the bar, we find a cosy corner table and I order a Manhattan, which makes me giggly and slips down almost before I realise. I insist on buying the next round, which is eye-wateringly expensive but well worth it, because I'm a Piña Colada convert! I tell myself it's a special night and I won't have to worry quite so much about rent now that I'm moving in with Jackson.

I assume we'll head off to the studios after that, but

just as we're leaving the bar, a crowd of people that Jackson knows walks in, so naturally we stay to chat a little. From the conversation he's having with a couple of the guys and a woman in a stunning sequinned mini dress, I gather they're on a work night out from a company Jackson occasionally does business with.

He introduces me simply as 'Roxy' – no mention of the word 'girlfriend', which I try not to mind about. We've only been going out a couple of months, after all, and maybe Jackson didn't want to be presumptuous. We join them at their table for a drink.

'Just one,' murmurs Jackson in my ear. 'Is that okay?'

I smile at him, feeling deliciously mellow. 'Of course.'

Naturally, the talk is mostly about business, so I smile and drift off, only half listening, just happy that Jackson is happy. He seems to be having a lot of chat with the woman in the stunning dress, who's called Lara. She keeps laughing and flicking her hair and touching his arm. But watching them, I just feel proud that he's with me. I know how important business is to Jackson and that any opportunity he has to mingle, he's right there.

After a while, I glance at my watch and realise the time is getting on. If we're not careful, we'll be late to the studios. But I'm happy to leave it in Jackson's hands – and the champagne cocktails that keep arriving are going down wonderfully well.

A little *too* well, I realise, when we finally make a move.

I stand up a bit too quickly, and have to cling onto Jackson because everything is spinning as if I'm on a ride at the fairground.

'Have a great time!' sings the girl in the sequinned dress, as we leave, giving Jackson a 'call me' sign.

I give her a thumbs-up because I can't make my mouth work and I nearly fall over. Jackson grabs me just in time and I smile up at him.

Where are we going again?

Through a haze of alcohol, I vaguely recall something about the TV.

Are we going to be interviewed on the telly? God, I hope not. On the other hand, maybe being three sheets to the wind will loosen me up a bit and turn me into a reality TV star overnight! But it actually doesn't matter where we're going as long as my gorgeous man is here to cling onto. Jackson will look after me! Jackson Cooper loves *me*, not that girl in the naff, sparkly dress he was talking to for ages!

At the TV studios, Jackson asks me if I need the bathroom, which makes me giggle and tell him I'm not ten. Then he takes my arm quite firmly and steers me up the steps to our seats. It seems to take quite a long time because I can't stop giggling and trying to make him stop and kiss me.

We finally arrive at our seats and I slump down happily and snuggle into Jackson.

Being with Jackson is making me fizz with happiness inside. My cheeks feel nicely flushed and my banter with him is rather witty (if I say so myself). I can't stop laughing at a man sitting further along the row in front. He's wearing a Christmas tree on his head – quite a tacky one, at that – and the person behind him taps him on the shoulder and asks him to remove it, which he does.

'Bah humbug!' I say, getting thoroughly into the Christmas spirit.

The woman in front of me turns and glares, and I make a shamed face at Jackson, but he just grins and squeezes my hand, which makes me even more in love with him than ever.

Feeling full of the joys, I lean my head on his shoulder and smile goofily to myself, drifting away from what's happening on stage and into the world of my imagination. I'm moving in with lovely Jackson tomorrow! The woman sitting in front is probably just jealous because she doesn't have a gorgeous, handsome, funny, intelligent man to make her life sparkle! And Flo is right. I need to have more confidence in myself. I should tell Jackson exactly how I feel about him . . .

'Ah, do we have a pair of lovebirds here?'

The man who had been on the stage talking to the audience has suddenly appeared in the aisle next to

22

us. He's leaning over me, thrusting a microphone at Jackson.

'So how long have you two been together?' he asks.

Jackson, cool and laid-back as ever, smiles and says, 'Not long enough for my liking.' I smile and snuggle closer, and there's a big 'aaah!' from the people around us.

Jackson kisses the top of my head, and in my cocktail haze, I feel quite weepy. I really am the luckiest girl in the world!

The TV host is looking at me now. 'Are you enjoying yourself tonight?' he asks.

The microphone veers towards me and my hazy brain takes in the fact that millions of people are probably watching the show at home and every one of them is waiting for me to answer. So I throw a big smile to the camera and announce, 'I'm having a fabulous time, thank you very much. I'm the luckiest girl in the world!'

'That's wonderful.' The TV host's eyebrows rise. 'And why's that?'

I attempt to get my tongue around the words, *Because I'm here with Jackson*. But it emerges as, 'Because I'm jeer with Hackson.'

The host nods. 'And is there anything you want to say to – erm, your man – on this date night to beat all date nights?'

My head spins woozily as Jackson smiles down at

me, and the microphone hovers expectantly in front of my nose. 'There is, acshully.'

For some reason, an image of Flo drifts into my head.

Flo thinks I can't be spontaneous. She thinks it's just not who I am. But maybe, with Jackson, I can become a braver person – the person I've always wanted to be!

I turn to Jackson, trying my hardest to focus. And there are *two of him*!

Lovely Jackson. He's been so patient with me and I really want to show him how much he means to me. And this lovely audience and the TV host are looking at me, waiting for me to speak, expecting something amazing.

I swallow hard. And then the words just tumble out of my mouth.

'Hackson Jooper, I love you. Will you marry me?'

There's a second's silence then the whole studio gasps with delight.

You could hear a pin drop as Jackson clears his throat. And I wait, misty-eyed, to hear the words we'll tell our grandchildren in years to come . . .

He's staring at me, with a frozen look on his face, as if he's never seen me before and I find myself drawn to his Adam's apple, which keeps bobbing up and down.

Finally, he leans towards the microphone and murmurs:

'Er, *no?*'

Chapter 3

It's amazing how quickly you sober up after your proposal of marriage is flatly turned down.

It's also amazing how fast you can locate an exit and flee the studio – even with double vision and two left feet.

Blundering down the front steps of the building, I'm praying for some form of transport to arrive and get me out of here. The last thing I want is to hang around here, waiting for a bus or a taxi, and risk Jackson catching up with me.

If he followed me out, that is.

Did he follow me out?

I glance back, not sure if I desperately *want* to see him or desperately *don't*.

I might get over the shame of it all – in about twenty years – if Jackson hotfooted it after me and told me he froze when I asked him to marry me and said the first thing that came into his head. And that really, now he'd had a chance to think about it, the marriage thing wasn't such a bad idea.

But there's no sign at all of Jackson, which hurts almost as much as the original rejection.

A bus lurches to a stop in front of me, so I jump on and sink into the nearest seat – before realising it's going in entirely the wrong direction. Stumbling off at the next stop, I vaguely recognise an important land-mark – our local kebab shop – at which point I realise I'd been on the right bus after all. The bus that is now disappearing into the distance.

I wrench off my heels and start to scurry along the pavement, dodging groups of people in their Christmas finery coming towards me. All I want to do is get home and pour out the whole ridiculous story to Flo – and ask her not to rent my room out to someone else because I'm not moving in with Jackson after all!

But of course when I finally arrive home and burst through the door, she and Fergus are snuggled together on the sofa. By the looks of things, Fergus is manfully sitting through Flo's favourite rom-com for about the two hundred and twenty-fifth time. (Fergus is lovely like that.)

Flo looks up questioningly to see me back so early.

'Bit of a hiccup. Don't ask!' I paste on a grin, implying a ladder in my tights or something equally harmless. Then I escape up the stairs to my room.

Sitting upright on my bed, hugging my knees, I stare at my feet and the tights that are blackened and full of holes from my desperate dash home. I dropped one of my gorgeous new shoes on the way but ran on like someone possessed, not caring. I wish I'd stopped now. There's a small smear of blood mixed with the dirt from where my foot pounded onto something sharp.

I reach down to touch the wound, and the sting intensifies a hundredfold.

Tears well up as the full horror of what I've done hits me with the force of a sledgehammer. I've just made the biggest tit of myself in the history of TV bloopers. I'll probably be on every episode of *When Proposals Go Wrong* for the next ten years, and that's only if I get lucky.

The nightmare scenario of the most cringe-making, toe-curlingly gruesome hour of my life seems to be playing on repeat in my head – presumably in case I might somehow, without the constant helpful reminders, forget it happened.

Like I'm ever going to forget tonight!

I flump face down on the bed. What on earth *possessed* me? You do *not* propose to someone unless you are one hundred per cent certain of the answer. *Especially* if you're doing it on *live TV*!

Flo knocks softly on the door.

'I'm asleep,' I call.

There's a pause. Then, 'Okay, but come and get me when you want to talk about it.'

'Okay,' I mumble into the pillow, feeling quite nauseous. The alcohol is making my head spin round and round.

Those bloody champagne cocktails! They should come with a warning: Danger. Drink at your peril. You might be forced to emigrate to escape the shameful consequences of your actions.

I scramble under the covers fully clothed, just wanting to disappear from *earth*, never mind the UK – perhaps taking a year's sabbatical on Mars – so that no human being will ever again clap eyes on the tragic soul who proposed to her boyfriend in front of six million people.

And received the answer: *Er, no?*

I lie there for an hour or so, trying not to think about the most mortifying experience of my life, but without a great deal of success. (It's like someone telling you *not* to think about a purple elephant. After that, it's all you bloody *can* think about.)

Then my mobile rings and it's Jackson.

Since I've been expecting him to ring ever since I fled the studio, I don't immediately pounce on it. Let him wait! In fact, I might not answer it at all. He could at least have phoned to make sure I was okay.

But then my emotions get the better of me. Perhaps . . . perhaps he's going to say he's sorry and that it was all a big mistake and of course he wants to marry me.

So I pick up. My voice when I answer sounds thick with tears.

And then blow me if he doesn't just sound like his usual cheery self – no apologetic note in his voice at all – as if I didn't just lay my emotions on the line with practically the whole of the UK watching!

This just plunges me into even deeper gloom.

'You didn't miss much,' he's saying. 'The programme was rubbish. Not a patch on the old *Blind Date*.' As if that's supposed to make me feel better – knowing that, instead of rushing out after me, he actually *sat through the entire rest of the show and even paid attention to it*!

When I remain silent, he says gently, 'Roxy, why did you do it? In front of all those people? I don't mean to sound harsh but did you really think the answer would be yes?'

My throat closes up. I want to end the call right then, but I suppose he deserves an answer. 'I don't know . . . maybe . . . you asked me to move in so I naturally thought you really cared.'

He laughs. Yes, actually *laughs*. 'Of course I care, Roxy. But I only suggested you move into my place as a *practical measure* because you couldn't pay the rent on Flo's flat.'

A practical measure?

'You're still welcome to move in – until you get yourself another job.'

I can't speak. My head is spinning and not in a good way.

'Don't get me wrong, I think you're great, Roxy,' he adds, piling on more humiliation. 'But I thought we were just, you know, having a good time?'

I manage to dredge up some spirit from somewhere. 'Jackson, could you just bugger off now and leave me alone?'

'What about the Winter Ball on Saturday? You *are* still going with me?'

I laugh incredulously.

'You've got your dress and everything. You're going to be the belle of the ball,' he says, turning on the charm. 'Please, Roxy?'

Tears threaten to break through. I'd been so looking forward to attending the Winter Ball with Jackson. It was something he organised for his employees every year and, by all accounts, it was pretty magical. I absolutely adored the dress I'd bought . . .

'Think about it,' he says. 'I really do care about you, Roxy.'

My throat is too choked up to answer.

So instead, I end the call.

* * *

For the next two days, my phone stays resolutely turned off as I retreat to the safety of the sofa to lick my wounds.

There's a little pile of 'essentials' scattered on the floor below. Tissues. An array of used coffee mugs. Giant box of fake After Eights, kindly donated by Flo after a trip to her favourite everything-for-a-pound shop. Plus a self-help book (that's no help whatsoever) called *Moving On After Yet Another Disastrous Break-Up*.

The Christmas tree I decorated with Jackson stands there in all its garish glory, unapologetic and impossible to ignore – a constant sparkly reminder of happier times.

At intervals, Flo – who's now been fully briefed on what happened – creeps in quietly, as if there's an unexploded bomb beneath the floorboards, and brings me messages from Jackson, who has resorted to calling on the house phone. The gist of them seems to be: *Are you coming to the Winter Ball? Or should I find someone else to go with me because I'm definitely not pitching up alone. Can you call me back?*

Which is all very touching but something is stopping me from phoning him back. I suppose, deep down, I don't think his gestures are grand enough. He must know how embarrassed and devastated I am after making such a plonker of myself at the show. And worse, having my proposal – however drunken it might

31

have been – flatly turned down. If I'd turned Jackson down like that, I'd be jumping through hoops now to make things right. A few phone calls from him don't really cut it.

The whole thing has also made me realise that Jackson has never felt about me the way I feel about him . . .

On the third day, I wake up feeling more positive.

Turning on my mobile, I decide that this time, when Jackson phones, I'll actually pick up.

I've had lots of time to think, and with the benefit of hindsight, I've concluded that it was very foolish and unfair of me to put him on the spot like that, proposing marriage in front of millions of people. No wonder the poor man said no! He must have thought he'd hooked up with a woman who was more than slightly unhinged. Maybe he still thinks that. But it hasn't stopped him phoning and trying to talk to me.

I stay in the house by the phone. Apart from wanting to be there when it rings, to be honest I'm a bit worried about venturing out after my infamous appearance on Saturday night TV. The story of my humiliation seems to have gone a little bit viral. I've spotted a fair few stories online – *with pictures* – detailing my hideous rejection on live TV and I know I shouldn't read them, but I can't seem to help myself. What if people recognise me as that sad, drunk woman whose boyfriend rejected her?

Much later, tired of waiting by a phone that never rings and needing some fresh air, I nip out for a walk around the block under cover of darkness. I feel certain there'll be a message for me on the home phone when I get back. But there isn't and my heart sinks. Perhaps Jackson's out of the country on business – as he often is – in which case he might phone tonight from his hotel.

By bedtime, there's still been no word and I'm starting to feel needled. Surely he hasn't given up on me already? I tell myself that if I hear nothing by lunchtime tomorrow, *I'll* phone *him*. Relationships are a two-way thing, after all.

The next afternoon, I take a deep breath and make the call. But to my surprise, after five rings, it goes straight to 'message'. Jackson normally answers immediately in a very businesslike voice, since nine times out of ten it will be an important work call. I leave a message asking him to ring me.

But then I decide I can't sit around waiting for a call from him. That will only drive me nuts. I'll nip out to the shops for milk and fresh supplies of chocolate. I haven't been out properly for days and, with a bit of luck, the world will have forgotten all about my prime-time blunder on national TV.

Yes, there were probably a good few sniggers when Jackson said, *Er, no?*

But no one is going to actually recognise me from the telly. Not now . . .

With new resolve, I head for the shower. Twenty minutes later, I get wrapped up in my coat and scarf, and leave the flat, emerging – after my self-imposed hibernation – with the vulnerability of a new-born lamb into the frosty December afternoon. It's already growing dark, which is good.

Far less chance of someone—

'Oof.' I collide with a couple walking past the gate and the man peers back at me.

He nudges his partner. 'Hey, it's her!' he says in a loud stage whisper. 'That woman who proposed on TV.'

'Is it?' The woman turns. 'Oh, yes! God, the poor soul. Do you think she'll ever get over it?'

'Nah. Scarred for life, I reckon.'

And they walk on.

I stand there, staring after them, feeling about as small as it's possible to feel. Turning, I fish out my keys to retreat back inside.

Then I stop.

The Winter Ball is just a few days away and I'd pretty much decided to tell Jackson I'd go with him, after all. What if he's been sitting at home, feeling as gloomy as

I am, thinking it's all over between us? Perhaps he was in a business meeting when I phoned and he hasn't even listened to my message yet.

I should give him another chance – leave him another message telling him I'm looking forward to wearing my new dress . . .

The idea brings a little surge of relief at the thought that it might not, after all, be the end for Jackson and me.

The Winter Ball would be the perfect opportunity to patch things up, smooth over the catastrophe of Saturday night and get back to the way things were.

Standing there in the street I phone his number, preparing my little speech in my head. I'll go for a bright and breezy tone, to let him know I'm back to my normal self and looking to the future . . .

'Jackson's phone,' breathes someone in what sounds like a French accent. An alluring *female* voice.

An icy hand grips my heart.

A series of giggles on the other end of the phone turns into full-blown shrieks of delight.

Then, abruptly, I'm cut off.

Chapter 4

I stand there, stunned for a moment, feeling sick. My legs feel wobbly so I sit down on the wall outside the house and stare for a long time at the Christmas lights strung over the windows of the café over the road.

After a while, the lights blur into one another, but I continue to sit there with my hands thrust deep into my coat pockets, thinking about Jackson and how it was never going to work out for us anyway. What with me scared to take the relationship to the next level and Jackson being a total babe-magnet.

It was a recipe for disaster. I just couldn't see it at the time.

I really thought that this Christmas would be different because I'd found Jackson and we'd be spending at least some of the festive season together. I'd been so confident of this, I'd even told Mum and Dad that they should book the winter Caribbean cruise they'd been wanting to go on for years because I'd be spending it with Jackson. And now, that's what they're doing. They leave in a couple of weeks and will be away until after New Year. So I really shot myself in the foot there!

The festive season of love and goodwill is here. And I will be all alone.

Why on earth did I imagine someone as clever and popular as Jackson could be serious about a no-hoper like me? I mean, thinking about it, what the hell have I achieved in my life so far – apart from a job at the biscuit factory?

I probably could have achieved more. But after the accident, my confidence hit rock bottom, and I've never really recovered. I suppose part of me still thinks I'm not good enough to try for something different.

That look on Billy's face when he broke off our relationship has stayed with me, resolutely refusing to disappear into the mists of time. It happened eleven years ago, when I was only nineteen, yet even now I can recall – as if it happened only yesterday – that heart-stopping mix of pity and guilt in his eyes.

But isn't it time I moved past that?

I've lost Jackson and now my future is an open book. A big fat question mark. Instead of living in fear, maybe I should see it as a golden opportunity to throw off the chains of the past and start living my life differently.

But am I too late, at the age of thirty, to start my life over again? To finally throw off the hang-ups that have held me back and maybe find a career that inspires me – instead of just working to pay the rent?

The first step is to get over Jackson. Because, clearly, he's already well on the way to getting over *me* . . .

Getting up off the wall, I take a deep breath and force my legs to move in the direction of the supermarket.

I'm done with humiliating myself over Jackson Cooper. It's time to move on . . .

Arriving at the supermarket, my throat is choked with held-back tears but I'm determined not to give in to them.

I head straight for the milk, then march purposefully into the home-baking aisle in search of Betty Crocker. She makes great chocolate cake mixes. She will save me from complete despair.

Funnily enough, the last time I was here, I was also on a search for cake mix.

Our irritating next-door neighbour, Edna Hartley-Pym, had knocked on our door, requesting cakes for her home-baking stall at the church hall's Christmas fayre. She's a difficult woman to say no to, so I promised her a homemade chocolate cake, which got her off our doorstep nice and smartly.

I thought I'd cheat with a Betty Crocker cake mix

but, to my horror, there were none to be had and the fayre was the following day. So I'm afraid I resorted to buying a Marks & Spencer concoction, roughing it up a bit in my Tupperware box to make it look like an authentic home bake.

Needless to say, Edna was well impressed.

Thankfully, the cake mix section has now been thoroughly restocked. I hover in the aisle, trying to choose between Devil's Food cake mix and Super Moist Party Rainbow cake, eventually solving the dilemma by throwing both into the basket.

My attention is caught by a woman further along the aisle who seems to be having a problem. She's trying to reach something on the top shelf and keeps jumping up but failing to grab it. The grunts she's making with the effort are growing more desperate by the second, so eventually, I go over and offer to help. (Being so tall, I'm used to people asking me to reach items for them from the top shelf.)

The girl turns, dashing her dark hair out of her eyes. 'Oh, would you? Thank you. It's the last bag and I really need it.' Her face is flushed with exertion. Or possibly anxiety.

'No problem. They didn't nickname me Beanpole at school for nothing!' I assure her with a grin, reaching up with ease and handing her the prize – a bag of self-raising flour.

'Oh, thank you!' she gasps gratefully. 'I run a catering business and, believe it or not, I've run out of flour.'

'Ooh, what's the name of your business?' I ask.

'Truly Scrumptious.'

'Great name!'

'Thanks.' She smiles warmly. 'It's just me, really, although my friend, Erin, sometimes helps out. I'm baking for a children's birthday party tomorrow so I need to get my hands on some flour. I can't believe this is the only bag left.'

'People must be making their Christmas cakes.'

She smiles, looking a little less flustered. 'Yes, it's that time, isn't it? I've got twenty Christmas cakes to bake for next weekend.' She holds out her spare hand. 'I'm Poppy.'

We shake. 'Roxy.'

'Nice to meet you, Roxy. Now, I really must get back. Those fairy cakes won't bake themselves, worse luck!'

She turns to go but, as she does, the bag of flour somehow slips out of her grasp. It falls to the ground, catching her boot buckle, which tears the bag open. The contents spill out across the floor.

Poppy stares at the mess in stunned disbelief, and I feel her pain. She looks as if she's about to sob her heart out right then and there, in the middle of aisle number seven.

'Have you tried the corner shop?' I ask quickly.

She nods. 'None left.'

'The supermarket on Bridge Street?'

'They're out of flour as well, believe it or not. There's been a problem with deliveries.'

I frown, racking my brains to come up with a solution. Poppy seems really nice. I can't just leave her here in bits like this.

'I've got flour at home that you can have,' I say, in a burst of inspiration. 'And I only live along the road.'

She glances at me, round-eyed and hopeful. 'That's so nice of you to offer, but I couldn't possibly . . .'

'No, really, it's fine. Come on.'

After paying for my groceries, we head back along the street and Poppy tells me all about her catering company. Apparently she's just won a contract to supply mince pies and festive gingerbread men to a local pop-up ice rink during the fortnight leading up to Christmas Day.

'That's brilliant,' I say, although I can't help noticing that Poppy doesn't seem overjoyed.

'Well, it is. But the problem is, my friend, Erin, who normally helps out, is off to Mexico on holiday.'

'So you've got to manage yourself.'

'Exactly.'

'I'm just here.' I indicate our blue front door and we turn in at the gate.

Poppy frowns. Then she peers at me. 'I don't suppose

you bake?' She smiles. 'The fact that you've got flour is a promising sign.'

I laugh. 'Oh well, the last time I made a chocolate cake—'

'Does she *bake*?' says a loud voice. 'Oh Lord, yes!'

We swing round and there stands my neighbour, Edna, wrapped up to go out, handbag over her arm. At eighty-two, she's a little deaf, hence the shouting.

Addressing Poppy, she says in her plummy voice, 'Dear Roxanne baked a chocolate cake for the church hall Christmas fayre last week and all I'd say is, *Nigella, eat your heart out!* Soft. Moist. Simply chocolate heaven!'

She beams at me.

I laugh. 'No, no, it was—'

'Now, don't be modest.' Edna wags a finger at me. 'It was utterly mouth-watering, believe me! My friend Celia bought it and made me try a slice because she thought it was just as good as a Marks & Spencer cake. And that's no exaggeration!' She taps the side of her nose at Poppy, smiles and walks off with a little wave.

I shake my head apologetically at Poppy. 'Really, she doesn't know what she's talking about.'

'Oh.' Poppy's face falls. 'The thing is, I really need some help, otherwise this whole event is going to be a complete disaster.' She shrugs. 'People *need* mince pies at Christmastime.'

I nod solemnly. 'And festive gingerbread men. Although shouldn't that be ginger people these days?'

She laughs. Then her chin wobbles and her pretty face crumples. 'Oh, God, sorry about this. It's ridiculous, really. I mean, of course people don't *need* mince pies. It's just, if I want the business to succeed, I've got to nail this contract.'

I fish out a hanky, which mercifully seems unused. I can't believe I actually *have* any clean ones left after my sobbing marathon of the past few days.

'Thank you, Roxy.' Poppy dabs her eyes, streaking her mascara. 'Sorry about this.'

'Hey, it's no problem. And if you need some help . . . well, I'm in between jobs at the moment, so . . .'

'Really?' Her dark brown eyes open wide. 'God, you have no idea how grateful I would be for an extra pair of hands.' She peers at me anxiously. 'Is it weird hiring someone I've only just met? Sorry, just thinking out loud. I mean, I wouldn't even be *thinking* of offering you the job if I didn't have a good feeling about you.' Her eyes light up. 'Perhaps you could do the desserts as well! I've said I'll cook for my boyfriend's family and friends at Christmastime, too, you see.'

'Oh, no.' I shake my head in horror. 'I couldn't possibly do anything like that.' I could probably throw a handful of stuff into a pan to make mincemeat, as long as I had specific directions – but make desserts? I don't think so.

'That chocolate cake you baked sounded fab!' There's more than a hint of desperation in her tone. 'And there'd be no set menu. You could just make the sort of puddings you normally do.'

Her face is a study in pleading. I can't bear to tell her the cake was a fake, and my pudding-making skills stretch only to opening up the box and cutting the contents into slices. On the other hand, I'm going to need a pretty hefty distraction if I'm planning to get over Jackson Cooper this side of the next millennium. And I suppose there's always YouTube if I get stuck.

'So I wouldn't have to make anything complicated?'

'Oh, no, no. Just simple things, like maybe a cherry chocolate mousse? Or a delicious cheesecake? Or a basic but wonderful lemon meringue pie?'

Simple things?

'Or cranberry cranachan?' Poppy laughs. 'Actually, now I'm insulting your abilities. I saw the recipe for that the other day and it's so simple, even a five-year-old could make it!'

My face performs a cross between a smile and a grimace. *I'd better steer clear of the cranberry cranach-thingy, then!*

'And obviously, you'll be a dab hand at making sweet shortcrust pastry,' Poppy rushes on. 'For the mince pies.'

I remember my efforts from my schooldays. 'It's been a while,' I say cagily, not wanting to spoil her mood because she's looking so much more cheerful than she was earlier.

'Oh, you'll be fine, Roxy. As you well know, there's just one big golden rule of pastry-making you need to remember . . .' She smiles, confidently expecting me to be able to answer the question that's now hanging in the air.

'Ah, yes.' My mind races. 'That big golden rule. The one that many people forget when they're making pastry.' *Or didn't know in the first place. Like me.*

She nods. 'Precisely. So they get a horrible result you'd break your teeth on!'

'Ha-ha, yes!' I shake my head to show I'm definitely not one of those ignorant people who bakes rocks.

'Oh, Roxy, that's brilliant.' Poppy's whole body seems to slump with relief. 'Thank you so much for agreeing to help.'

I smile, thinking maybe I should enlighten her as to the full extent of my lack of baking know-how. But I have a feeling that even if I said, *Last time I made mince pies, I set myself and the entire street on fire*, she'd probably wave it away and say, *Oh, these things happen!*

She frowns anxiously. 'It would just be for the fortnight before Christmas, though. Would that be okay for you?'

'Yes, that's fine. Where's the ice rink, by the way?'

'On the shores of a lake about ten miles from here.'

'Oh yes, I know where you mean.'

She nods. 'I'll be staying at my boyfriend's place which is right nearby. It's lovely. It's called the Log Fire Cabin and is set among fir trees on the banks of the lake. Really picturesque. Especially when it snows, which hopefully it will.' She glances up at the sky.

I rub my arms. 'It's definitely cold enough for snow.'

'It is, isn't it? I keep imagining snow drifting down on the skaters. So romantic.' Her expression turns wistful and sort of sad.

'It sounds lovely,' I agree.

'So you're definitely up for it?'

'Erm . . .' I stare off into the distance, thinking. If I went to work for Poppy, I'd have nothing to lose and quite a lot to gain. It would give me a much needed financial boost – plus, it would give me something to do so I wasn't just moping around the house, trying not to think about Jackson and his alluring new woman with the sexy French accent.

My heart tumbles into my boots at the thought of the two of them together. But I force a smile. 'I'd love to help.'

Poppy looks delighted. 'It's all going to work out perfectly.'

I nod with a little less conviction.

I guess I'll have to teach myself how to bake – and fast!

A week later, having crammed as many online baking tutorials as possible into my brain, I'm heading out on the road that leads to the Log Fire Cabin.

As I skirt Guildford, I'm aware of everything gearing up for the festive season. Jolly lights and decorations adorn every house, and one even has a huge blow-up Santa perched on their roof, about to climb down the chimney. It's just a shame my own excitement over Christmas has taken such a complete nosedive.

My Grand Live TV Humiliation has had some of the heat taken out of it due to the fact that, contrary to my fears, not many people have recognised me as that saddo off the telly who was rejected by her boyfriend. This is great. In about a decade or so, I might even have forgotten all about it myself.

I've been trying really hard to put Jackson out of my mind, with mixed success. Every time I start remembering the good times we had, I force myself to replay the shock I felt hearing that woman's seductive voice answering Jackson's phone. I thought about hoping it was his sister but that didn't work for two reasons. One, she didn't sound how a sister would sound. And two, Jackson doesn't have a sister.

Part of me still misses him like crazy. But I think it's

more the *idea* of him that's left a hole in my life, rather than the actual physical person. Because I've since realised that we weren't hugely compatible. He hardly ever laughed at the things I thought were funny. Or my jokes. In fact, I've started to wonder if he ever actually listened to me at all.

One thing in particular will ensure the process of getting over him isn't too dragged out: with a bit of luck, I will *never* have to see Jackson or the inside of a TV studio ever again!

Chapter 5

Poppy has asked me to meet her at the pop-up ice rink, which has been set up a little further along the lakeside track from her boyfriend's Log Fire Cabin.

Apparently there's a rather swish boutique hotel, owned by a woman called Sylvia, right next to the ice rink site. It was Sylvia's idea to bring skating to the local community this Christmas – and it's Sylvia who's ordered the hundreds of mince pies Poppy and I will be baking in the run-up to Christmas Day.

When I turn off the main road onto the lakeside track, which has recently been laid with tarmac, all I can see are trees on either side, sparkling with frost in the winter sun, and glimpses of the lake to my left. The Log Fire Cabin has been so cleverly merged with its surroundings that I give a gasp of surprise when I suddenly see it.

It's a stylish modern wooden construction on two levels that blends in beautifully with the surrounding trees and countryside. It looks big enough to house quite a few guests, but according to Poppy, her boyfriend Jed has booked some rooms in the hotel, as a sort of overflow. As well as making hundreds of mince pies and Christmas gingerbread men, we'll be cooking every night for ten people.

That's ten portions of dessert!

Every time I think about that, I get an uneasy, fluttery stomach.

Driving past the cabin, I see the hotel and the ice rink up ahead and, a minute later, I'm entering the big makeshift car park in a field that serves visitors to the rink.

As I park, I glance around, trying to spot Poppy.

A week has passed since I rescued her with a bag of my own flour. And now, it feels as if she's rescuing me.

The past seven days haven't been great, and that's an understatement.

Flo came in one night last week, full of agony over whether to tell me the latest news about Jackson. I wheedled it out of her, although I could tell it was going to crucify me to hear it. Sure enough, what I suspected was true. Jackson had started seeing someone else.

She plopped down beside me on the sofa and gave me a hug and the rest of her bar of Cadbury's Dairy Milk, which I considered true friendship indeed. Flo's parents were whisking her and Fergus off to New York for the festive season to celebrate their engagement, and I knew I'd miss my best friend.

'I think you had a lucky escape,' Flo murmured, and I nodded, determined not to cry, and tried to look on the bright side.

I was undoubtedly better off without a guy who could move on to his next girlfriend with such indecent haste . . .

I find Poppy and we stand for a while, leaning on the barrier, watching the skaters making their way around the rink. Some of them carve their way across the ice with confidence while others wobble, grim concentration etched on their faces. The rest are progressing at a snail's pace, clinging to the sides.

I'd definitely be a clinger-to-the-sides – but since I'm here to work, thankfully I won't have to set even one solitary skate on that treacherous surface. It's nice to just relax and observe—

'Let's have a go,' says Poppy suddenly.

I turn, startled. 'What? No.'

'Come on. It's fun.'

'But . . . we've got baking to do, haven't we?'

Thousands of mince pies!

'Well, yes, but you've just arrived, Roxy. I'm not going to throw you in at the deep end straight away.' Poppy grins. 'I set aside a few hours to show you around and get you settled in.' Her smile slips slightly. 'And to be honest, I could do with some fun.'

My face must be a picture of panic. But Poppy's already striding over to the place where you hire the skates, so I suppose I have to follow.

'You'll be fine,' she reassures me as we each imprison our feet in a pair of battered-looking metal monstrosities.

I smile, the way you have to if the boss tells you to do something.

Before I know it, Poppy is leading me onto the ice by the hand and telling me to hold onto the side and push off on my right foot. This is easier said than done. Even remaining in an upright position is terrifying enough as skaters swish past us, showing off. (Or so it seems from my position of shaky vulnerability.)

When I finally manage to move a skate, it feels about as safe and secure as stepping onto a tightrope stretching across the Grand Canyon. I wobble furiously, grasping onto Poppy's hand, then I try to move the other skate and find myself, seconds later, crashing to the ice on my bottom.

That pain is like no other. But Poppy is grinning down at me. 'Everyone falls at first. It's how you learn. In a week, you'll be flying around the ice like Torvill and Dean. Honestly.'

She shows me how to get up by rolling onto my

knees first. Then she holds out her hand and I'm on my feet again – except they don't feel like my feet at all. I feel as if I'm strapped into weapons of torture.

'Poppy? Can I have a word?' A large blonde woman bundled up in a fake fur is beckoning her over. 'I've done some projections. We need to talk mince pies!'

Poppy smiles. 'No problem, Sylvia. I'll see you in the café?'

The woman called Sylvia gives her a thumbs-up and Poppy looks apologetically at me. 'Will you be okay? This should just take a minute then we can continue the lesson. We'll be over there.' She points to a pretty, white summerhouse-type construction. It has a serving hatch under a pink stripy awning and lots of tables and chairs in front of it. It's presumably a temporary café to cater to the ice rink visitors.

'Er . . . sure.'

'Just try and do a circuit of the rink, holding onto the side, and I'll be back before you know it.' She skates to the edge and jumps neatly off the rink like a professional.

I attempt a smile but I'm quaking inside. I feel like a prize idiot, standing there with a forced grin on my face, not knowing how the hell I'm going to actually move even an inch from the spot.

Why do people think this is fun? Are they all masochists?

Sighing, I glare down at my skates, willing them to

do the right thing. But they wilfully disobey and slide in opposite directions, so, next second, I'm back on my bum with an agonising bang.

'Are you okay? Can I help you up?'

I glance up into the face of a guy with a friendly smile. He looks about my age and, more importantly, he looks as if he can actually stand without wobbling.

'That's so kind of you.' I smile up at him and roll over onto my knees as Poppy taught me. 'If you could just give me a hand, I'll get out of these alien things and onto solid ground.'

'I could take you round if you like,' he offers. 'I can't promise to stay on my feet myself, but I'm sure that, between the two of us, we could prop each other up?'

I shake my head firmly. 'No, thank you. I've had enough for one day.'

'Are you here with anyone?' He glances around as he helps me up.

'My new boss. She's in the café, I think, talking business.'

'Leaving you to sink or swim?' He grins.

'Or crash.' I pause for a while to navigate the stepping-off-the-ice bit, which looks a little tricky. The relief when I'm on solid ground is huge. 'Actually, she didn't just abandon me. Well, she *did* – but I think she expected me to be grown-up about it and not freak out like I did.'

I smile at my rescuer but he's gazing at me with a slight frown on his face.

'This might seem like a weird question,' he says. 'But don't I know you from somewhere?'

My heart sinks.

'Er, no, I don't think so.'

Great. Someone else who witnessed my total humiliation on live TV! Will I ever be able to live that disastrous night down?

'Right.' He nods and doesn't pursue it, much to my relief. 'I'm Alex, by the way.'

'Roxy.' We shake hands.

'Short for Roxanne?'

I nod. 'My mum's a Sting fan.'

'Ah. Great classic, that. Rooooox-anne.'

'Yes, shame it's about a sex worker, though,' I say drolly, and he chuckles and acknowledges my jest with a nod.

We lean on the safer side of the rink edge and watch the skaters flying by.

'It's not easy, this skating lark,' he murmurs. 'I haven't done it since I was a teenager. I've got used to spending Christmases in Australia on the beach.'

I glance at him in surprise. 'So you emigrated?'

'Yeah. I studied at uni here, then Mum and Dad decided they wanted to live in sunnier climes, so I went with them. That was eight years ago.'

That explains his tanned face and neck, and possibly the lighter streaks in his dark blond hair, I think, glancing at him. 'I suppose there's not much opportunity for pop-up festive skating rinks in Australia.'

He grins, showing two rows of nice white teeth. 'None at all. Actually, one of the things I've missed living over there is the British seasons.'

I nod solemnly. 'Yes, I can see how you would long for a cold, sleety walk along a British beach. You'd get sick of warm, golden sands and barbecues and swimming in the ocean pretty quickly, I'd imagine.'

'Been there, done that, got the T-shirt,' he says in a bored voice.

We look at each other and laugh.

'So are you here to stay? Or will you be going back to Australia?'

'I'll be heading back to Oz after Christmas. I work as a GP in Melbourne for my sins.'

I sneak another glance at his shaggy blond hair. 'I bet you surf.'

He turns and grins at me. 'So I'm a walking cliché, am I?'

'No! I just meant you *look* as if you do – with your tan and your . . . your – um – beach hair.'

'My beach hair? God, is it that bad?' He looks really worried and I rush to apologise.

'Sorry, no, it looks absolutely fine.' I feel myself flushing up in confusion.

He grins lazily at me. 'Hey, it's okay, I'm only joking. As a matter of fact, I do surf. I live right next to the beach so it would be rude not to, really. And a haircut is at the very top of my list of things to do today.'

An expert skater narrowly misses ploughing into a novice, who's trying to get up off the ice, and both Alex and I say, 'Ooh,' at the same time.

'And people do that for *fun*?' I murmur, really feeling for the poor learner skater who seems to have been completely abandoned by her show-off boyfriend.

Alex shrugs. 'Once you learn the basics, you start having confidence in your ability to do it, and that's when it becomes fun.' He turns. 'So do you live near here?'

I nod. 'I share a flat the other side of Guildford, but I've just started a new job here.'

'Doing what?'

I grimace. 'Baking.'

'Why the face?'

'Er, because I *can't* bake. My mum, bless her, worked full-time and hated domestic stuff so most of the time we had fish fingers and chips for dinner and shop-bought cakes. Needless to say, I *didn't* help her to stir cakes from being knee-high to a grasshopper. So now, I'm not really sure where to begin.'

He laughs. 'Does your new boss know this?'

'No. But it's fine. I've been online. I now know how to make a basic Victoria sponge cake and an apple crumble. So I should be okay. I'll just do variations on the basic theme.'

He nods slowly, studying me with laughter in his eyes. 'And where is this place you're working?'

'It's just along the road there, by the lake. You can see it through the trees.' I point. 'It's that gorgeous chalet-type building over there. The Log Fire Cabin.'

His eyes open in surprise. 'You're working for Poppy?'

I frown at him. 'Yes, but how did you—'

'Did I hear my name mentioned?'

I nearly jump out of my skin at the sound of Poppy's voice. *How much did she hear of my conversation with Alex?* I was planning on breaking the news gently about my lack of baking skills but maybe the cat's out of the bag now.

'Hey, Poppy,' says Alex, 'I just scraped your new assistant here off the ice. I think she needs to brush up on her skills a little.'

He gives me a huge, knowing grin and I flush scarlet. It's fairly obvious he's not just talking about the skating.

But Poppy seems totally unaware. 'Roxy rescued me in the supermarket when I was weeping over a bag of flour. Thank God. Because she might just have saved my bacon.'

'Or your mince pies,' points out Alex.

Poppy nods. 'Speaking of which, I've got the five hundred for tomorrow's delivery to box up – plus we've got two hundred gingerbread men to ice. We'd better get cracking, Roxy!'

She starts walking off. 'See you at dinner, Alex!'

I glance at Alex, perplexed.

'I'm staying at the posh hotel here,' he explains. 'But I'll be over at the Log Fire Cabin most nights. Poppy's boyfriend, Jed, is one of my best mates from uni. We're having a sort of Christmas reunion while I'm over here.'

'Oh. Right. Well, I'll probably see you later, then.'

'You probably will. With a haircut.' Alex grins as I hurry after Poppy.

On impulse, I call back, 'There's nothing wrong with beach hair,' and he gives me an impressed thumbs-up as if he totally agrees.

I've been dreading meeting all the guests at the Log Fire Cabin. Having to talk to them and think of something interesting to say. But it feels a little less daunting now that I've met Jed's friend, Alex.

It will be nice having a friendly face around the place . . .

Chapter 6

Driving back along the road to the Log Fire Cabin, Poppy gives me a run-down of what I'll be doing during my days here.

'I really feel like I'm dumping you in at the deep end,' she says, apologetically. 'If it's too much, just say so.'

'No, honestly, it's fine.' The more hours I can spend at the Log Fire Cabin each day, the less time I'll have to kick my heels at home, moping about Jackson, so I'll get over him much faster. That's the theory, anyway.

'I haven't spoiled your Christmas plans, I hope?'

I shake my head and explain about Mum and Dad going off on a cruise. 'My flatmate, Flo, is away, too, with her family. They're spending the festive season in New York.'

'Ooh, lucky Flo!'

'I know.'

'So . . . I thought if you could make the desserts, I'll

concentrate on the main courses and we can do the starter together. How does that sound?'

'Good,' I say, as my stomach turns several somersaults in quick succession. *Isn't there a dessert called Eton Mess? That sounds right up my street.*

As I park outside the house, I ask her how she first met Jed and her serious expression melts into a faraway smile.

'He phoned me, thinking I was his brother's girlfriend, Clemmy. He got the wrong number, you see. So he left a message inviting me – well, *Clemmy* – for Christmas. And, well, I phoned him back and told him he'd got the wrong number and we chatted . . .' Her face is glowing just thinking about it.

'So what happened?'

'Well, I thought that was that. But there was something about his voice I really liked. And then I happened to be at the station when he was meeting Clemmy off the train.'

She shoots me a glance, her cheeks colouring up. 'When I say I "happened" to be there, I actually went to the station deliberately. I suppose I was curious to see Jed in person. And it all sort of fell into place after that.'

'Did you talk to him?'

'Yes. He found out I was setting up my dinner party business and he just happened to need a caterer for over the Christmas holidays – so that was it!'

'How romantic.'

She beams at me. 'It was. I couldn't quite believe it when we finally got together.'

'And that was two years ago? And you've been together ever since?'

Her smile slips. 'Two years, yes,' she murmurs, almost as if she's forgotten I'm there.

'Do you live at the Log Fire Cabin with Jed?'

There's a pause. Then she turns. 'No, we don't live together. I have my own flat in the village, although I stay over at Jed's place once during the week. And most weekends.'

'Lovely.'

She nods. 'Of course it makes sense for me to stay here every night until the baking contract ends at Christmas. But after that, it's back to my own place!' She smiles but it doesn't quite reach her eyes.

As we walk in the imposing entrance, with its modern, oak wood staircase rising up to the first-floor bedrooms, the man himself – Jed Turner – runs downstairs. Seeing Poppy, his handsome face spreads into a beaming smile.

'Hey, you.'

'Hey,' she responds with a shy smile.

'And you must be Roxy. I hope she's treating you well?'

'Oh, yes. Very well.' I smile and we shake hands. Then

he takes Poppy into a loose cuddle and plants a lingering kiss on top of her head.

She relaxes fully into his embrace for just a moment. Then she pulls away. 'Right. We have two hundred gingerbread men to ice.' She reaches up and plants a quick kiss on his cheek. 'Let's go, Roxy.'

She walks briskly along to the kitchen and I follow in her wake, turning back to smile at Jed. He's standing there with his arms folded, staring after us, a pensive look on his face.

Icing gingerbread men turns out to be even more tricky than I'd imagined, and I need four tries – and much embarrassed laughter on my part and giggles on Poppy's – before she deems me proficient enough to work on my own. I'm painfully aware that I'm slowing up the proceedings. But if Poppy is worried, she doesn't show it. She just keeps making encouraging remarks and praises me to the skies when I finally get Santa's red suit with white trim and black buttons almost perfect. He looks a little cross-eyed, but she doesn't seem to mind about that.

'Right, if we get these done by five, we can run through the recipe for the mince pies to get a head start for tomorrow. Then we can start on dinner. I've told them eight o'clock tonight because I knew we'd be working up to the wire.'

I nod, focusing on getting Santa's pupils in the right place this time.

'You're very welcome to stay for dinner,' she says suddenly, and I glance up. 'You might as well. There'll be plenty.'

She's smiling encouragingly.

'Oh, no. I really need to get back. But thank you.' *Flo will be desperate to know how today went!*

'Is there anything at all to read around here?' says a voice.

We both turn to find a statuesque girl in her early twenties standing in the doorway, chewing gum in a rather bored fashion. She's wearing a short, silky, pale lilac dress and skyscraper nude heels, and her hair flows down over her shoulders in sculpted honey-blonde curls.

'I'm not being funny but is it always this tedious in the countryside?' She crosses her arms and gazes around sulkily.

'Oh, hi, Sophie,' says Poppy. 'Roxy, this is Sophie. She's going out with Jed's friend, Jack. Sophie, this is my new assistant, Roxy.'

I smile at Sophie. 'Hi.'

She hitches her mouth up fractionally, flicks her eyes over me and continues chewing. 'Well?'

'Oh, books, yes,' says Poppy. 'If you go through to the study along the hall you'll find a big bookshelf—'

'I don't mean *books*.' She looks so horrified, I want to giggle.

Poppy raises her eyebrows questioningly.

'*Cosmo?*' snaps Sophie impatiently. '*Harper's Bazaar? Vogue?*'

'Ah, sorry, no. I'm afraid I don't buy fashion magazines.' She suddenly colours bright red and glances at me with a grimace that I don't understand. 'I mean, I do *sometimes*.'

Sophie eyes Poppy's outfit of blue jeans and a plain pink T-shirt. 'Perhaps you should read them more often. You might pick up some tips.' She smiles to show she's just being helpful.

If Poppy is annoyed, she doesn't let it show. Instead, she beams at Sophie. 'Roxy, Sophie here is a very important person in the world of fashion magazine publishing. She's the editor-in-chief of *Dazzle*.'

'Oh. *Dazzle?* Wow, that's amazing. I used to read it all the time.' I'm genuinely impressed. Come to think of it, Sophie is dressed impeccably – as I guess she should be, representing such a stylish magazine as *Dazzle*.

'But you don't read it now?' Her tone is a little accusatory.

'Er, well, sometimes I do,' I say awkwardly. *Dazzle* is pretty much all fashion, which I was well into in my teens. But since the accident, my twenties have been much more about covering up . . .

Sophie is looking quite put out. But maybe that's

just her normal expression. Still, better not mention I only ever flick through *Dazzle* now when I find a copy in the dentist's surgery.

'My mum insists on giving me her back copies of *The People's Friend*. Any good?' offers Poppy. I glance at her. She's gazing innocently at Sophie but I'm fairly certain she has her tongue firmly in her cheek.

Sophie doesn't even dignify this with a reply.

'How's the hotel?' Poppy asks. She turns to me. 'Sophie and her boyfriend are staying at the same place as Alex. You know, when I first came here, it was just a sad, rundown old cottage. And look at it now! A gorgeous boutique hotel! Sylvia's done a superb job transforming it, don't you think?'

'It does look lovely,' I agree. 'Especially all decorated for Christmas.'

Sophie wrinkles her perfect nose. 'It's okay I suppose, although the rooms are quite small. It's not a patch on The Lawns,' she adds, naming a five-star hotel twenty miles from here. Renowned for its elegance and attention to detail, it also boasts a Michelin-starred chef. 'We stayed there a few nights ago.' Sophie gives a theatrical sigh. '*So* romantic. The bedrooms are big enough to host a party!' She picks up one of the mince pies and holds it aloft, examining it with her pinky finger in the air. She takes a tiny bite, chews doubtfully, then drops the rest in the bin.

Walking out, she calls back, 'A moment on the lips, a lifetime on the hips.'

Poppy and I stare after her with our mouths literally hanging open.

'What a bloody cheek! That woman thinks she's royalty just because she edits a fashion magazine,' mutters Poppy once she's gone. 'And as for her romantic night at The Lawns – excuse me while I puke!' She shakes her head wearily. 'I'm just not in the mood to hear about love's young dream at the moment.'

I heave a sigh. 'I know what you mean.'

I'd like to ask Poppy about her relationship with Jed but I definitely don't know her well enough yet – and she *is* my boss, after all.

'God, I'm starving. What time is it?' Poppy glances at her watch, then crosses the kitchen, pulls the fridge door open and peers inside. She brings out a Tupperware box and sniffs the contents. 'Kedgeree leftovers. Would you like some?'

'No, thanks. You go ahead.' I grin as she gets a fork and starts chomping through the fish and rice concoction in the box. 'Wouldn't you prefer it hot?'

She grins. 'Not bothered. I can't seem to stop eating these days. It must be the worry.'

'Worry?'

She shrugs. 'That I won't be able to fulfil this contract. There's so much depending on it. I want to take the business to the next level – perhaps even start employing a couple of full-time staff. But if this doesn't work out . . .' She shakes her head and munches faster.

'It'll be fine. We'll do it.' I try to sound reassuring, although I have absolutely no idea if it *will* be fine.

'I thought we could have trifle for dessert,' she says. 'I found a box in the cupboard. Nice and quick.'

I feel a big surge of relief. *Yes! I can make trifle from a box! We have it every Christmas when I'm at Mum and Dad's!*

Poppy presents me with a lovely cut-glass bowl, the box and a tin. I pat the canned fruit cocktail happily. *You can't go wrong with a tin!*

'Shall we make the custard from scratch?' she asks.

I stare at her blankly then glance at the box. I didn't know you *could* make custard from scratch.

She nods. 'I know, I know. You're right. Far too time-consuming! Let's just stick to the packet variety.' She opens the trifle box and looks inside, drawing out the packets of jelly and custard that I happen to know you just add hot water to. Even *I* can do that!

Poppy grins, pops the packets back into the box and hands it to me. 'There you go!'

And there, indeed, I went. With a huge feeling of relief.

I make the trifle in no time, according to the instructions, and when Poppy asks me to whip some cream for the top, I casually ask where she keeps her 'balloon whisk'. (I learned about balloon whisks when I was watching cookery demos on YouTube.)

Peeling a load of prawns for the starter is easy by comparison.

Every time I need to go to the fridge for something, I peer at my trifle with pride.

First dessert made. And I think I got away with it!

From about seven o'clock, there are lots of comings and goings out in the hall but I'm too busy trying to present the prawn cocktails with panache (like they do on *MasterChef*) to pay much attention. Soon, the kitchen is filled with the delicious aroma of Poppy's lasagne and, before I know what's happening, she's loading the starters onto a large tray and carrying them through to the dining room.

I watch them go like an anxious mum dropping her kids for their first day at a new school. When the dishes come back empty with no report of complaints, a feeling of sheer relief rushes through me, making me feel quite light-headed. Maybe I'll be able to do this!

When it comes to dessert, Poppy insists I should carry my trifle into the dining room myself. It will be a good chance, she says, for me to meet all the guests.

I'm a little nervous but at least I already know Jed and Alex, and I've met Sophie. In fact, I'm quite looking forward to Alex seeing my beautiful trifle because then he'll realise I'm not quite such a flop in the kitchen, after all . . .

My hands feel a little sweaty from nerves so I run them down my jeans a few times and pick up the bowl. Walking through the hallway, I'm concentrating so hard on not tripping over any rugs that I'm not even looking at the diners.

'Presenting . . . Roxy's trifle everyone!' says Poppy.

I look up and meet Alex's eye. He gives me a big encouraging smile and a sly wink, which bolsters my confidence. He's had the haircut he promised. It suits him short.

My gaze slides to Sophie. She's eyeing the trifle with a wary look as if she's worried I might poison her. Her head is resting on the shoulder of the man next to her.

A second later, my eyes collide with his and my heart nearly leaps out of my chest.

'Jackson?' I gasp, my knees turning to blancmange.

'Roxy?' growls Jackson, shock written all over his handsome face.

The blood rushes to my head and I think I might keel over.

I manage to save myself but not the trifle, which slides out of my damp grasp and lands on the wooden floor with a spectacular, rainbow-coloured crash.

Chapter 7

Flo can't believe it when I get back and break the news about Jackson.

She makes me sit down in the best armchair and supplies me with a large glass of wine to combat the shock. I refuse her chocolate offering because my insides are in complete tatters. But as she listens to my story, she systematically unwraps and eats three Mini Rolls, one after the other.

'He just turned up at the Log Fire Cabin with his new girlfriend and you had to serve him dinner? You had no warning whatsoever?' Her eyes are round with disbelief.

I rake my hands through my hair and stare at my flatmate in anguish. 'I can't go back there, Flo. Imagine having to face him every day, and know that he's tucked up every night with the delectable Sophie at that bloody boutique hotel!'

She nods in sympathy and holds out the Mini Roll plate.

I shake my head. 'Thanks, but I think I might be sick.'

'So that French girl who answered his phone . . .?'

'A one-night stand? Before he got with Sophie? Oh, God, I don't know!' I wail, grabbing a Mini Roll in desperation.

'The bastard doesn't waste much time,' murmurs Flo.

'I know. But how can I let Poppy down? She's relying on me.'

Flo frowns. 'Listen, hun, all's fair in love and war. You have to do what you have to do. And if you can't face the thought of seeing Jackson and *Sophie* every day during the festive season, you'll just have to tell Poppy you've changed your mind.'

I nod. 'I think I'll have to. I'm sure if I explain why, she'll understand. She's such a lovely person.'

Later, in bed, I lie there wide awake, thinking back to the catastrophe that was the trifle incident. Jackson looked just as shocked to see me as I was to clap eyes on him. In a way, it was quite fortuitous that I dropped the trifle because it meant that, in the ensuing kerfuffle of getting it all cleaned up, we were able to skate over the fact that we'd been far more than just acquaintances. Sophie kept shooting me funny looks when she thought I wasn't watching, so she obviously suspected something. I was just glad no one at that table had apparently seen my tragic proposal of marriage on live TV . . .

Unless they were being diplomatic and just pretending they hadn't.

Next morning, I'm feeling totally drained from the emotion of the day before. I sit at the kitchen table, huddled in my dressing gown, drinking tea and trying to psyche myself up to phone Poppy and explain it won't be possible for me to continue at the Log Fire Cabin. My heart sinks every time I imagine her reaction. But Flo is right. It's all about self-preservation. I have to do it.

My mobile rings, making me jump with fright.

Poppy's name appears.

I look at Flo, who's buttering toast, and groan. 'Here goes.'

'Hi, Roxy? Listen, you're going to hate me but I'm going to have to ask you to manage on your own today.'

'Oh? Is something wrong?'

Poppy groans. 'I'm not well, Roxy. I don't think those kedgeree leftovers I ate yesterday agreed with me. I keep thinking I'm going to throw up.'

My heart sinks. Can I really let her down when she's feeling so rotten? 'Poor you. So . . . you need me to make the mince pies and the gingerbread Santas?' I shrug helplessly at Flo.

Maybe I could just go and help out today, until she's feeling better. Then I'll tell her I can't continue . . .

'Oh, Roxy, I'd be so grateful. I'll pay you double time.

Because obviously it's not fair on you when you've only just started. Uh oh, hang on, gotta dash!' She hangs up abruptly.

I turn to Flo. 'What could I do? She's ill.'

Flo shakes her head. 'You'll never get over Jackson if you have to keep on seeing him.'

I heave a sigh. 'Don't worry. Now that I've got over the shock of seeing him again, I'll be absolutely fine.'

Flo looks dubious, to say the least.

'Honestly, I'm struggling to remember what it was I saw in him.' I shrug. 'Jackson who?' I give her a big smile and rise to my feet to go and get ready.

Escaping from the kitchen, I sag against the wall and stare up at the ceiling. The storm of emotion I'm feeling at the thought of returning to the Log Fire Cabin is worrying, to say the least.

If I'm this much of a mess now, it will be a hundred times worse when I'm back there . . .

Driving along, my whole body is literally quaking at the thought of bumping into Jackson again.

It's an odd mix of feelings, though. Because amongst the stomach-churning dread of seeing him again, there's a weird little breathlessness going on – similar to the elated feeling I always got when I was due to see him again.

I take a couple of deep breaths to calm myself down.

Jackson is with Sophie now. There's no future for him and me whatsoever, so I need to just turn up at the Log Fire Cabin and do what I can to help Poppy. Then, once Poppy's feeling better, I'll explain the tricky situation I'm in with Jackson and she'll totally understand that I can't possibly continue there . . .

I'm approaching the turn-off but my hands are trembling so much, I fumble with the indicator and the motorist behind me flashes his lights.

Turning off, I pull into the side of the road leading to the lake and the Log Fire Cabin, and switch off the engine. Then I stare ahead at the frost-encrusted pine trees lining the road. They look just like a Christmas card and I feel as frozen as they are – with indecision.

I could turn the car around and head home, and phone Poppy to explain. But then I think of how she'll feel, losing the contract. The way we met in the supermarket definitely felt like fate. And fate has also led me back to Jackson.

I'm not a huge believer in destiny, but it's quite an extraordinary coincidence that I should run into Poppy who just happens to be hosting Christmas for Jackson! Maybe it's not a coincidence at all. Maybe some things really are meant to be. In which case, shouldn't I just go along with it instead of fighting it all?

Starting the engine, I'm still not sure what I'm going to do.

But as the road is too narrow to turn the car around right there, I have no option but to drive onwards, towards the Log Fire Cabin. And then my fate is sealed because Alex is walking towards the front door as I draw up, and he gives me a wave.

I wave back and drive into one of the parking spaces, nausea washing around in the pit of my stomach.

Alex waits for me and holds the door to let me in first.

'You came back,' he says.

I'm about to make a jokey reply when I catch something in his expression and, in a flash of clarity, I realise. *He knows.*

'I wasn't sure you'd actually *be* back,' he murmurs, with a slight air of apology. 'Not after last night . . .'

We linger in the hallway and I can sense he's saving me from having to talk about it with others listening in.

I force a smile. 'Yes, well, as far as shocks go, that was pretty much off the chart. Seeing Jackson. Or *Jack*, as you all call him. And I did wonder if I could face coming back. But hey, Poppy needs help. I couldn't let her down.'

He nods slowly. 'I knew I recognised you but I couldn't think from where.'

'You wouldn't be the first person who's said that to me in the time since that horrible night! And I guess you won't be the last.'

He frowns. 'Sorry, I never thought of that.'

'Don't apologise. At least you were subtle about it and didn't follow me along the high street singing a rowdy, Bridget Jones-style rendition of "All By Myself".'

'That actually happened?' He looks aghast.

I smile grimly. 'Oh, yes.' I quail inside at the memory. They were just teenage girls having a laugh but still . . .

I have to ask him. 'Has Jackson said anything to you – about knowing me?'

Alex shakes his head.

His reply makes me feel cold inside. The fact that Jackson hasn't even told his closest friends about our relationship makes me feel even smaller than I already did. Which is saying something.

'It's probably difficult for him, though, with Sophie here,' Alex points out. Tears well up but I blink them away quickly and force a smile. 'That's true.'

We stand there, rather awkwardly, for a moment. Then Alex murmurs, 'Listen, if you ever feel the need to get away – from *anything* – remember I'm on hand to give you a skating lesson.'

He gives me a sly, sideways grin and, against all the odds, laughter bubbles up inside me. 'God, I can't imagine ever being *that* desperate. But I'll bear it in mind.'

'You do that. Poppy's upstairs, by the way. She said to tell you to go straight up.'

We turn at the sound of footsteps from behind us.

It's Jackson and my heart swoops.

In the second our eyes meet, before I look away, I take in his long legs in the faded jeans, his bare feet that he hated but I loved, and the blue checked shirt I bought him for his birthday back in October.

'Hi Roxy. Good to see you again.' He gives me one of his dazzling million-watt smiles that always turns my knees to jelly. Today is no exception.

I mutter a hello, feeling awkward as hell, in total contrast to Jackson, who seems to be taking my sudden appearance at the cabin completely in his stride. He does actually look genuinely pleased to see me.

'Poppy will be glad you're here,' he says smoothly.

I catch a waft of his familiar cologne and it almost floors me.

'Hope you're not monopolising her, Al,' he comments jokily to his friend. 'Roxy's got work to do.'

I'm not sure what Alex's response is because I'm already fleeing past him up the stairs. If I have to keep dodging out of Jackson's way like this, it's going to be one very long fortnight . . .

Chapter 8

Poppy is in bed, propped up on her pillows, looking pale. She groans when she sees me.

'I should have known eating two-day-old kedgeree would give me a gippy tummy. I'm so sorry about this, Roxy.'

'Hey, it's fine. Are you feeling any better?'

She nods. 'A bit, thanks. The symptoms have worn off at least. But I think I should stay away from the kitchen for a while, just in case any germs get transmitted.'

'Well, no problem, that's what *I'm* here for.' I sound far more confident than I'm feeling. 'You can direct proceedings from the comfort of your bed.'

She smiles. 'Thank goodness I had a meltdown over that burst bag of flour. If I hadn't, we'd never have met – and *then* what would I have done? At least we already made a start on the next order of mince pies yesterday.'

'True. We made a hundred and eighty.'

'Well remembered.'

I screw my eyes up, calculating. 'So that's just another . . . three hundred and twenty to make today?' I smile brightly to conceal the panic that's surging up at the very thought. We haven't even discussed the gingerbread Santas!

Poppy grimaces. 'I guess that's about the size of it. Look, just do your best, Roxy, but don't feel pressured. I can always get up very early tomorrow morning to make the rest.'

'Can I bring you anything before I start?'

'No, thanks. Jed's been really sweet, actually. He keeps popping in to make sure I'm still alive.' She smiles fondly. 'He's nipped out but he said he'd bring me back some magazines to relieve my boredom.'

I grin. 'Not content with *The People's Friend* from the skating rink kiosk, then?'

'Oh, God, no!' she says in a plummy voice, doing a fairly impressive impersonation of Sophie. 'It has to be *Harper's Bazaar* or *nothing*!' She attempts a laugh then clutches her stomach miserably. 'Jed and I were supposed to be taking part in a pairs skating contest at the rink on Tuesday night, but I'm not going to be able to do it.'

'You might be feeling better by then.'

She sighs. 'Hopefully. But I'd already decided I'm far too busy to take part, even though it would have been fun. I've asked Jackson and Sophie to fill in for us.'

I swallow miserably. They'll make a very glamorous pair on the ice. Jackson seems to be good at everything he turns his hand to, so it wouldn't surprise me if they were to win.

'We'll all go down there and watch. Sylvia's closing the rink to the public for a couple of hours on Tuesday evening so the contest can go ahead.'

'Sounds great,' I lie.

She shrugs. 'It's Sylvia's way of getting a bit of publicity for the local businesses involved in her ice rink venture, including Truly Scrumptious, of course. Every business has nominated a couple to represent them – so for us, that will be Jackson and Sophie.'

'Right, well, I'd better get started.' I paste on a smile, having heard quite enough already about Jackson and Sophie, and head for the kitchen.

But, as I run down the stairs, I tell myself it's only a fortnight and the money will come in very handy indeed. And Poppy is so easy to get along with. I keep having to remind myself that she's actually my boss.

I make it to the kitchen without running into Jackson again. Closing the door behind me, I breathe a sigh of relief and go in search of my ingredients.

For the next few hours, I immerse myself completely in making the delicate sweet pastry the way Poppy demonstrated the day before, and following the recipe for her special apple, cinnamon and mincemeat filling. While the huge block of pastry chills in the fridge and the gorgeous fruity compote bubbles on the hob, filling the kitchen with the aromas of apples and Christmas spices, I take a look at the gingerbread recipe. It can't be *that* hard with the instructions in front of me, can it? And it would take the pressure off Poppy. Imagining how pleased she'll be if I've made a start on the gingerbread Santas, I decide to take the initiative and try to bake a batch myself.

I sift together the flour, ginger and cinnamon and pour them into the bowl of the food processor, then I cut the butter into the mix – feeling like quite the professional – and whiz until it starts to look like breadcrumbs. Adding the sugar and big dollops of deliciously gooey golden syrup, I set the mixer off again but more slowly this time, like Poppy did the day before. Then I roll out the dough and carefully use the special cutter to make lots of perfect Santa shapes, which I lay on a series of greased baking trays.

Once they're in the oven, I decide that, if Poppy were here, she'd be suggesting a break for a cuppa. I put the kettle on and decide to go up and see if she would like one. But first, I clear off my work surface, my eyes lingering on the golden syrup spoon lying in the mixing bowl. A quick glance at the door and then I'm over by the window, staring out at the frosted lake scene, slowly licking the golden syrup spoon clean.

I close my eyes in the stillness of the warm kitchen, enjoying the very moreish taste of the syrup on my tongue and thinking about Jackson. I heard him in the hallway with Sophie earlier. She was complaining about the lack of things to do in the countryside and Jackson was making fun of her for being a townie.

'What's up with *you* this morning, anyway?' I heard Sophie say, just before the front door closed behind them. 'You seem remarkably cheerful. Normally I can't get a word out of you in the morning until you've had at least three coffees!'

'Caught you!' A male voice cuts into my thoughts and I spin round guiltily.

Jackson?

But it's Alex standing in the doorway.

Arms folded, he grins at me. 'Don't worry, that's an extremely necessary ritual. I doubt the mince pies would turn out right if you didn't lick the spoon.'

I smile back. 'That's an interesting theory. Do you bake much yourself?'

'Never. Although I'm excellent at operating a microwave.'

I nod, pretending to be impressed. 'Raymond Blanc, eat your heart out!'

'There's nothing wrong with Pop-Tarts.'

'Definitely not.' I adopt a solemn expression. 'It's a little known fact but Pop-Tarts are actually the new cupcakes.'

We laugh and I say, 'I'm making tea. Would you like one?'

'I'll have a strong coffee if there's one going.'

'Okay. I'll bring it through.'

'Thanks, Roxy. That would be great. I'll be in the living room.' He flashes me a grin and disappears.

The aroma of ginger filling the kitchen reminds me that my baking needs to come out of the oven. Carefully, I transfer the Santa biscuits to several large cooling trays, overlapping them slightly to fit them all on. Most of them have turned out fine, much to my surprise. There are just a few that have caught slightly at the edges.

After that, I make some tea and take it up to Poppy. She's sunk into an exhausted sleep, curled on her side, so I just leave it on her bedside table and return to the kitchen to make Alex's coffee. At the last minute, I waft one of the biscuits in the air to cool it faster, then I quickly make up a little icing the way Poppy showed me yesterday and give the Santa a funny, cross-eyed expression. Then I pop it on Alex's saucer, hoping he'll appreciate my artistry!

Just as I'm emerging from the kitchen, the front door opens and Sophie walks in, followed closely by Jackson.

'Oh no, we couldn't *possibly* use the hotel for a fashion photo shoot,' Sophie is saying. 'We'd need to completely redecorate first. Those *curtains* in our *bedroom*!'

'I think they're quite nice,' murmurs Jackson. 'They match the quilt.'

'Well, *precisely*! That's my point entirely.'

They catch sight of me, waiting there with a fixed smile on my face. 'Hi, Roxy,' says Sophie. 'Hey, were you named after that sex worker in the Sting song?'

Jackson glances down at his feet.

I smile brightly. 'I was, actually. Mum liked the song but I don't think she listened to the words properly.'

Sophie's ice-cool gaze sweeps over me.

'If you want to go Christmas shopping, we'd better leave now,' says Jackson shortly. 'Town will be murder if we leave it any later.'

I swallow. It's obvious he can't wait to escape.

'Ooh, can we go for coffee at that little place we found?' Sophie slides her hands coyly up over his chest and round his neck. 'Pretty please?' she begs in a little-girl voice.

He smiles and kisses her nose. 'Yes, of course we can.'

'Great! I'll just get my bag from the living room.'

'Could you take this through to Alex, please?' Smiling pleasantly, I hold out the cup to Sophie.

She stares at it for a moment. Then she spots the

cross-eyed gingerbread Santa on the saucer and her eyes widen. 'Are you really serving *that* up?'

Shaking her head and ignoring my request, she clatters off along the hallway.

Jackson meets my eye awkwardly and takes the cup for Alex himself. He frowns down at the Santa. 'Er, you might need more practice doing the icing, Roxy. His face doesn't look quite right.'

I shrug. 'He's supposed to be cross-eyed.'

'Really? But . . .' He looks genuinely puzzled.

I shake my head and retreat to the safety of the kitchen. God, this is awful. I need to stay out of Jackson's way, but it's so difficult when he's liable to pop up at any moment.

I'm removing the block of sweet pastry from the fridge to start on the next batch of mince pies when the door opens, and when I turn, Jackson is standing there.

'Roxy.' He takes a step into the room and my foolish heart starts beating in double-quick time. 'I just wanted to say how sorry I am for the way things ended.' He holds out his arms in a shrug of bemusement. 'I honestly couldn't believe it when you said . . . er . . . *that* in front of the cameras. Naturally, I was flattered. Who wouldn't be? But I'm sure, once you sobered up, you realised it was all a bit premature?'

He walks over and, before I know what's happening,

he's enveloping me in a hug. 'But hey, we can still be friends, can't we?' he says into my hair, as I stand there, my arms at my sides. He steps away from me. 'It was great while it lasted, though, wasn't it?' He winks at me and walks calmly out of the kitchen.

I stare after him, dumbfounded at the cool way he just dismissed our relationship as something that was 'great while it lasted'. I'd thought it was pretty special. More fool me! He'd displayed no sadness over the fact that it hadn't worked out for us. And he clearly had no conscience at all over the speed with which he'd moved on to his next conquest – before I'd barely had a chance to draw breath!

When the door opens again, I almost jump into next week with shock.

But it's Poppy this time.

'Sorry, Roxy, did I startle you?'

'No, it's fine. You look a bit better,' I say truthfully, as my racing heart rate slowly subsides.

She nods. 'I think I'm getting there. Thanks for the tea, by the way.' She surveys the results of my efforts with a delighted smile. 'Wow, well done, you!'

'Thank you. I enjoyed doing it.' I'm actually more surprised than Poppy that my baking turned out okay. Not that I'm about to admit this to her.

She frowns. 'Aren't you too warm in here with the oven blasting all the time?' Poppy herself is wearing just a short-sleeved T-shirt with her pyjama bottoms. 'Take your cardy off and I'll hang it on the peg over here.'

She puts her hands up as if to start removing it for me, and in a panic, I twist away.

She stares at me in surprise.

Feeling stupid, I try to make a joke of it. 'Sorry, it's just I'm a bit of a wuss. I tend to feel the cold. Even when it's warm,' I add, confusing even myself.

My heart is racing. Stripping off my top layer to reveal the sleeveless T-shirt beneath would mean I'd have to talk about the accident – and that's something I never, ever do. Just the thought of revisiting the horror of that night is enough to make me feel nauseous and light-headed. The nightmares are bad enough . . .

'Oh. Okay.' Poppy shrugs lightly. 'By the way, Jed's decided to take everyone out for dinner tonight, so once you've iced the gingerbread Santas and made a few more mince pies, we can just kick back and relax.'

'Don't you want to join them for dinner?' I ask, as my heart rate gradually returns to normal.

She pats her stomach and grimaces. 'I'm not sure I can face food quite yet.'

For the rest of the afternoon, Poppy rests in her room and I work as quickly as I can to finish tomorrow's order. I'm obviously much slower than Poppy but I know that, as long as I keep going, I'll get there. Even if I'm still making mince pies at midnight!

The radio is tuned to a station specialising in music from the nineties and every now and then an old classic comes on that has me singing along as I work away, icing faces onto Santas, rolling pastry and sliding gleaming baking trays in and out of the oven. As darkness falls beyond the large picture windows of the cosy, lamplit kitchen, and the glorious scent of ginger and warm golden syrup fills the room, I'm feeling a little calmer after my encounter with Jackson.

They say baking is good therapy and I can vouch for that myself now. When you're focusing on measuring out ingredients, stirring, folding and blending them carefully, tasting as you go and breathing in the scrumptious aroma of home baking, all thoughts and stresses seem to float from your mind. For that small window of time, all that matters is getting as perfect a result as you can. And it's so satisfying when the goodies emerge from the oven, warm and golden – and looking surprisingly edible.

Soon after seven, as I'm still icing my small army of gingerbread Santas, Jed pops his head round the door and asks me if it would be easier for me if I moved into the cabin for the Christmas period. He leaves me to think about it and I quickly realise that it makes sense. If we're going to be super busy baking Sylvia's huge order every day, it would be so much better if I wasn't having to waste precious time driving home in the evening and back the next day. If I'm here in the morning, we can just get started straight away.

Half an hour later, Jed leaves to take Jackson, Sophie and Alex out for dinner. I hear his murmured exchange with Poppy in the hallway as he goes, then she appears in the kitchen and asks me if I've decided to stay.

'Are you sure there's room for me?'

She nods. 'Even after Jed's Uncle Bob and Gloria arrive with Ruby the day after tomorrow, there'll still be one spare bedroom. We thought Ruby's brother, Tom, would be coming but he's going to his girlfriend's for Christmas instead.'

'Who's Ruby?'

'Oh, she's lovely. She's Gloria's seventeen-year-old daughter. A bit boisterous but great fun. Uncle Bob's wife died but he started seeing Gloria a few years ago. I like her a lot. She's a real character.'

'Who else is coming for Christmas?'

'Ryan and Clemmy are due here tomorrow morning.'

I screw up my eyes, thinking. 'And Ryan is Jed's brother?'

Poppy nods. 'And Clemmy's his girlfriend. She's heavenly – you'll like her. She's not a bit like Sophie.' She shakes her head. 'I don't know what Jack sees in that girl.'

You and me both, I think to myself. *Apart from the fact that she looks like a model.*

'So will you stay?' Poppy looks at me expectantly.

'Well, if you're sure. I suppose it makes sense.'

My stomach feels uneasy at the thought. It might make practical sense but living here will make it a hundred times more difficult to avoid Jackson!

'Good. That's sorted, then.' Poppy looks pleased. 'I can lend you some stuff for tonight and you can nip back home and pack a bag tomorrow.' She tries to suppress a yawn. 'Sorry, I'm shattered, yet I've done nothing all day. Once you've finished here, I'm going to show you your room, then I'm going to open a bottle of wine for you and make myself a lime and soda.' She grimaces. 'Good for a tummy that's still slightly delicate. Then we're going to crash out in front of the log fire!'

Chapter 9

True to her word, an hour later, we're lounging on a huge, squashy sofa by the roaring log fire in the stylish living room, and I'm hugging an enormous, balloon-shaped glass that seems to have barely anything in it, but actually contains almost half a bottle of wine. I know this because I watched Poppy pour it out.

'I bet you decorated this room,' I say, glancing at the fairy lights winking along the mantelpiece and the glorious Christmas tree, decked with shiny red and gold baubles and cute tartan bows.

She grins. 'Got it in one. Jed's useless at stuff like that. Cheers!' she says, leaning over and clinking my glass. 'Thanks again for agreeing to come and work for me. You saved my bacon!'

I take a sip of the white wine. It tastes completely delicious – like honeyed gooseberries. 'It's a pleasure.'

And I really mean it. Poppy is so easy to get along with and I'm discovering baking skills I never knew I had. If only Jackson wasn't around, making me jumpy all the time . . .

'Did you never want to do anything else, Roxy? Apart from working at the biscuit factory?' Poppy asks with a curious frown.

A feeling of dread creeps over me. Conversations about my choice of job can sometimes lead to tricky questions that I don't want to answer. And I like Poppy too much to want to lie to her. So I shrug and say airily, 'I liked working at the factory. It was a good, steady job – until I was made redundant.'

She nods thoughtfully, but I can tell she's not fooled by my blasé attitude. 'So did you start there straight from school, then?'

'Er, not quite.' I swallow hard. We're straying into wildly uncomfortable territory here. 'I had a few – um – problems which delayed everything. But then I got the job at the factory so everything worked out fine in the end.' I paste on a bright smile. 'So you've been going out with Jed for two years?'

Her eyes go all dreamy and I breathe a sigh of relief that we're off the subject of me. 'Yes. The happiest time of my life. I knew as soon as I met him that he was a really solid bloke – kind, thoughtful, funny.'

'And rather good-looking.'

'There is that, yes.' She grins and leans her head back against the sofa, staring up at the ceiling. 'Jed's lovely. I suppose he's my ideal man, really. We make each other laugh.' She swallows and her smile fades. 'But nothing ever works out the way you think it will.'

'What do you mean?' I ask.

'Oh, just that we seem to be on completely different pages. I'd like to be galloping along to the happy-ever-after, but Jed is still messing about in chapter one. And that's fine, of course. Everyone's different. But after two happy years together, you'd think – I don't know . . .' She shrugs.

'That there'd be some talk of the future?' I suggest.

She turns her head towards me. 'Exactly.'

'But there isn't?'

'Not a whisper. He neatly deviates from the topic every time I touch on it, and I still don't feel I can leave any stuff at his house.'

'What – not even a toothbrush?'

'Well, a toothbrush. But nothing else. These few weeks that I'm staying here are purely for convenience. Even Jed can't object to that when I'm working out of his kitchen!'

'Perhaps he's just nervous of the whole commitment thing. It doesn't mean he's not still crazy about you.'

'I suppose.' She sighs heavily. Then she smiles. 'So what about you, Roxy? Got a lovely man in your life?'

'Oh, well, er . . . not at the moment.' I feel my face

go from normal to pillar-box red in a matter of seconds.

Poppy smiles. 'Are you sure?'

'Well . . .' *Should I tell her about Jack?*

'Hey, listen, I don't mean to pry,' she says quickly.

'No, it's fine. It's just – well, it's all a little bit awkward. You see, my ex is actually here.'

Her eyes open wide in astonishment. '*Here?* Oh God, do you mean Alex? He's *such* a lovely guy. I knew he and his long-term fiancée had called off their engagement, which was why he decided to come here for Christmas. But I didn't realise it was you!'

'No, no, not Alex. It's – erm – Jackson.'

'Jackson?' She looks puzzled. 'Oh, *Jack!* Wow, you and Jack were an item?'

Nodding, I take a large gulp of wine. Unfortunately, I manage to breathe in simultaneously, the liquid goes down the wrong way and I start coughing furiously.

Poppy starts slapping me on the back until eventually my spluttering calms down enough to talk. 'It was really embarrassing the way it ended. On live TV.'

'*Live TV?*' Poppy looks horrified. 'What on earth happened, Roxy?'

So I tell her the story, which I haven't told anyone except Flo. And she nods and shows all the emotions – intrigue, amazement, shock – that I would expect. Except that she doesn't laugh, for which I'm really grateful. Because, so far, that's been the response of everyone who's recognised me as 'that poor girl off the telly'.

Those encounters made me feel wretched and stupid. But after I've unloaded it on Poppy, I actually feel better about the whole thing. I can see the funny side myself, instead of just feeling like the butt of the joke.

'Crikey, that was so brave of you,' she murmurs. 'I know *I* could never propose on live TV. No man's worth endangering your pride! Not even Jed.'

I grin. 'It wasn't brave, it was stupid. And alcohol played a massive part.'

'Well, maybe in retrospect it was a bit rash,' she agrees. 'But sometimes in life you have to take a risk. And you did! You and Jack, eh?' She shakes her head. 'So are you over him now?'

'Oh, yes.' My face is already so hot, I could probably fry eggs on it. So the lie sneaks through.

Poppy keeps shaking her head. 'What on earth did you think when you walked in and saw him at the dining table?'

'I nearly fainted. My life flashed before me and—'

'You dropped the trifle! Oh my God, I thought you were just a bit nervous!'

There's a ring at the door. Poppy frowns. 'They can't be back already.'

I listen to her socked feet padding along the hallway

to the front door. Then she's shrieking a greeting and welcoming some people inside – a man and a woman by the sounds of it.

My heart sinks a little. I've been having such a lovely time chatting to Poppy. Now I'll have to make polite chit-chat with a couple of people I've never met before. I decide I'll retreat to my bedroom as soon as I decently can and leave them to talk. That way, I can also avoid having to see Jackson and Sophie when they return. I can say I'm really tired after my early start, which is absolutely true . . .

The arrivals are Jed's brother, Ryan, and his girl-friend, Clemmy. They were supposed to be getting here tomorrow but decided to pitch up early for some reason. As soon as Clemmy bustles in, her scarlet coat flapping open around her ample curves, her heart-shaped face wreathed in smiles, I find myself relaxing. When Poppy introduces us, Clemmy heads straight across the room towards me, tripping over a coffee table leg but managing to stay upright.

'Careful,' says Poppy with a giggle.

'Oops! What am I like?' laughs Clemmy, pushing back her abundant reddish-brown locks.

'The world's most accident-prone woman?' grins Ryan. I can tell from his slightly goofy expression that he adores her.

'Delighted to meet you, Roxy,' she says, enveloping

me in a big, perfumed hug. 'Poppy tells me you've saved her life with your wonderful mince pies!'

I smile at her. 'Well, I wouldn't go that far.'

'*I* would,' says Poppy firmly.

'Well, I can't wait to try them!' beams Clemmy.

Poppy opens another bottle of wine and brings through a plate of the mince pies in question. Clemmy promptly tries one and says it's so delicious, she absolutely has to go back for seconds.

I laugh, feeling absurdly pleased. 'They *are* quite small. I think you need at least two to really appreciate them!'

Clemmy nods. 'I couldn't agree more.'

I sit and listen to Poppy and Clemmy chattering nineteen to the dozen about their plans for Christmas, while Ryan injects a good-humoured comment every now and again, when he can actually get a word in edgeways.

Ryan's quite different to Jed in appearance. While Jed is tall with thick, dark chestnut hair, Ryan is shorter with close-cropped blond hair and more of a rugby player's build. Their dry sense of humour is the same, though.

At one point, the focus turns to me, and whether my family mind that I'm working at Christmas, and I explain that Mum and Dad have decided to go somewhere warm for a change this year.

Then I hear a key in the lock and my heart lurches into my throat. I've left it too late to escape to my room!

In the commotion that follows, with everyone greeting each other, I fix on a smile and start making my way towards the stairs. Hoping to avoid announcing to all and sundry that I'm off to bed, I murmur this to Poppy and she smiles and tells me to sleep well.

'See you in the morning, Roxy,' she calls, as I'm half way up the stairs.

I turn to reply but, instead of meeting Poppy's gaze, it's Jackson's face I immediately zero in on. Sophie is clutching onto his arm and saying something laughingly into his ear. But Jackson is staring up at me with a look of such open affection in his eyes that my heart lurches. For a second, it feels just like old times, when we were together.

Then someone laughs and I'm snapped back to reality.

Pulling myself together, I smile weakly at Poppy. 'Yes. See you then. I'll be up nice and early to get started.'

Turning, I manage to make it up the rest of the stairs without stumbling, despite the suspicion that Jackson's eyes are following me all the way . . .

Chapter 10

The room Poppy has given me is lovely. It's all white walls, soft cream carpet and pale grey shabby chic – from the king-size bed frame and headboard to the free-standing wardrobe and chest of drawers.

After taking a quick shower in the en suite, I put on the pretty pink pyjama set Poppy has laid out on the bed for me, smiling at the way the sleeves and the bottoms are a little too short for my long limbs. Then I dive into the comforting folds of the crisp white bed linen.

Propping up the pillows, I relax back and glance around the room. It's elegant and yet it feels cosy, too – just like the rest of the Log Fire Cabin – but I can't help wondering if I've made a big mistake, agreeing to stay here over the Christmas period. When Jackson is staying here, too . . .

Breathing deeply in an effort to calm myself down, I detect the subtle aroma of lavender and when I glance at the bedside cabinet, I see there's a scented candle on there in a crystal holder, sitting beside a small stack of *The People's Friend*. I smile, thinking of Sophie's disgust, and imagining Poppy's amusement as she placed them there for me.

Lavender is credited with magical sleep-inducing properties. But the benefits seem to be bypassing me completely. It's long after midnight before I finally feel myself drifting off . . .

I'm trapped in a room, staring at nothing but inky-black darkness. The air is thick and acrid and I'm fighting to breathe.

Even as I fumble blindly for the door, finally locating the cold metal handle, I know it will be locked. I can hear someone moving around on the other side and my heart leaps in hope. But when I try to shout for help, no sound emerges.

Panic surges like a scream in my ears.

It feels as if a pillow is being pressed against my face, suffocating me. I try to claw at it but, with a sickening shock, I realise there's nothing there. My heart crashes against my ribcage as the terrifying truth dawns.

I'm going to die . . .

I hear music. Faint at first, it grows louder – a monotonous jingle playing over and over again. The pitch-black darkness gives way to grey shapes – shapes I begin to recognise. And I realise the sound I'm hearing is the morning alarm on my phone.

Shivering, I emerge from the nightmare, drawing in great gulps of air and clutching my throat. Warm tears slide into my hair as I stare up at the bedroom ceiling, waiting for my heart rate to return to normal.

After a while, I glance at the clock and realise I need to get up. But my limbs feel heavy as I force myself out of bed and head for the shower. It always takes a while to feel normal again after one of these horrible, recurring nightmares . . .

After showering and dressing, I go in search of Poppy.

She's not in the kitchen, so I climb the stairs to her room, noticing on my way that it's started to snow. Large flakes are drifting down past the window and, when I look out, I see it's starting to settle prettily on the branches of the fir trees. Staring at the Christmas card view from the half-way landing window, I suddenly spot Poppy outside.

Hunched into a big padded coat, she's walking along the lake's edge, staring out across the flat grey water. I run back down to the kitchen and I'm about to knock on the window, but something about the way she's now standing, shoulders slumped, stops me. Perhaps she's still not feeling well.

The snow is falling more heavily now and she must be getting wet but she doesn't appear to notice. She turns at that moment and waves when she sees me standing at the window. Then she crunches quickly back over the snow-crusted grass to the French windows.

I open the door for her. 'Ooh, you must be freezing. Shall I make you a coffee to warm up?'

'That would be lovely,' she says, stamping her welly boots on the mat.

I busy myself with the kettle. 'How are you feeling today?'

I catch her dejected look when I turn, but she immediately fixes on a smile. 'Oh, much better, thanks. I'll just go and take these wet things off.' And she disappears.

We drink our coffee, chatting about the order for tomorrow, and Poppy, who's still looking really tired, says, 'As long as we start baking by twelve, we should get the order done easily between us.'

'But are you sure you're okay?'

'Oh, yes, I'm fine. It wasn't the kedgeree at all.' She swallows and gives me an odd look. And then Alex comes into the kitchen at that moment and says he's going skating if anyone's interested.

Poppy suppresses a yawn. 'I'm going back to bed for a while. But Roxy could do with a lesson or two.'

'Or twenty,' says Alex, leaning back onto the breakfast bar and folding his arms.

'Times by a hundred,' agrees Poppy.

'What cheek!' I pretend to be massively insulted. 'I'll have you know I'd be a total natural. If I'd been christened Jane Torvill.'

'Have fun.' Poppy gives a little wave, collects her cup and heads upstairs. I watch her go, wondering if she needs someone to talk to. But I don't really feel I can ask. She is my boss, after all.

So instead, I accept Alex's offer to manoeuvre me around the ice.

It turns out I'm much better at it this time.

Well, when I say 'much better', what I really mean is: this time, I'm able to stand on the ice for a full minute before fright makes my knees start to feel as useless as a chocolate fire guard.

Alex makes it fun, though, keeping up a daft running commentary as if we're skating in the Olympics.

'So how's the situation with Jackson?' he asks.

I jerk backwards a little but he steadies me. 'We've – um – had a chat and we're fine.'

'Sophie's . . . interesting. She couldn't be more different to you.'

I laugh. 'You mean she looks like a stunning supermodel.'

He shoots me a look. 'I didn't mean that. Although she is exceptionally beautiful, I'll grant you.' There's a pause, then he says, 'You don't have much confidence in yourself, do you?'

An image sails into my head – Billy giving me the devastating news that meant our relationship was over – but I push it away and plaster on a smile. 'Neither would you if you'd made a plonker of yourself on live TV.'

'Hey, you don't have the monopoly on making an arse of yourself, you know.' He grins. 'I've wished for the floor to swallow me up on many an occasion.'

Afterwards, we grab a hot drink at the coffee stall and Alex gets us two spare seats from separate tables that are spread out over the grass. We sit hunched in our coats, warming our hands on the paper cups, and somehow we end up talking about our first serious relationships. Well, Alex does. I neatly evade the subject of my own disaster with Billy by joking that I come out in a rash at the mere mention of his name.

'We weren't right for each other. I can see that now,' says Alex, obviously quite happy to talk about his own first love, a girl called Judith who he met at uni. 'She didn't get my sense of humour at all and she hated stepping out of her comfort zone. I kept wondering if she'd be fun to grow old with.'

'Really?'

'Yes, I mean, what if I wanted to throw caution to the wind and go backpacking in Outer Mongolia at the age of seventy-three?' He grins. 'Would Judith throw a wobbly and insist I stay at home to creosote the fence?'

I start to laugh. Then, as we're getting up to go, I spot who's heading towards us, and my heart does a leapfrog in my chest.

It's Jackson and Sophie, arm in arm. She's smiling up at him, her razor-sharp cheekbones aloft with bliss, as if she's just been told the wonderful news that eating chocolate counteracts the calories in cake. Jackson cups her face in his hands and tenderly kisses the tip of her nose, and my heart contracts painfully because he used to do that to me too.

They're so wrapped up in one another, they don't even notice Alex and me until we practically bump into them.

Sophie's smile snaps out like a light when she sees me, which makes me wonder if Jackson has told her we used to be an item. Or maybe she's just the sort of girl who hates any sort of female competition.

In the split second before Jackson and Alex start bantering about who's better on the ice, his eyes swivel from me to Alex and back again.

Then Sophie is dragging Jackson onto the ice. 'Come on, darling. Let's practise our routine for the pairs competition. We need to get it absolutely right.'

I really don't want to watch them but some masochistic tendency keeps my feet pinned to the ground.

Alex grins appreciatively as Jackson and Sophie skate to opposite ends of the rink, then on Sophie's signal start skating towards each other, building up speed, until they meet in the middle and perform a spectacular spin, hands gripping each other's waists. They circle on the spot for so long, I feel quite dizzy just watching them. Then they wrap their arms around each other and skate several times round the rink, performing lots of cute moves and semi-lifts.

'Not bad,' laughs Alex when, flushed and smiling, they join us at the side of the rink.

'Yes. Very good,' I add hurriedly, while actually experiencing a disturbing urge to get on the ice and 'accidentally' collide with Sophie so she lands with a crash on her dinky *derrière*.

Try as I might, I just can't help the desire to escape their joy as fast as social etiquette allows. So, leaving Alex chatting, I head off along the path round the lake, not looking back, feeling dangerously close to tears. I would never have signed up for this if I'd known I would have to face Jackson and his new girlfriend at odd hours of every day!

Alex catches me up when I'm almost at the cabin. 'Sorry. Got held up.' He grins, slightly out of breath from running after me. 'Sophie wanted to know what pre-skating "fuel" I'd taken on board.'

In spite of myself, I find myself smiling. 'Are you an

aeroplane? What did you tell her? I doubt she'd approve of a nice big plate of Coco Pops.'

'Oh God, I didn't mention *them*. I just said that, as far as fuel goes, I happen to be a diesel man.'

'Did she laugh?' I ask, laughing.

'No, she just looked at me strangely and suggested I should take my diet seriously if I don't want to keel over before I'm sixty.'

'She does have a point.'

'I know. And I do eat my veg. But man cannot live on liquidised broccoli alone.'

'Very true. We should be aiming for a *balanced* diet.'

He grins. 'A beer in both hands. Absolutely.'

When I open the door, I hear the clanking of saucepans in the kitchen. Poppy must be up and about.

'Right, I'm off back to the hotel,' says Alex.

I glance at him in surprise. 'Did you just walk me home?'

He shrugs and I'm sure I spy a little bit of a blush. 'No big deal. Just wanted your company for a little longer, that's all.' He winks and heads off, back up the road.

'See you later,' I call after him, and he raises a hand without interrupting his stride.

I strip off my outdoor stuff and pad through to the kitchen in my socks. Poppy is preparing the beef for tonight's dinner. She turns and says, 'Hi, I thought I'd make an early start and get dinner prepared ahead of time. I don't know what you were thinking of making for dessert, but I've got the ingredients for a chocolate bombe here if you like?'

I glance at her, startled.

A chocolate bomb?

For one bizarre second, I think the bomb must be intended for Sophie.

'Have you made a chocolate bombe before?' Poppy asks.

'Er, no, actually. But if you give me the recipe, I'll have a – erm – I'll get it done no problem at all.'

She thumbs through a cookery book and slides it over. I'm relieved to see that bomb has an 'e' on the end. But I'm *not* relieved to see that a chocolate bombe is a very classy-looking dessert – the glossy kind served in Michelin-starred restaurants by waiters wearing white gloves. The one in the book is decorated with amber-coloured bits of something or other, described as 'shards' in the caption.

'Oh, don't worry about the sugar work,' says Poppy, catching my worried look. 'I know we haven't really got the time for fancy stuff. Just do the cake.'

'Right.' I give her an enthusiastic thumbs-up, while at the same time my heart sinks at the list of ingredients, which appears to be almost as long as my arm.

Thanks to YouTube, I can make a cake that involves flour, butter, sugar, eggs and possibly cocoa powder. But this concoction is altogether more sophisticated.

'Enjoy the skating?' Poppy asks. 'Alex is good company, isn't he?'

I smile. 'Yes, thank you. And yes, he is. He's very sweet.'

She gives me a knowing look and for a second I panic, wondering if she might be thinking of match-making, which is obviously the very *last* thing on my mind.

To change the subject more than anything, I blurt out, 'Are you sure you're up to this?' She might be feeling better but she still looks exhausted.

She glances at me in surprise, and for a moment, I think she's going to nod and say, 'Yes. Why wouldn't I be?'

But instead, she heaves a shaky sigh. Abandoning the ingredients in her bowl, to my horror, she leans over the counter, her face in her hands, shaking her head.

'What's wrong?' I'm by her side, but she just keeps shaking her head, not looking at me.

'Is it the job? Are you stressed about it?' I lay my hand gently on her back. 'Because I'm certain we can handle it between us.'

Tears are leaking out between her fingers.

'It's not the job,' she whispers at last. 'It's Jed. I don't think we're going to make it.'

I stare at her bent head. 'What do you mean? Don't you feel the same about him any more?'

Her voice cracks. 'That's the problem. I love him even more than I did at the start. But I'm just not sure he feels the same way about me.'

'Really?' My head whirls in confusion. 'But I've seen you together. It seems to me like Jed's crazy about you.'

'Appearances can be deceptive,' she says tightly.

I tear off some kitchen roll and she straightens up and blows her nose hard then dabs at her mascara. She's stopped crying, as if saying the words that have been weighing her down has released some kind of pressure.

'We've been together for two years,' she says, her voice still thick with tears. 'You'd think there would be *some* talk of the future, but there's nothing. In fact, it's worse than nothing because Jed avoids the subject altogether. We haven't even been away on holiday together – although he says that's because he's so busy at work. And we *definitely* have no plans to move in together. Whenever I so much as *hint* at it, he starts talking about something else. Every time. It's as if he doesn't want to make any commitment at all to me.'

She looks at me, her eyes full of hurt. 'And the thing is, that would be fine, as long as I thought his feelings on this would change at some point.' She shakes her head sadly. 'But I'm starting to think they never will. So what's the point?'

I stare at her, wanting to say the right thing. 'Two years isn't *that* long to be together. Perhaps Jed just wants to be sure . . .?' I grimace a little because it sounds feeble even to my ears.

'Yes, but I don't even feel I can leave clothes here. Plus, we haven't had sex for ages.'

'Maybe he *is* just really busy?'

She nods slowly. 'The architect's practice he took over from Bob is thriving but it means he has to work late. A lot. He's taken some time off to help me get prepared for Christmas. But usually, he just comes home, eats and falls asleep. So it sort of makes sense that we don't see each other during the week. There wouldn't be any point.'

'Well, there you are, then. You're worried over nothing. It's just life getting in the way – the way it always does.'

'Yes, but it's not just that . . .' Tears spring to her eyes again and I glimpse a flash of real panic in her face. 'I understand that you can't rush things in a relationship and I'd never want to put pressure on Jed to commit too soon. Christ, I'd be happy just going along like this, to be honest. It's just . . .'

'It's just what?'

The door opens and we both swing round.

It's Sophie, her shiny blonde hair swinging like a shampoo advert. Dressed in tiny purple shorts and a little white vest top that shows off her perfectly flat, tanned midriff, she jogs daintily into the kitchen.

'Hi, Poppy! Put this up on your fridge, will you?' Running on the spot and completely ignoring me, she hands over what looks like a large glossy photo. 'I'm thinking of signing to a modelling agency so I had some pictures taken, and I thought you could put one up on the fridge. You know, to stop you snacking and putting more weight on.'

Poppy glances at me then looks away quickly. 'Gosh, thanks, Sophie, how thoughtful of you,' she says.

Sophie shrugs modestly. 'Well, what's the point of being editor-in-chief of a popular woman's lifestyle magazine if you can't spread your knowledge and help people to improve themselves?'

I glance over Poppy's shoulder at the photo.

Sophie looks stunning. She's staring out to sea, reclining on a lounger on a sunny tropical beach, which is presumably a fake background in a photographer's studio. The bikini she's wearing is practically non-existent and shows off her magnificent body to perfection.

'You look great,' says Poppy, discreetly wiping her hands over her tear-tracked cheeks. 'But won't being a model clash with your job on the magazine? Being editor of such a popular publication must be fairly full-on, I imagine.'

An odd look comes over Sophie's face. '*Editor-in-chief*. Yes, it is. But I can handle it, no problem at all. As a matter of fact, my staff think I'm amazing. I heard my deputy telling someone I'm like Wonder Woman and Margaret Thatcher, rolled into one!'

'The Iron Lady,' murmurs Poppy, staring at her.

'What do you mean?' snaps Sophie, leaping straight on the defensive.

Poppy frowns. 'Margaret Thatcher's nickname was The Iron Lady?'

'Oh. Right. Well, anyway, if you could pin that up.'

I watch as Poppy obediently uses a fridge magnet to stick the photo in place.

It's impossible not to stare at it in awe. 'How on earth do you stay so slim?' I ask in wonder.

'It takes effort.' She assesses my figure. 'You'd never make a model because you're too top-heavy. You're tall enough, I suppose, but your legs are out of proportion to your body. They're too short.'

'Right.' I catch Poppy's eye and she pulls a cross-eyed face behind Sophie's back.

Sophie swings round. 'And you'll always have a tendency to put on weight, Poppy, especially if you carry on baking for a living.'

Poppy's smile freezes.

'But hey, cheer up!' Sophie stops jogging on the spot and does a few impromptu leg stretches. 'Even *ordinary* people can make a difference to the way they look by starting a health regime.' Her eyes light up. 'Actually I've decided I'm going to write a book called *The Way to a Heavenly Face and Body*. I've been planning a little presentation on it, so I could practise it on you all after dinner one night. How about that? You'll pick up loads of tips.'

'Well, I . . .' Poppy glances at me, looking about as enthusiastic as I'm feeling at this suggestion for post-dinner entertainment.

'Great! That's settled, then.' Sophie beams at her. 'You'll enjoy it. The book's going to be all about tackling those really troublesome areas.' Sophie's eyes flick across to me. Her eyes travel downwards, hover on my top-heaviness before landing on my pitifully short legs.

'Are you and Jackson looking forward to the pairs skating contest on Tuesday night?' Poppy asks.

'What? Oh, that. Yes, we've practised a little routine that's quite dramatic, actually. Jackson says I'll be the star of the show in my crystal-encrusted skating dress.' She gives a smug little smile. 'The beauty of being editor-in-chief is you get access to lots of lovely clothes! Right, going for my run. Toodles!' With a little wave, she jogs off.

Poppy looks thoroughly depressed. 'Bloody crystal-encrusted skating dress! Oh God, and a lecture on "The Way to a Heavenly Face and Body"?' She sighs. 'I just can't wait.'

I'm not feeling much perkier. 'I really could have done without that run-down of my physical failings. Especially by *her*!'

Poppy nods in sympathy. 'A tendency to plumpness, indeed! I mean, she's absolutely right, of course, but still . . .'

'It must be really hard work, though, staying that "perfect".' I use my fingers for quotes. 'At least we enjoy our food.'

'So you're saying I *am* plump?' demands Poppy, putting her hands on her hips. 'Well, I guess this is my watershed moment where I decide enough is enough and I need to go on a starvation diet so I can meet society's stringent but hugely debatable ideas on what female physical beauty actually is!'

'What?' I stare at her. 'No! I didn't mean . . .'

I catch the mischievous glint in her eye and we both burst out laughing.

'You're easy to wind up,' says Poppy. 'Of course I'm not going on a starvation diet. I'm not going on *any* diet because they don't work. You just end up putting it all back on again and a little bit more besides.'

I nod. 'Absolutely right.'

I pause, then add, 'I'd still love to look like *that*, though.'

We both stare gloomily at the photo on the fridge as I nurture fond thoughts of using Sophie as a dartboard.

Poppy doesn't reply and, when I look over, I'm shocked to see tears rolling down her face.

'Oh, Poppy, don't let Sophie get to you. I'm totally ignoring her remarks about my stumpy legs,' I lie.

'You haven't got short legs.'

'Well, you're not in the least bit plump! And I'm sure Jed thinks you're absolutely perfect just the way you are.'

To my alarm, this only serves to increase Poppy's sobbing.

'It's not Sophie,' she gasps between sobs.

She turns to me, her face full of anguish. 'Oh, Roxy, I've got myself into an impossible situation and I just don't know what I'm going to do.'

Chapter 11

'Hey, come on. Sit down.' I guide Poppy across to the breakfast bar by the window and she heaves herself onto one of the high stools. Grabbing more kitchen roll, I sit opposite and wait for her to calm down.

Finally, she looks up. But still she hesitates, as if she can't bring herself to say what's on her mind. Then she heaves a long, despairing sigh.

'I'm pregnant.'

Her words seem to reverberate around the room.

There's silence in the kitchen except for the clock on the wall, ticking out the seconds until I reply.

I'm not sure what to say. 'Oh, how wonderful!' doesn't exactly seem appropriate, given that Poppy is currently breaking her heart at the very idea of having a baby, so I simply reach across and lay my hand on hers.

She attempts a watery smile. 'Sorry. I shouldn't be loading this on you.'

'Of course you should. You can't keep something like that a secret. I take it Jed doesn't know?'

At the mention of his name, her face crumples again.

Oh, God, maybe it's not Jed's baby!

'He doesn't know.' She stares at me urgently. '*Please* don't tell him, Roxy!'

I shake my head. 'I won't breathe a word. I promise. It's up to you when you want to break the news.'

'I only found out yesterday. I did a test because I couldn't understand why my sickness bug wasn't going away.' There's a ghost of a smile on her tear-stained face as she lays a protective hand on her belly. 'I've always wanted to be a mum. And Jed will make the perfect dad.'

Relief trickles through me. *It is Jed's baby!*

'So . . . you're pleased, then?'

She heaves a sigh. 'My head's all over the place. Jed's made it clear he's not ready for the whole commitment thing, and I'm just really worried that, if I break the news that we're having a baby, he'll feel obliged to do the honourable thing and ask me to move in with him. He's such a lovely guy, I know that's what he'd do. But . . .' She swallows hard and stares miserably out of the window at the snow falling over the lake.

'But then you'd never know if he was with you because he really wanted to be,' I say slowly.

She turns and nods. 'I'd always be thinking he only wanted me because of the baby, and I don't think I could bear living like that.' She shrugs. 'The last thing I want to do is make the man I love feel trapped.'

I sigh. 'But you know you have to tell him, right?'

She looks up, her eyes full of panic. 'No! Absolutely not!'

'But what will you do? Wait and hope that he asks you to move in *before* he finds out about the baby?'

She shrugs.

'But that's crazy,' I say softly.

Poppy's chin wobbles but her look is determined. 'So I'm crazy.'

The front door opens and we hear voices in the hallway. Ryan says something in his deep voice and Clemmy starts laughing. They must be back, full of high spirits, after having lunch together in Guildford. Poppy quickly wipes her hands over her face and flicks at her hair, then goes to wash her hands at the sink.

We make a right pair. Here's Poppy thinking Jed doesn't care enough to make a commitment to her. And here I am *knowing* that's true of Jackson.

The familiar ache is still there, no matter how much I've tried to ignore it. *Will I ever be able to think of Jackson without feeling that my world ended in that blasted TV studio?*

A second later, my hopes that Clemmy and Ryan will walk straight past the kitchen door are dashed.

'Hi, folks!' Clemmy bursts in, her face radiant with happiness. And possibly wine. 'Ooh, it always smells so gorgeous in here. Doesn't it, Ryan?'

'Good lunch?' I ask.

Her smile widens. 'Blissful, thank you, Roxy.' She flicks a coy glance at Ryan. 'And I'm not just talking about the food and the company.'

Ryan is wandering over to the pan with the home-made mince pie filling and peering in.

'Don't you dare,' says Clemmy, laughing.

'Just looking.' Ryan turns and holds up his hands, grinning. 'Honest.'

'Actually, it should be *me* holding up my hand,' says Clemmy. She has her hands very obviously behind her back and looks as if she's about to burst with excitement.

'Ta-dah!' She produces her left one with a theatrical flourish. 'We only got *engaged*!'

There's a beat of silence.

'Oh, wow, that's fantastic!' I burst out, as Ryan comes to stand beside her, smiling bashfully. 'Isn't that great, Poppy?'

I glance at her nervously.

But she manages a broad smile. 'That is the best news ever. Congratulations, you two!'

She walks over and hugs them both. Then Clemmy rushes over and hugs me, too, and the atmosphere is charged with emotion.

'We'll have to have a party to celebrate,' says Poppy.

Clemmy sighs with pleasure. 'Could I be any happier?'

Ryan puts his arm round her, a proud grin on his face. 'Clem actually went down on one knee in the restaurant.'

'*You* asked *him*?' Poppy's mouth drops open. 'Good for you, girl!'

I try to nod with enthusiasm but it's not easy with images of my own disastrous proposal playing in my head like a horror movie.

'Yep. We went and picked out a ring straight after. And she's already made plans to go wedding dress shopping,' Ryan says. 'I have a feeling you two might be roped in.'

'Just try stopping me!' says Poppy brightly, her smile pinned in place, and I can feel her pain. 'If you could just excuse me for one second while I grab my phone from the other room.'

Hurrying out, she calls back, 'Such amazing news! I'm so happy for you!' before the door clicks shut behind her.

I hear Poppy's footsteps running up the stairs, although thankfully, the lovebirds are far too wrapped up in the moment to notice.

* * *

I escape upstairs as soon as I can.

Poppy is sitting on top of her bed, propped up on pillows, looking pasty-faced and sad. When she sees me, she grimaces. 'God, I'm so sorry, Roxy. You must think you've come to work for a complete fruit loop! I'm not usually like this, honestly. I think it must be pregnancy hormones.'

'How far along are you?' I ask, sitting on the end of the bed. 'Have you worked it out?'

She smiles bitterly, rubbing her temples. 'Since sex is a bit of a rarity these days, I've been able to pinpoint the exact day. I'm six weeks and four days.'

'Headache?'

She nods. 'It's really thumping. I'm so pleased for Ryan and Clemmy. I love them both and they're so good together. But . . .' She swallows hard, unable to continue.

I smile sadly in sympathy and she says, 'By the way, I keep meaning to say, I don't know how you're surviving here.'

'What do you mean?'

'Well, if I'd turned up at a strange place and realised I had to serve food to and practically live with my ex, I think I'd have totally freaked out and run a mile by now.'

I smile wryly. 'I did consider that. But you were so stressed out about the job, I didn't want to leave you in the lurch.'

She puts her head on one side and smiles at me, her eyes filling with tears.

'Hey, don't go getting all emotional on me, now. I needed the job and I will survive the experience!'

'Thank you, Roxy. I'm so grateful. I've been so wrapped up in my own stuff, I didn't really think about how bad it must be for you. I would totally understand if you couldn't stick another minute here. Really, I would.'

It would be so easy to agree with her and call it quits, especially now I know Poppy understands exactly why I'd be leaving. But something is stopping me, although I'm not quite sure what.

'You know what? Bugger Jackson Cooper! Why should I let a man scare me away from a job I'm enjoying!'

She beams. 'Hey, good for you. And listen, there's someone far better than Jackson out there for you, I'm certain of it.'

I smile dutifully. I wish I could be so sure of that.

'He's the loser in all this.' She shakes her head. 'Imagine choosing stick insect Sophie over you. The man's an idiot.'

I laugh. 'I appreciate your support. I really do. But I think there might be lots of men out there who'd totally disagree with you.'

She sighs grumpily. 'Well, if that's the case, the world must be full of shallow, idiotic men!'

Chapter 12

My chocolate bombe is not going well.

In fact, looking at the shape of it, fresh out of the oven on the cooling rack, it's less 'chocolate bombe' and rather more 'brown sludge cow pat'. Why has it gone so *flat?*

I glance at the clock. Have I got time to have another go?

But it's already nearly seven and Poppy wants to serve dinner at eight. I'd be cutting it really fine. Unless . . . unless I make lots of chocolate icing and pile it high on top to make up for the shortfall in the height of the cake?

This seems like a good idea so I rush around gathering the ingredients. Everyone likes chocolate butter icing, don't they?

The butter is hard from the fridge so I bung it in the microwave for a bit to soften it. When it emerges, it's still hard as a lump of granite in the middle while the edges are starting to pool into liquid. But I dump the whole lot into a bowl anyway then pour icing sugar on top. *What the dinner guest doesn't see . . .*

Blending in the icing sugar and cocoa powder seems to be an art in itself. The way I do it is clearly the wrong way because puffs of the stuff rise up everywhere. It's a very messy business indeed and, soon, there appears to be more of it on the work surface than in the bowl. But I've made a whole load of chocolate icing, so there should be enough . . .

I've just finished dolloping the lot on top of the cake and fashioning it into a dome shape when Poppy walks into the kitchen, looking a bit better. At least she has some colour in her cheeks now.

She stares at my unique take on a chocolate bombe. 'Wow. Interesting. I've never seen it made quite like that before.'

'Oh, yes, I always present it like this.' Warmth suffuses my cheeks. 'The chocolate icing really – um – complements the cake bit.'

I study it anxiously. If only the great mound of icing wasn't actually leaning slightly to one side, as if trying to slide off altogether with embarrassment.

Poppy's head is on one side, looking at the cake. 'Actually, do you know what would make it even better? If we take off just *some* of the icing?'

I nod. 'Excellent idea. I suppose the ratio of cake to icing is – erm – a little out of proportion.'

Poppy quickly takes a palette knife, smooths off the top four inches and drops it into a bowl. 'There.' She stands back and nods approvingly. 'Perfect.' She dips her finger in the bowl and licks icing from her finger. 'Mmm. Lovely.'

'Yes, that's much better,' I agree. 'It's obvious who the real cook is around here.'

She grins. 'Don't be so modest, Roxy. You're brilliant.' She nods at the new-look dessert, which – being flat as a pancake – now resembles a cow pat even more closely than before. 'I'm sure *that* will go down a *bombe* with everyone.'

'Boom boom!' My nervous cackle makes me sound like a witch.

I persuade Poppy to let me tell everyone she has a bad headache and is lying down.

'Don't worry. I'll serve up,' I rashly announce, sounding far more confident than I actually feel. In reality, I'm quaking inside. Just the thought of Jackson's smile following me around the table as I deliver the starters makes me go all fluttery and breathless. I wonder if he really has told Sophie we used to be together? Even if he hasn't, she'd probably still look at me frostily, as if I'm a slightly unhygienic pet who might jump up at her at any moment.

I can tell Poppy is relieved she doesn't have to sit through the happy chat at dinner.

The talk is *all* of Ryan and Clemmy's engagement.

Luckily, Jackson is sitting on the same side of the table as me so I don't have to worry about meeting his eye.

Jackson himself doesn't seem at all bothered that I've hijacked his Christmas break by turning up here so unexpectedly. After our initial awkward meeting, he's been quite laid-back about my presence. I just wish I could feel the same way.

In the kitchen, I put the finishing touches to Poppy's main course, and Clemmy helps me to bring the dishes out.

Sophie looks dismayed when I put down her plate. 'Oh, red meat?' She's sitting on my left with Jackson on her other side. 'Did you know meat sits in your gut for about a hundred and fifty days after you've eaten it?'

'Would you like me to get you something else?' I ask.

'Such as?'

I rack my brains, trying to think what's available. Oh God, I'm supposed to be a cook! I should be able to provide an alternative dish if requested.

'Erm, beans and sausages on toast?' There was definitely a tin of those in the cupboard. 'With a twist of cracked black pepper?' I add, in an attempt to make it sound sophisticated.

Someone makes a noise that sounds suspiciously like a snigger, and turns it into a cough.

Sophie stares at me as if I'm something nasty on her shoe and doesn't even bother to answer. Carefully sawing off about one square inch of meat, she pushes the rest firmly to the side of her plate.

Alex catches my eye and my mouth curves up in silent response. For an awful second, I think I might get an attack of the giggles and not be able to stop, so I have to look away quickly and think of something tragic.

Abandoned kittens.

By the time we reach the dessert course, I'm starting to feel very nervous about my chocolate bombe.

Apparently, I had every right to be.

When I place it in the centre of the table, Sophie takes one look and starts to laugh. 'Christ, what's that? A flattened manure heap?'

'That's quite funny for you,' comments Jackson.

'Oi!' Sophie sends a razor-sharp glance his way. 'I'll have you know I'm renowned in the boardroom for my wit and playful good humour!'

I catch Alex's eye and his eyebrows rise fractionally.

'Well, I vote we give it a wide berth altogether. It's obviously got enough sugar in it to kill everyone.' She shudders delicately.

'I think that might be a *bit* of an exaggeration,' says Jackson wryly. 'Although I have to agree it has an air of the dung heap about it.' He peers round Sophie and grins at me. 'It reminds me of that—'

He suddenly remembers where he is and stops.

My heart is beating fast as I rise, with a face like a burning furnace, to cut the blasted thing into pieces. I know exactly what Jackson was going to say. I once attempted a chocolate sponge cake that sank almost without trace when it came out of the oven. So I slathered it in chocolate icing and tried to pass it off as a tray bake.

'It reminds you of that *what*?' demands Sophie, looking sharply from me to Jackson and back at me.

I groan inwardly as I cut into the dung heap, which actually turns out to be surprisingly light in texture. I just want to run away, it's all so bloody awkward.

'Well I, for one, can't wait to try it,' says Alex. 'And thank you, Roxy, for making my favourite Australian dessert! I didn't think you were paying attention when I told you about it.'

I glance at him, wondering if I'm actually losing my mind.

Maybe nerves are killing off my brain cells, because I have no recollection whatsoever of discussing desserts with Alex. We've talked about lots of other things – but definitely not Australian puddings!

'It's an Ayers Rock Ganache,' says Alex casually, addressing Sophie. 'My granny used to make it all the time, and I have to say, you've reproduced the look brilliantly, Roxy.'

I gulp. 'That's – erm – great! I'm so glad, Alex.'

He smiles and nods. 'My granny would be impressed. A large piece for me, please.'

When I hand him his plate, I give him a big smile of gratitude.

Sophie looks a little sceptical at the 'Ayers Rock Ganache' but at least it silences her. And actually, the cake turns out to be surprisingly moreish, once everyone gets over its scary appearance, with Ryan, Clemmy and Alex going back for seconds.

'Should you be eating that?' says Sophie suddenly, as Clemmy tucks into her second slice with gusto.

Clemmy pauses with a forkful half way to her mouth.

'I should have thought you'd want to slim down for your Big Day. Isn't that what all brides-to-be do?'

There's a brief and rather awkward silence.

'Why would she want to lose weight?' asks Ryan, looking genuinely puzzled. 'She's perfect as she is.'

Clemmy flushes. 'Aw, thanks, you.' She nudges Ryan and pops the food into her mouth. 'Maybe I ought to try and get fit, though. I keep meaning to. Perhaps I'll start running.'

'Really?' Ryan glances at her in surprise.

Clemmy smiles, remaining remarkably good-natured considering Sophie's just told her she's fat. 'Sophie has a point. A wedding is the ideal time to start a health and fitness kick.'

'Precisely,' says Sophie smugly. 'Although, really, the pursuit of fitness should be an everyday thing. Not just for special occasions.'

'Well, maybe I'll start tomorrow,' says Clemmy, ever eager to please.

Sophie nods. 'Well, no bride wants to *wobble* down the aisle, do they?'

'*Sophie!*' murmurs Jackson.

'What?' She swings round to him in indignation. 'What have I said?'

He sighs. 'It isn't *every* woman's goal in life to be a size six! And actually, I agree with Ryan. Clemmy looks great as she is.'

Clemmy flushes. 'Thank you, Jackson. That's lovely.' She turns appeasingly to Sophie. 'But I think I will start being more active.'

Sophie gives Jackson a 'there, told you so' sort of look. Then her eyes light up. 'Ooh, I know! How about we feature you in the magazine? When were you thinking of getting married, Clemmy?'

'Oh, probably not until next Christmas.'

'Perfect! So that gives you plenty of time to get in shape using my new fitness regime. We could run lots of "before" and "after" photos. And my new book would get a lovely plug!' She frowns. 'Mind you, you'd have to make sure you kept the weight off so that the wedding day pictures look stunning.' She smiles at Clemmy. 'What do you think?'

'Oh, well, I'm not sure.' Clemmy looks less than thrilled at the prospect of featuring in *Dazzle*.

'Where are you doing it?' Sophie asks.

'Sorry?'

'Where's the venue?'

'Somewhere nice and cheap,' grins Ryan.

Clemmy admonishes him jokily with a look. 'We were thinking the registry office and Jed kindly suggested we could have the reception here, in a marquee.' She smiles at Jed.

'Oh, no, surely not!' Sophie looks appalled. 'It's your big day. You can't spend it in someone else's *house*!'

Clemmy laughs and glances around. 'Well, it's a bit more than just a house . . .'

Sophie leans forward. 'Where would you get married if you could choose any venue?'

Clemmy hesitates, quailing under the pressure.

'Go on. Use your imagination. Anywhere in Britain! Where would it be?'

'Anywhere in Britain?' says Clemmy. 'Oh, well, that's easy. Maple Tree Manor. I went to a friend's wedding there and it was absolutely glorious. But it's *way* out of our league.'

'Maple Tree Manor?' Ryan whistles. 'We'd have to take out a small mortgage just to pay for the food!'

Sophie frowns up at the ceiling, thinking.

Then she focuses on Clemmy with a bright smile. 'Okay, do the magazine feature –' She pauses for effect '– and the company will *cover the cost of the venue and the food*. You'll have a free wedding at Maple Tree Manor, the venue of your dreams!' Sophie sits back with an air of triumph and folds her arms, not once taking her eyes off Clemmy's face.

Clemmy turns brick red with confusion. She looks at Ryan, who shrugs his shoulders. He's such an easygoing guy, I'm guessing he doesn't mind either way and is happy to leave the decision to his fiancée.

'That sounds amazing,' says Clemmy slowly, turning back to Sophie. 'But can you do that?'

Sophie laughs. 'Of course I can. I'm the *editor-in-chief*. I get the final decision on everything.'

Clemmy swallows, looking torn. 'I don't know. I mean, it sounds wonderful. But I'm – I'm not sure I'm brave enough to appear in the magazine. Would I have to take my clothes off for the "before" pictures?'

'No, no, of course not. We'd probably just need shots of you at the gym or in your running gear.'

Clemmy laughs nervously. 'I'll need to *get* some running gear first!'

'Don't do it if you don't want to, Clemmy,' says Jed, and there's a murmur of agreement around the table.

Tentatively, Clemmy says, 'Could we – Ryan and I – have time to think about it, Sophie?'

'Sure.' Sophie shrugs lightly. I glance at her profile. She sounds relaxed, but there's a certain steel about her mouth that suggests this feature idea of hers is important to her.

For the first time, I wonder how much pressure Sophie is under to keep *Dazzle* readers coming back for more. And also how much pressure there is for her to *look* the part of a beauty and fashion magazine editor-in-chief. She represents everything that *Dazzle* has to offer in the way of style and sophistication. I guess a day in tracksuit bottoms, a hoodie and no make-up isn't often an option for her.

Clemmy flashes Ryan a look that reveals she's a bit scared but excited at the same time.

'I'd love to see Maple Tree Manor,' I say. 'Is it far from here?'

Clemmy shakes her head. 'Just about twenty miles.' Her eyes light up. 'We could go there and have a look around. You, me and Poppy.' Her eyes flick to Sophie. 'And you as well, of course, Sophie,' she says swiftly.

'Uh oh, looks like it might be on, then, Sophie,' smiles Ryan.

Clemmy digs him playfully in the ribs. 'I've not decided yet. But there's no harm in looking, is there?'

I grin at her. 'Absolutely not.'

'Would *you* ever propose to someone, Roxy?' she asks, beaming across the table at me.

I stop chewing in shock. *Where on earth did that come from?*

The room falls silent as my head whirls madly around. I'm painfully aware of Jackson sitting on the other side of Sophie. I really could have done without this reminder of my night of shame.

Clemmy's face falls. 'Sorry, Roxy, I didn't mean to ask such a personal question. That's just me and my foot-in-mouth problem.'

I shake my head. 'No, no, it's fine. You just caught me off guard, that's all.' I glance at Alex, who's looking at me with a tense expression on his face. He's the only one here – apart from Jackson – who actually *knows* I've made a fool of myself in that respect.

I could tell the truth and embarrass everyone around the table, especially Jackson.

Or . . . I could show Jackson I'm completely over him by laughing it off.

I draw in a deep breath. Then slowly, I say, 'I *did* once propose to someone. But he turned me down.'

'Oh.' Clemmy gasps in horror.

'But then I woke up and it turned out to be just a scary nightmare!'

Everyone laughs with relief. All except Jackson, who – when I flick a glance in his direction – is just staring grimly down at his plate. For just a second, I feel a surge of victory over him. Just for once, it's *him* who's feeling awkward, not me!

'I just can't believe,' says Clemmy, 'that I actually plucked up the courage to ask Ryan the question in the first place. I never thought I could be that brave.'

'It was brave all right!' says Jed with feeling. Then he grins and raises his glass to her.

I glance at Jed curiously. Does he mean *he* wouldn't be brave enough to propose to Poppy? Or does he just not believe in marriage? There's definitely something going on there.

Clemmy puts her palms to her hot cheeks and smiles radiantly around the table. 'But I'm so glad I did it now.'

She turns to Ryan. 'Imagine how awful it would have been if I asked you and you said no. Honestly, I'd have wanted to *die*!'

'I'd never have said no, Clem.' Ryan takes her hand, gazing at her with an adoring smile. 'I think you knew that. Otherwise you wouldn't have asked.'

'Well, maybe.' Clemmy snuggles happily into his shoulder.

I glance quickly at Jackson. He's sitting back in his chair looking perfectly relaxed, whereas all this talk of proposals is making my temperature soar – and not in a good way.

I stare down at my lap, feeling sick. We're only a fortnight into December, which means I've got another *eleven days* of this awkwardness to endure.

It could turn out to be the longest Christmas ever . . .

Chapter 13

The next day, I get up earlier than usual and drive to the flat to collect clothes and essentials for the rest of my stay at the Log Fire Cabin.

Flo has already flown off on holiday and the place feels oddly cold and a bit bleak. It makes me suddenly glad I'm spending Christmas elsewhere – even if it *is* with Jackson Cooper!

On the drive back, my mind turns to the morning ahead.

It's the day after the chocolate bombe disaster – and, unfortunately for me, another day means another dessert. I mention to Poppy that I'm thinking of making an apple crumble for tonight and she nods thoughtfully and says, 'That sounds good, Roxy. Although I'm sure you could dream up something a little more exciting that shows off your culinary flair at its very best!'

'Erm, right,' I croak, nodding.

Hiding my panic-stricken face, I bend down to the oven to check the latest batch of mince pies.

Bugger!

Apple crumble is the only pud I've learned to make. But Poppy thinks it's too dull.

What the hell am I going to do?

She's going to find out I'm an absolute fraud and then our blossoming friendship will be over. The thought of this makes me feel quite sad. We've only known each other a few days but I feel as if we've been friends for a long time. I *so* don't want to let her down . . .

At lunchtime, when Poppy drives to the supermarket for fresh supplies, I slip into my coat and wander outside, crunching across the frost-covered grass to the lake with a mug of tea in one hand and a ham sandwich in the other. The snow that fell yesterday didn't lie but the forecasters are predicting heavy falls later in the week.

I stare across the water, hoping for inspiration. Poppy told me to text her with any ingredients I need for tonight's dessert – but I've no idea what I'm making, so I can't.

'Penny for them?' I jump as Alex's voice cuts across my mounting panic.

I turn and he says, 'Sorry. Didn't mean to scare you.'

'I was far away,' I tell him gloomily. 'Trying to decide

whether to attempt to make chocolate fudge cake or opt for the alternative.'

'Which is?' He cocks his head on one side.

'Run for the hills. Because, let's face it, anything fancy I attempt is going to be a disaster.'

'It might not be.'

I cross my eyes at him. 'Two words. Chocolate bombe.'

Alex laughs. 'Probably best to stick to what you know.'

'But I only know two recipes. Victoria sandwich cake and apple crumble.'

'So make an apple crumble. I love that. It's my favourite.'

'Poppy thinks it's not adventurous enough.' I heave a despondent sigh.

Alex nods slowly. 'So . . . do them both.'

I stare at him. 'What do you mean?'

'Make a cake with apples and slap some crumble on top.'

I laugh. 'Wow, you make it sound unbelievably tempting.' But my mind is ticking over. I'm not convinced it will work but, since I can't think of anything better, it's probably worth a try.

'Help me out? Please?' I beg, and he shrugs and follows me back into the kitchen. 'I need to check if we have the ingredients.'

'Okay, what do you need?' He rubs his hands together then picks a couple of dessert apples from the fruit bowl. 'We 'ev ze apples. Now we need ze flou-eerrr and ze butt-eeerrr.'

I dash to the cupboard, giggling at his terrible French accent, suddenly feeling so much better. With Alex's help, maybe – just maybe – I can rescue the situation and come up with something edible!

Soon we have a variety of ingredients assembled, although Alex keeps 'helpfully' producing other stuff from the cupboard.

'A leetle Worcester Sauce perhaps? Or a dash of maple syrup?'

I shake my head. 'Stop making me laugh. This is serious. I've got to get it done before Poppy gets back.'

'Okay, my leetle slave driv-errrr.'

'Actually, that's not a bad idea,' I say, grabbing the bottle of maple syrup from his hand and plucking a jar of cinnamon from the cupboard. We use cinnamon with apples in the mince pies and they go together so well. Maybe this combination will raise my crumble cake to delicious heights, too!

'Nuts?' says Alex.

'You definitely are!'

'Not me. These.' He tosses me a bag and I squeal, just managing to catch it.

'Pecan nuts. Nice. Hey, I think we're getting somewhere.'

He grins. 'We make a good team.'

'We do.' I smile shyly at him and my heart does a funny little leap – probably with relief because I'm no longer doing this on my own.

The door opens and Jackson walks in. 'Sounds like *someone's* having fun in here. Can anyone join the party?'

I glance at Alex and we grin sheepishly at each other.

'Alex was just helping me with tonight's dessert,' I tell Jackson, feeling slightly deflated at the interruption.

'Well, now that I've given you the benefit of my massive expertise,' quips Alex, heading for the door, 'I'll leave you to it, Roxy.' He turns at the door with a smile that doesn't quite reach his eyes and leaves the kitchen.

And I stand there awkwardly with Jackson. It's strange but I feel a little guilty – almost as if I shouldn't have let Jackson see how much fun I was having with Alex. Which is ridiculous, of course, because Alex and I are just friends and I have nothing to feel guilty about . . .

'I didn't know you were such a great baker, Roxy,' says Jackson, surveying the ingredients on my worktop.

I smile up at him and decide to brazen it out. 'Oh, yes. My crumble cake has won prizes. You're in for a treat tonight.'

'Right. Well, I'd better let you get on. And can I say

I'm *very* much looking forward to my dessert, Roxy.'
He gives me one of his dazzlingly white smiles and the
hint of *double entendre* in his tone makes my cheeks
sizzle.

At the door, he pauses. 'Glad to see you're getting on
so well with Alex,' he remarks with a raised eyebrow
and walks out.

I stare at the closed door and almost want to laugh.
Is Jackson jealous?

Thinking about Alex and me bantering away, then
Jackson walking in on us, is making my head spin. I'm
feeling strangely fluttery inside and I've no idea why.
Unless it's just the weirdness of the situation.

But remembering I have to produce tonight's dessert
is more than enough to focus my mind – and soon,
I'm whipping up cake mix and adding chopped apples,
maple syrup, cinnamon and nuts to the mix. Then I
set to making the delicious crumble as a topping for
the cake. As a final touch, I finely slice another apple
and lay the segments in a pattern on top, then top with
a few knobs of butter and a generous sprinkling of
brown sugar.

Then I pop my concoction into the oven and cross
my fingers firmly.

By the time I hear Poppy walk in through the front
door, the aroma of sugary, buttery apples and cinnamon
wafting through the house is unbelievable. I just want

to try a slice now! I only hope it looks as good as it tastes.

'Gosh, that smells absolutely gorgeous,' says Poppy as soon as she walks in. 'What is it?'

I'm in the process of taking the cake out of the oven and I freeze, thinking I should have thought of a name for it. But then as soon as Poppy claps eyes on it, all crisp golden crumble and apples on top, she exclaims, 'Oh, clever you! It's an apple crumble cake!'

I smile triumphantly, amazed it's an actual thing. With an actual name. I didn't just make it up, after all! I'm so relieved, I feel like dancing a Highland fling around the kitchen.

'What are you going to serve it with, then?' Poppy asks enthusiastically, and I gulp.

'Er, cream probably. Or maybe ice cream. Yes, definitely ice cream.' I never thought about what to serve it *with*!

On her way out, taking some of her shopping upstairs, Poppy winks. 'Knowing you, Roxy, it won't just be boring old vanilla!'

'Of course not.' I laugh a little too loudly at this. Then, as soon as she's gone, I dash to the freezer to see what flavours we have.

Yup, as I suspected.

Nothing but boring old vanilla.

Now what do I do?

Immediately, I think of Alex. If it hadn't been for him, I'd never have managed to invent a cake that had apparently already been invented! Perhaps he can pull something out of the bag again . . .

Quickly, before Poppy comes back, I dash into the living room where Alex and Jackson are sprawled, watching some football on TV.

They both turn.

'Er, Alex, can I borrow you for a minute?'

He rises off the sofa with a grin and says, '*Absolument!*' in his terrible French accent.

'Something wrong with the cake?' he asks when we're out of earshot of Jackson.

'No, it's fine actually.'

We exchange an impressed grin and do a victorious high-five.

'I need something to serve it *with*,' I say, gazing at him anxiously. 'Something very delicious.'

He nods, thinking. 'Ice cream.'

'We've just got boring old vanilla.'

He shrugs. 'Could be nice. Or what about caramel sauce?'

'We don't have any.'

'So make some.'

'Are you joking?' I give him a look that suggests he's several scoops short of a full bag of flour.

'No, I'm not, actually.' He laughs. 'I'm sure my mum

makes it for her sticky toffee pudding. I think it's just sugar and butter. Look it up online.'

Poppy's bedroom door closes and we hear her footsteps on the stairs. I nudge Alex and hiss, 'Thank you. Now could you make yourself scarce, please? Hurry up!'

He salutes, gives me a big wolfish grin and departs before Poppy arrives.

I feel oddly breathless and giggly, as if I've just taken part in some secret, undercover operation in a *Carry On* film. Quickly whipping out my phone, I check online and, sure enough, the recipe for caramel sauce seems fairly easy. I think even *I* could do it! There are only three ingredients: sugar, butter and cream. And luckily, we have them all.

'Fancy a walk around the lake?' asks Poppy, coming back into the kitchen. 'I'm shattered. I think I just need some proper fresh air. And you look as if you've been mad busy ever since I left.'

'Oh, I have,' I agree, with feeling. 'Yes, a walk would be great.'

I can make the caramel sauce later.

It's a cold, crisp afternoon. A sharp frost has touched the fir trees and the grass with a diamond glitter, and we wrap up extra warmly to head out.

'Have you thought any more about telling Jed?' I ask carefully, as we walk along the side of the narrow tarmac road. 'About the baby?'

'No.' She shoots me a worried glance. 'You haven't said anything to anyone, have you?'

'No, of course not.'

We walk in silence for a while, our breath emerging in the icy air like little puffs of smoke. The sound of Christmas songs drifts across the lake from the ice rink, making me feel a little sentimental and reminding me that Mum and Dad will be celebrating Christmas on board a ship. Normally, by this time, I'd be looking forward to travelling down to the south coast to spend the festive period with them. This year will be strange.

'Come on, Clemmy!' calls a bossy voice. 'Little bit faster!'

Poppy and I turn at footsteps behind us. Sophie is jogging along the road with that distinctive spring of hers that for some reason always reminds me of an Easter bunny bobbing along. Clemmy is bringing up the rear, huffing and puffing, lagging a long way behind.

'It'll all be worth it when you can slip into that size six wedding dress!' calls Sophie encouragingly. 'Hello, ladies,' she calls as she springs past. 'Fancy joining us? You could nip that post-Christmas flab in the bud, before it even gets the *chance* to stick to your hips!'

'Er, no, we're fine, thanks,' says Poppy.

'Maybe another day,' I add.

Sophie laughs. 'Yes, that's what they all say – and that day never arrives! Clemmy, pick your feet up, for goodness sake! You're rolling along as if you're on casters.'

Clemmy eventually catches us up, but she's almost too knackered to speak. 'All I've had is broccoli and celery juice. How can I exercise on *that*?' she pants, and raising her hand a few weary inches, she staggers on. Bobbing Sophie is now just a spot in the distance.

'Poor Clemmy. She loves her food so much,' says Poppy.

'She must really want that wedding venue to put herself through this torture!'

'The running, you mean?'

'No, having to be Sophie's whipping boy!'

Poppy groans in agreement. 'Why does she have to look so *cheerful* when she runs?'

'I know. It's just not natural.'

Poppy decides to take a turn around the rink but although I get into my skates, I opt to just lean on the observers' side of the rail and watch.

I hear a male voice nearby and my heart nearly leaps out of my chest.

Jackson?

I glance around but he's nowhere in sight and, eventually, I conclude I must have been imagining things.

At first, after we broke up, I'd see Jackson everywhere. A tall man in a familiar navy coat striding along the high street. The guy with cropped, dark hair ahead of me in the queue at the supermarket. A face in a magazine with that brilliant smile that lights up the room. Of course it was never actually him. But every time, my heart skipped a beat. And apparently it's still happening!

I just wish I could get over all that nonsense once and for all.

The trouble is that at one point I really did think Jackson and I were forever.

And then, as reliably as clockwork, my throat is aching, remembering the good times we shared . . .

'Hi, there!' It's Alex at my shoulder. 'How's the inventor of the fabulous Ayers Rock Ganache and Apple Crumble Cake?'

I laugh. 'Thank you for coming to my rescue – on both occasions.'

'I think you got away with it,' he murmurs, ramping up the act by glancing behind him furtively, as if someone might be listening in.

'That chocolate bombe turned out all right, I thought.' I give him a superior look.

He nods. 'I thought the judgements were very unfair. It definitely wasn't a manure heap. More a big pile of – anyway, we'll not get into that!' He's grinning broadly so I whack him on the arm.

'And I thought you were on my side,' I wail, pretending to be upset.

'I am, I am. It actually tasted great.'

I shrug. 'I suppose it's a good lesson in not judging a book by its cover.'

'Or a strangely flat Australian land formation by its chocolate icing?'

Smiling, I dig my hands deeper in my pockets against the cold. 'I thought Sophie was going to get hysterical with laughter at her own manure heap joke.'

'It was actually a very good cake,' says a deep male voice behind me, making me jump.

Jackson.

This time, it really is him. I wasn't imagining it.

He smiles from Alex to me and back again. Then he glances down at my skates. 'How about a turn around the rink?'

'Oh, no. I'm rubbish. I'll just stay here and watch.' I make shooing movements with my arms, hoping he and Alex will both hop onto the ice and leave me alone.

But Jackson isn't a man to take no for an answer.

He grins at Alex and grabs my hand, and before I can even think about protesting, he leads me to the entrance. Then he steps onto the ice and, turning to face me, takes hold of both my hands and pulls me onto the rink with him. I jerk backwards but he steadies me. I feel the warmth of his hand as grips my waist and then we're skating together – or rather, he's propelling me along and I'm clutching onto him for dear life, most of the time not even having the chance to practise what Poppy has taught me about pushing off on alternate feet. He's whizzing me around the ice and, after a while, I find myself relaxing into it and beginning to feel quite exhilarated.

Jackson's hand around my waist is giving me the confidence to take chances. He's the leader in this ice skating partnership, just like he always was in our relationship.

The icy breeze in my face as we sail around the perimeter of the rink pinches my cheeks and makes them glow. I'm glowing inside, too, safe in the steady support of Jackson's arms, and when he smiles down at me, my heart lurches as it always did. It's almost like we've whisked back in time and are a normal couple again. I can almost forget Sophie even exists. I just want to fly around the ice in Jackson's arms forever . . .

I glance at the faces along the perimeter railing and catch Alex standing watching us.

He has a strange expression on his face and when I wave, it takes a second for him to wave back. The next time we circle past him, I give him a big cheesy smile and he's ready this time with an enthusiastic thumbs-up.

'Don't just stand there,' Jackson calls to him. 'Get on the ice.'

I'm trying to turn round to see what Alex's reaction is, without losing my balance completely, when I suddenly find myself guided to an abrupt stop. My back is to the perimeter railing and Jackson is staring down at me with an intensity that takes my breath away.

His arms are still around me, even though I'm no longer in danger of falling, and my heart gives a giant leap. I thought this spin around the ice was just for old times' sake, but the expression in Jackson's dark blue eyes right this moment is suddenly very far from casual and friendly.

'I've missed you, Roxy,' he says, raising his voice above the sound of Slade's 'Merry Christmas Everybody'. He grins lazily. 'I don't mind admitting you scared me half to death when you asked me to marry you. And I thought I'd managed to put our relationship behind me and move on. But finding you here has made it all come flooding back. The memories of being together. And now . . .' His piercing blue eyes locked on mine reduce my knees to jelly, just like they always did.

I gulp. 'And now?'

'Now I can't stop thinking about you.' He stares down at me with such sad longing, my whole body starts thrumming with a breathless joy I thought I'd never feel again.

Jackson has missed me. He thought he could move on without me but now he can't stop thinking about me.

I stare up at him, struck dumb by his fairytale declaration – on the ice of all places. So romantic! He lowers his head and my heart goes into overdrive because I know he's going to kiss me . . .

Then, suddenly, I catch sight of Poppy on the other side of the rink. She's standing still on the ice, staring over at me, and the shock on her face brings me sharply back to reality. I twist away from Jackson, deftly evading the kiss.

What the hell am I even *doing*, allowing myself to be swept away by him all over again? The last time I kissed him in front of an audience, it ended in total disaster. Granted, the audience that time was somewhere in the region of ten million, as opposed to the fifty or so milling around the rink today. But who's to say the same thing won't happen all over again?

Jackson looks a bit taken aback at my squirming away from him. I guess it doesn't happen to him very often.

I move further away from him on the pretext of looking at my watch. 'What about Sophie?' I ask casually.

He shrugs. 'What about her?'

'You've just told me you missed me. Do you think that's fair on Sophie?'

He grins. 'Chill out, Roxy. I like Sophie but it's early days. Things aren't that serious yet.'

'I doubt she sees it like that.' *They're spending bloody Christmas together! How much more serious does it get?*

'Maybe. But she'll get over it.'

'So does that mean you think we *were* in a serious relationship?'

'It was as serious as any relationship I've ever had. You were special to me, Roxy, and you could be again.' He shrugs. 'If you wanted to be.'

The look he gives me makes my heart lurch. But there's a little warning voice in my head telling me not to fall for his charm because it can only end in disaster.

Remembering Poppy, I glance anxiously around the rink, but she's nowhere in sight.

'Come on. Let's get out of here,' Jackson says suddenly, grabbing my wrist and pulling me in the direction of the exit.

'What?' I try to resist. 'But where?'

He shrugs. 'Anywhere. We'll go for a drive, far away from here, so we can get reacquainted.' There's a mischievous smile on his face that I always found impossible to resist. 'Come on. You know you want to.'

I shake my head. 'No, Jackson. I'm working this afternoon.'

'But surely you deserve a lunch break? Tell Poppy you need to go shopping into Guildford.'

'I can't.' My heart is hammering, being so close to him, but the warning bells are clanging even louder now.

He puts his arm around my waist and tries to turn me round, but the sudden movement is fatal. My blades slide from under me and down I go, crash-landing onto the ice, which brings the tears to my eyes.

Jackson grins down at me, holding out his hand to help me up. But landing so hard on my bum has brought me back to reality in more ways than one. I don't know how to take Jackson's declaration that he wants to be with me again. Part of me wants to fling myself into his arms and forget everything that happened post-proposal. But there's something about the manner of his approach that makes me wary. I'm not exactly fond of Sophie but the poor girl doesn't deserve to be dismissed as casually as Jackson just did. And I also can't help wondering if Jackson's sudden ardour has something to do with the fact that he caught me having fun with Alex in the kitchen.

Ignoring his outstretched hand, I roll over onto my knees, the way Poppy taught me, and get myself back on my feet. 'I have to get back to work now, Jackson.'

His smile slips. 'Okay. Have it your way,' he says, folding his arms. 'See you later, Roxy.'

Abandoned at the edge of the rink, I watch him go with a slightly sinking heart. I'd forgotten Jackson's tendency to sulk when he doesn't get his own way. On the other hand, he's just poured out how he felt about me, so I can hardly blame him for feeling disappointed I have to go back to work.

I glance at my watch. I need to find Poppy and head back to the cabin. Suddenly, I spot her at the kiosk, handing in her skates, and foolishly, I decide to save time by crossing the rink instead of skating round the perimeter.

I'm half way across, on my achingly slow, perilous journey, when a hefty rugby player type skating backwards to impress his girlfriend fails to see me and crashes into my side. We manage to stay upright and he skates on. But a second later, I lose my tentative balance and down I go.

I sit there, looking around for Jackson, trying to summon the strength to get up. But this time, it feels like a mammoth effort. All the feelings stirred up by Jackson's declaration seem to have rendered me weak as water, and I feel suddenly on the verge of tears.

Then suddenly, out of nowhere, he's there at my side, holding out a hand – and I'm reaching out gratefully and being swung in one easy movement to my feet.

I look up at him with a grateful smile, feeling safe again.

And it isn't Jackson at all.

It's Alex.

Chapter 14

'You keep having to rescue me!'

He grins. 'I know. I'm hoping it might turn into a full-time job.'

'The demand is definitely there.' I rub my shoulder woefully. I banged it quite hard when I landed on the ice.

While Alex is bending down to pick up a stray glove someone's dropped nearby, I glance swiftly around the ice, trying to spot Jackson. But no luck.

'He's gone back to the hotel,' says Alex.

'Jackson?' I ask with an innocent expression, although my blushes must give me away instantly. 'Oh. Right.'

Great. Sophie's probably in their room, taking a shower after her run with Clemmy. No, no, I do not *want to think about that!*

My feelings are confusing me. Something tells me getting back with Jackson would be a big mistake, so why did my heart leap with joy when he told me he'd missed me? It shouldn't bother me that he's with Sophie in their hotel room now – but it actually does.

A weight of despair descends, almost knocking me back down on the ice again. Then something occurs to me that makes me feel even worse. In all the emotional upheaval, I'd forgotten that Poppy probably wasn't the only one to see our 'almost-kiss' in the middle of the ice. Alex must have witnessed me making a show of myself, too.

I swallow miserably. I really like Alex and I mind very much what he thinks of me – and his opinion certainly can't be very high at the moment. What if he thinks I'm trying to steal Jackson away from Sophie?

The whole situation is just a big mess, I think, as I rub my aching shoulder distractedly.

'Are you injured?' Alex frowns. 'Perhaps I should take a look at that shoulder?'

'No!' I shrink back in horror.

He looks taken aback, as well he might. Then he smiles in a puzzled way and says mildly, 'I am a doctor, after all.'

I give my head a little shake, feeling stupid. 'Yes. Of course you are.' I force a laugh. 'Sorry! The shoulder's fine.'

He nods slowly. 'Okay.'

I'm aware he's still wondering what he said to provoke such a dramatic reaction in me – and it suddenly hits me that I'm weary of hiding the truth from everyone. Perhaps I should just tell Alex about the accident? Then he'd understand.

But next second, I know I can't.

Old habits die hard . . .

'I'd better go,' I tell him, catching sight of Poppy standing at the edge of the rink, waiting for me. He puts his hand on my waist and guides me niftily through the passing skaters in her direction.

Walking back with Poppy, the conversation is a little strained and I know she must be wondering what on earth is going on. So, eventually, I bring up the subject.

'By the way, when you saw me in a clinch with Jackson just then, it really didn't mean anything.'

'Are you sure?' She peers at me.

'Absolutely. We were . . . just talking about old times.'

She smiles in sympathy. 'It would be only natural if you still had feelings for him.'

I sigh. 'I suppose I do. I've tried hard to tell myself he's history, but I guess I've never really stopped loving him.'

'And does he feel the same?'

'He said he missed me and he can't stop thinking about me.' My heart rate quickens at the memory.

'Well, maybe you'll get back together,' says Poppy softly.

A little surge of happiness rushes up at the thought. But it's not that simple.

'He needs to tell Sophie it's over first.'

She nods. 'He does.'

We walk along in silence for a while, each of us deep in our own thoughts.

Then Poppy groans. 'Oh God, I've just remembered. Sophie threatened to try out her presentation on us tonight. For the health and beauty book she's writing.'

'Perhaps she's forgotten.'

Poppy makes a hilarious cross-eyed expression. 'We can only hope.'

Just as we're arriving back at the cabin, a car comes hurtling towards us along the narrow road.

Instinctively, I grab Poppy's arm and we dive into the ditch, only for the driver of the car to slam on the brakes and make an abrupt left-hand turn into the parking area in front of the Log Fire Cabin. The car screeches to a halt, the door opens and out tumbles the driver.

'It's Ruby,' says Poppy. 'Oh God, she must have passed her test. I forgot she turned seventeen this year. There'll be absolutely *no* stopping her now.'

I glance at her to see if she's joking but she actually looks worried.

Next second, the passenger door opens and an older woman with amazing, copper-coloured hair staggers out. 'For fuck's sake, Ruby! And you know I don't normally swear!' She flumps against the side of the car and stares at the sky for a moment as if offering up a prayer for the miracle of still being alive.

'Oh, chill out, Mum,' grins Ruby. 'You didn't expect me to drive at a steady thirty miles an hour, did you? Where's the fun in that?'

'No, but I didn't expect the bloody wheels to actually *leave the ground* when we went over those humps back there!' She pushes herself away from the car. 'Christ, I need a drink!'

'Hi, Gloria. Great to see you both.' Poppy walks over and Gloria perks up. Poppy does the introductions, trying in the process to hug Ruby, who squirms deftly away from her.

'Thank goodness. Some sane, normal people,' Gloria remarks, giving the side of Poppy's face a little tweak and smiling at me. 'Not like my daughter, whose main hobby seems to be scaring me half out of my wits.'

'You're *already* half out of your wits, Mum, so what would be the point?' quips Ruby. She turns to Poppy and says in a loud stage whisper, 'Mum's started going through the *Big M* and it's turned her a bit weird.'

'Ruby!' Gloria glares at her, wafting her leopard print scarf vigorously in front of her face as her cheeks bloom with a ruddy glow.

Ruby grins. 'Can we go in? Has Uncle Bob arrived yet?'

* * *

I'm relieved to be in the kitchen with Poppy all after-noon, away from the possibility of bumping into Jackson again. Although with Ruby popping in every now and again for a cold drink or a gingerbread Santa, the kitchen is no longer the peaceful place it's been since I arrived.

'That girl will drive me utterly batty!' mutters Gloria when she comes in to make yet another cup of her strong black coffee. 'She's at drama college, Roxy, and she's decided she wants to be a stunt person in films.'

Poppy turns to me. 'Bob's an architect and he designed this really smart five-storey office block – and Ruby frightened Gloria to death by deciding to abseil down the front of it as a publicity stunt.'

Gloria groans. 'Oh, don't remind me. My heart was in my mouth. She was only sixteen.'

Poppy laughs. 'But the pictures in the newspaper were great.'

'What's that? Talking about me again?' Ruby walks in, glued to her phone and followed by Sophie.

'It's all good,' I reassure Ruby. 'I was hearing about your abseiling.'

She frowns. 'That's kids' stuff. I really want to try tombstoning but Mum nearly had a heart attack when I suggested it.'

Gloria fixes her with a glare. 'Don't you *ever* . . .'

Ruby sighs, flinging open the fridge. 'Is there any

cider? No, Mum, I'm not going to do the tombstoning thing. I'm actually not that stupid, believe it or not. Too many people have met grisly deaths.'

'Tombstoning? What on earth is that?' asks Sophie.

'Oh, jumping off cliffs into the sea,' says Ruby. She stares at Sophie. 'Is your skin *actually* that smooth or is it down to cosmetics?'

Sophie gives a smug smile. 'It's mostly down to the healthy diet and exercise programme I'm developing. I'm going to write a book about it.'

'A book? Wow.' Ruby nods, looking impressed. 'I like to swim.'

Sophie nods approvingly. 'Swimming is excellent exercise. One of the best, in fact.' She frowns. 'Gloria, older women shouldn't drink coffee that strong. Especially if they're going through the menopause and, judging by those horrendous hot flushes, it's clear that you are. You should give it up immediately and drink chamomile tea instead.'

Gloria finishes stirring two heaped teaspoons of sugar into her coffee and takes a sip, raising the cup to Sophie. 'Well, you know what? Bugger that. There's precious few joys in life as it is. Why on earth would I start giving them up just because I'm getting older?'

'Because it shows in your face?' Sophie runs her fingers from her nose to her chin. 'You have lines here that make you look far older than you probably are,

Gloria, and that's partly because your skin is completely dehydrated.'

There's an awkward silence as everyone tries not to look at Gloria's lines.

Even Ruby seems dumbstruck for once.

Poppy laughs. 'Gosh, it sounds like you're starting your presentation already, Sophie!'

Sophie ignores her. 'Caffeine's *really bad* for deep lines, Gloria. You need to drink more water to plump out the wrinkles. Especially around your eyes, where the skin is paper thin and more prone to the ravages of time.' She shrugs. 'It would help you lose weight, too.'

'Really? Well, thank you, Sophie,' says Gloria smoothly. 'Maybe I will drink more water. Now, any chance of a mince pie, Poppy, love?'

'Of course.' Poppy loads some on a plate and starts handing them round, just as Ryan walks in.

'Anyone seen Clem?' His eyes light up. 'Ooh, mince pies.'

Poppy laughs. 'How is it that you always arrive at the exact moment food is being served!'

Ryan grins. 'I've got a nose for stodge.'

Everyone takes a mince pie, except Sophie who gives her head a distasteful little shake.

'What presentation are you doing, Sophie?' asks Ruby, looking fascinated, in between munches.

Sophie flicks back her hair. 'I'm writing a health and beauty book and I did offer to give a talk on the content, but I get the feeling no one's very keen.'

'Oh.' Ruby studies Sophie thoughtfully for a moment. 'Well, I'd *love* to hear your talk,' she says.

Sophie blinks at Ruby. 'Oh. Well, in that case, I'll do it.'

Poppy catches my eye and we exchange a grimace.

'Great!' Ruby sticks up her thumb. 'Wow, and you're writing a book? How cool is that?'

Sophie shrugs. 'Well, I do happen to be editor-in-chief of one of the country's most trend-setting publications. I really *ought* to be able to write.' She gives a modest, tinkly laugh.

Ruby frowns. 'Hang on. You're Sophie Fairfax? Editor of *Dazzle* magazine?'

Sophie gives a little nod, at which point Ruby's mouth hangs open with amazement.

The door opens and Clemmy bursts in, panting. Her cheeks are red with the cold and there are huge sweat patches under the sleeves of her pink sweatshirt, despite the chill of the day outside.

'Hi, Gloria! Ruby! Bob's just arrived – and he says he wants to throw an engagement party for us, Ryan! Isn't that lovely of him?'

I can't help a worried glance at Poppy. But she smiles and says, 'Fab! Roxy and I will do the food.'

Clemmy shakes her head. 'You don't need to, Poppy. There's this amazing place called "The Enchanted Forest" that's opened a few miles from here. It's really magical and romantic at night, apparently. All fairy lights in the trees and that kind of thing. Bob knows the owner and he's going to book a function room there for the party. Won't that be brilliant? I was thinking fancy dress would be fun.'

Ruby, who's been studying Sophie thoughtfully ever since her lecture to Gloria on premature ageing, hops off the stool. 'Sounds good. I'll go as Evel Knievel.'

Clemmy's face falls. 'Oh, I was hoping we could dress up as our favourite movie and we all have to guess who we are.'

Ruby grins. 'You and Ryan could go as Beauty and the Beast.'

'Hey, you!' grins Ryan, pretending to box her ears.

'I don't think Evel Knievel starred in any movies,' murmurs Ruby. 'I suppose I could go as Wonder Woman instead.'

'As long as you don't go leaping off any tall buildings,' warns Gloria. 'Or any buildings at all, come to that.'

'Who will you go as, Sophie?' asks Ruby.

'Well, I'm not sure.'

Ruby frowns for a second, thinking, then she points at Sophie. 'Elsa from *Frozen*,' she says decisively.

'I'll go as *Pretty Woman* – the early days,' says Gloria

gloomily. 'She prances around with not much on at the beginning, so I'll be able to keep the hot flushes to a minimum.'

'I'll disown you if you do that,' frowns Ruby. 'And anyway, you look nothing like Julia Roberts.'

'Thanks, darling daughter.'

Ruby heads for the door with her phone attached to her ear. 'Chloe?' she says as she wanders out. 'The oldies are throwing a fancy dress engagement party. Yes, Clemmy and Ryan got engaged. Oh, and guess who's staying here? You'll actually *never* guess so I'll have to tell you. Only the editor of *Dazzle* magazine!'

I hear the front door opening and I find myself straining to listen.

Ruby's voice drifts through. 'Oh, hi, Uncle Bob. And you must be Jackson. They're all in the kitchen.'

My heart leaps into my throat. I can't face Jackson right now – especially not with Sophie in the room.

But when they come into the kitchen, Poppy and Gloria immediately start greeting Bob, who's just driven up from London, while Jackson joins Sophie.

'Roxy, this is Jed's Uncle Bob,' says Poppy. 'He and Jed are partners in the business. Bob, Roxy is my own personal Christmas angel. She pretty much saved my life by agreeing to help out.'

Bob gives me a warm smile and shakes my hand. 'Did she indeed? Well, it's very nice to meet you, Roxy.'

I smile shyly at Poppy's fulsome praise.

Bob seems lovely. He's a bit older than Gloria – in his sixties – but despite the greying hair, he seems a lot younger than his years, probably because he exudes a lovely lively energy. Poppy told me that Gloria got divorced five years ago and met Bob a little over a year ago in her home town of Newcastle when she was on a night out with 'the girls'. Bob was in the same pub having a drink after a business meeting. They couldn't be more different, according to Poppy, but the relationship seems to be working.

In the chat that follows, Jackson and Sophie are drawn into the introductions – and with a sigh of relief, I duck out of the kitchen and escape to my room.

Chapter 15

I fling myself down on the bed and lie there, staring up at the lamp shade.

Thoughts and feelings are haring around inside my head like a whirligig dryer on a windy day.

Ever since Jackson confessed his feelings for me on the ice earlier, my insides have been in total uproar. I never thought I'd hear him say he regretted losing me.

I'd imagined it so many times in my head: Jackson realising he'd made a big mistake and begging me to give him another chance. And in those imagined scenarios, I'd always taken him back. Because everyone deserves a second chance.

But how would I feel if he actually finished with Sophie to be with me?

Now, staring up at the ceiling, I'm realising the answer to that question is nowhere near as straightforward as I thought it would be.

Am I just using my guilt over Sophie as an excuse

to keep holding back from a proper, full-on relationship with Jackson? The way I dreamed up excuses all the time when we were a couple so I could avoid getting too close?

I did with Jackson what I've always done in relationships.

I told myself it was too early to have sex; that I wanted to wait at least three months before being properly intimate with him, because, then, the relationship would have a much better chance of lasting.

Hot tears well up.

Who the hell was I fooling? It was all just an excuse.

It's time I faced up to the painful truth: even though I was devastated when it all went wrong with Jackson, there was a tiny part of me that was actually relieved when we went our separate ways.

Because it took away the biggest fear of all . . .

My gorgeous dog, Gus, came into my life when I was twelve.

As an only child, living in a little seaside hamlet three miles from the nearest village, I led a fairly solitary existence. I had some good friends but seeing them after school was difficult, and I think Mum and Dad thought a dog would be good company for me.

From the moment they brought two-year-old Gus the Border terrier home from the shelter, I loved him with my whole heart. We bonded instantly. He was the best friend a girl could have and he went everywhere with me.

On that fateful night – the night when everything changed forever – I was staying over at Flo's house. It was early September and Flo's family were having a barbecue. They'd invited around fifty guests, including some of our old friends from school, and I took Gus along with me. It was my nineteenth birthday and I remember being really excited because I'd just been accepted onto an accountancy training course with a big firm, based in London. I'd be starting with them later that month, and I'd arranged to stay in London during the week and travel home at weekends. I knew I'd really miss Gus so I wanted to make the most of the time I had left before London beckoned.

I remember we had a great night. All our friends were buzzing with a mix of excitement and apprehension about their future, me and Flo included. It seemed we were all on the threshold of a brand new life.

If I'd known what that would entail for me, I wouldn't have been quite so gung-ho and happy.

Everyone had gone by midnight. I helped clear up, then Flo's mum made tea and we all went to bed.

The fire broke out in the early hours of the morning.

I was in a deep sleep and woke to the sound of Flo banging on my door and calling my name.

As soon as I opened the door, I could smell the blaze. But I froze for a second, still half-inhabiting the world of dreams. Perhaps *this* was a dream?

Then Flo shouted, 'Come on, we need to get out!' She reached for my arm and pulled me over the threshold. And her terrified expression galvanised me into action.

A bolt of panic surged up inside me as I stumbled after Flo, down the stairs. Smoke was already drifting up to the first floor and we were both coughing as we reached the front door and ran out into the safety of the garden.

A second later, though, when I stood in the garden and saw the flames licking the side of the house, a bolt of shock punched through me.

Gus!

I glanced wildly around me but there was no sign of him, so I shouted for him.

Nothing.

My heart in my mouth, I stared at the burning building, knowing deep down what I could barely acknowledge to myself.

Gus must be still in the house.

Before anyone could stop me, I raced for the front door and ran along the hall, calling his name frantically and looking in every room along the way. The door to the kitchen was wide open, the fire raging within. The crackle and smell of it chilled me to the bone but I knew that if Gus had been in there he'd have run out by now. So at least he was safe. I was about to go and search for him upstairs when I heard a noise.

It was so faint above the harsh crackle of the fire. But I heard it.

The breath caught in my throat.

Gus was in the little utility room! No doubt on the hunt for dog biscuits, he must have got trapped!

I hesitated for just a second. Then, spotting a route by the window that hadn't yet been ignited by the flames, I took my chance and dived through. I wrenched open the door to the utility room, gasping with pain as the flesh of my hand met the blistering metal of the handle.

Gus bolted out, barking, and disappeared into the flames.

I screamed out his name in a panic, and at that moment, I was knocked to the floor by something heavy. I landed on my front and the burning object fell on my back. Pain seared through me. A pain like nothing I'd ever felt before. My clothes were on fire and in my state of shock I was fighting to get the thing off me, not knowing what it was, pushing at it even while the searing pain made me scream in agony.

Even when at last I managed to roll away, onto my back to try and put out the flames, I was unwittingly throwing myself closer to the heart of the fire. The intense agony and blazing heat had reached an unbearable pitch.

I just remember a dark shape running in and shouting my name.

And then everything went black.

I remember waking up and feeling panicky because I was trapped. I cried out and tried to move but I couldn't. Faces hovered over me. One of them, a young woman with dark hair, kept saying my name and telling me it was all right and just to lie still. I'd been in an accident and I was in hospital. But things would be okay.

I knew something bad had happened but my head was swimming – due to the medication, I found out later – and I felt as if I was reaching into a thick fog desperately trying to reclaim scraps of memory. The painkillers I was on were very strong and dulled more than the physical agony of the burns.

But I remembered stumbling after Flo down the stairs. Watching the fire. Trying to get to Gus. Letting him out of the utility room and shouting at him when he ran towards the blaze . . .

'Gus!'

What had happened to Gus? I needed to get to him but I couldn't move for these stupid bandages wrapped so tightly around my arm and shoulder.

The brown-haired nurse was there in a trice.

'My dog. What happened to my dog?' I pleaded.

She frowned. 'Your dog? I don't know, Roxy. But we can ask your parents.'

'Where are they? Mum and Dad?' It suddenly occurred to me that they weren't here with me. Why was that? 'And Billy?'

'Shh, it's okay. Just relax,' soothed the nurse. 'They're waiting outside. They'll be in to see you soon.'

'But I want to see them now. They can tell me about Gus,' I wailed.

I think the drugs must have knocked me out again. But when I woke, Mum was sitting by the bed. She looked grey and tired, as if she'd aged ten years overnight. 'Roxy,' she whispered, and a tear ran down her cheek as she leaned towards me and gently held my hand.

Seeing Mum, tears started slipping down my face, too. 'Is Gus all right?'

My heart was in my mouth as I said it, and the relief when she nodded was overwhelming.

She smiled. 'The little rascal must have been terrified, shut away in the utility room. When you let him out, he shot straight outside, bless him. Flo's dad said he was like a bullet out of a gun!'

I laughed and it turned into a sob, at which point the nurse came and gently suggested to Mum it was time I had a nap.

'Did Flo's dad get me out?' I asked, remembering the dark shape leaning over me.

'He did. And your dad and I don't know how we'll ever be able to thank him enough.' She's smiling through her tears. 'Now just you relax, my love, and I'll bring Dad in to see you later.'

'What about Billy? Does he know?'

She nodded. 'He's desperate to see you but it's close family only just now. I promise he'll come in just as soon as he can.'

I lay there after she'd gone, thinking I could bear any amount of pain now I knew that Gus was all right.

And Billy would be coming to see me soon, I was sure.

Billy was great. Once I was out of intensive care and back on the ward, he came in to cheer me up every day, usually bringing little gifts for me, like magazines and grapes and, once, a gorgeous bracelet with a little jade charm that he said was the colour of my eyes.

He'd just started his course at Manchester University and I was missing him desperately. But he got the train back home every other weekend and I had no worries about our love surviving the separation. He'd be home for three whole weeks at Christmas and I planned to make it really special for us.

I lived for Billy's weekend visits – especially when the hard and often excruciatingly painful physiotherapy began. When I felt like giving up, it was the thought of Billy that kept me pushing forward.

I was determined to work as hard as I could to get better. I knew I'd have to have skin grafts on my back, shoulder and right arm, but once they were done, I'd be able to get myself back to the way I was before the accident shattered everything. They were holding my place for me at the accountancy firm because, obviously, I'd missed the start date. But I knew I'd get there so I was determined not to worry and just work hard at the physio.

Billy was making new friends and enjoying his course, and I was really pleased for him. One weekend in early November, he came home all excited about a trip away to Dubai he and his mates and their girl-friends were planning.

'It's next month,' he said, glancing at his phone. 'You'll be okay by then, won't you?'

I gazed at him in dismay. 'I don't think so, Billy.'

'Really?' He put his phone down on the bedside cabinet and I saw he'd changed his screensaver to a group photo, presumably of people he socialised with at uni. 'But I thought you were making good progress with the physio?' He looked genuinely puzzled.

'Well, yes, I am. But it's going to take months, not

weeks, before I'm able to do normal things again – like go away on holiday.'

'Oh. Right.'

He looked so disappointed. I reached for his hand. 'We can go to Dubai ourselves, just me and you, once I'm better?' I smiled. 'I might even be able to treat you, once I'm earning on my accountancy course.'

'Yeah, yeah, of course.' He shrugged, as if he wasn't bothered either way.

'So you don't mind too much that we can't go this time?'

He shook his head. 'You need to concentrate on getting better, Roxy. That's the main thing right now.'

I smiled and leaned over to kiss him. I was under no illusion at all that my road to recovery was going to be a slog. Thank goodness Billy understood.

While he was away fetching coffee, I picked up his phone and looked at the screensaver photo. Billy was in the centre and, even though I'd never met them, I already recognised his new friends, Evan and Mark and their girlfriends, Rachel and Tilly, from photos Billy had shown me. There was a girl with long, strawberry blonde hair that I didn't recognise, and I made a mental note to ask Billy about her.

It was so frustrating only being able to see Billy every other weekend when he came back from uni – and always in hospital at that! But looking at that group shot just made me even more determined to get better soon.

I smiled. It wouldn't be too long before I'd actually be *in* those photos, with Billy and his new friends.

It was a great incentive to keep working hard at my physio.

With injuries like mine, if I didn't exercise every day, I knew my body would start tightening up and I'd gradually lose my ability to move. So, despite the frequent pain and the frustration I felt at being confined to a hospital bed while the trees beyond the window turned the most glorious russet shades, I managed to stay fairly upbeat and positive.

But there was one thing I was avoiding.

I hadn't asked to look at the burns on my back.

I was used to the nurses changing the dressings every day, and I'd grown accustomed to the way my arm looked. But I knew that my back had taken the worst of the flames.

Then one day, when they were unwrapping the bandages, I asked to see the full extent of the damage. The two nurses exchanged a doubtful glance so I said, 'You know, I've got to see it some time, so it might as well be now.' I honestly would have given Meryl Streep a run for her money the way I said it so casually. The nurses would never have guessed the turmoil I was in at the very thought.

So I finally got to see. And immediately wished I hadn't.

My back, which had been smooth and unblemished, was now a horrific mass of scar tissue. The damage was all the way up to my shoulder blades and it snaked around my right shoulder and down my arm.

I felt a whoosh of light-headedness and really thought I was going to faint.

That was the moment I knew I'd been kidding myself. I was never, ever going to be the person I was before the accident. My body was broken. My carefree days were over.

One of the nurses looked up at a movement behind me. Her face froze. 'Billy,' she said.

My heart jolted in my chest. Oh God, I'd never have wanted him to see me like this – not without some warning. And not until the scars had at least had a chance to heal. But at least he knew how bad it was. He'd seen me at my worst and now we could move on . . .

I didn't turn round. Mainly because any movement really hurt and I always had to psyche myself up for it first. But Billy ducked out anyway while the nurses replaced the dressings and my loose nightgown. Then they left me and Billy came back in and sat down on the chair by the bed, staring down at the floor, his shoulders hunched, as if he was avoiding looking at me.

I reached for his hand. 'It's okay, Billy. It looks worse than it is. Honestly. I can hardly feel it now.' I was desperate to reassure him so he'd feel more at ease. 'The skin grafts will take a while to heal but I'll soon be back to normal.'

He looked up and gave me a stiff smile. 'Of course you will, Roxy.'

Over the next few weeks, I found myself thinking a lot about a holiday with Billy, just the two of us. I figured if we booked it for early summer that would give me enough time to heal and start getting back to leading a normal life. Knowing Billy would be coming in to visit on the Saturday morning, I got Mum to bring in some holiday brochures so we could look through them together.

I was feeling upbeat and excited when Billy walked onto the ward that morning. He helped me into a wheelchair and pushed me along to the communal lounge area that was conveniently empty.

He settled me in a chair and sat down beside me.

'I thought we could book a trip to Dubai for next year?' I said, flicking eagerly through one of the brochures on my lap and showing him a hotel I'd picked out.

He took it and looked at the page.

'What do you think?' I asked.

He gave a vague nod and continued to stare at the

brochure. I wondered if something had happened because he seemed distracted, as if he wasn't even looking at the hotel.

I took the brochure back. 'Sorry, you've only just got here. There's no rush. Have a think about it and when you come back in a couple of weeks, we can plan something, okay?'

'I won't be here in a fortnight.' He mumbled this at the floor so I almost didn't catch it.

'Oh?' I glanced at him in surprise. 'Is something happening at uni?'

He swallowed and examined his nails before he finally raised his eyes to mine. 'It's the Dubai weekend?'

My heart plummeted. *He was still intending to go?*

Billy shrugged. 'I'd already booked and paid for the flights. It would have been a shame to waste them,' he said, rubbing his nose and looking strangely shifty.

I thought about this and I quickly realised he was right.

Of course I hated the thought of not being able to go on a Dubai adventure with Billy and his new friends – but it would only be this once.

'Okay,' I nodded slowly. 'That makes sense. I can come the next time.' I smiled and took his hand, feeling pleased for him after my initial shock. Spending every other weekend visiting me in hospital wasn't exactly the excitement of the century. 'You'll have a great time, I'm sure.'

Then something occurred to me. 'What about my ticket? Is someone going in my place?'

There was a beat of silence.

'Erm . . . Natalie?' he said.

'Who's Natalie?'

'You know. Natalie? She's the best mate of Evan's girlfriend?'

'Oh? I've never heard you mention a Natalie.'

He frowned. 'Really? I'm sure I told you about her.' He flushed awkwardly.

I shook my head. 'You definitely didn't. But it doesn't matter.'

I thought of the girl with strawberry blonde hair in Billy's screensaver photo. Was that Natalie? Why had Billy never mentioned her? He was always talking about the other guys. So why not her? And why was he currently doing his best to avoid my eye?

Panic stabbed me in the gut.

But I told myself to stay calm. I was being over-sensitive. Billy loved me. We'd been crazy about each other ever since we got together two years ago.

Then Billy heaved a sigh and said, 'We need to talk, Roxy.'

I glanced at him in alarm, my heart in my mouth.

At last, he managed to look at me. 'I've . . . been

seeing Natalie. She's fun and we get on. And it's just – I don't know – *easy* with her.' He held out his arms as if it was all as bewildering to him, this turn of events, as it was to me.

I stared at him, unable to believe what I was hearing.

'Sorry, Roxy. I didn't know how to tell you. But I think it's for the best.' He forced a smile. 'You need time to recover. And I've got exams, so I can't keep coming back at weekends. It's much simpler if we just go our separate ways.'

I swallowed. 'How long have you been seeing this Natalie?' I asked, my voice cracking.

'Not long.' He glanced down at his hands. 'About a month.'

'A *month*?'

He shrugged, looking sheepish, but said nothing.

'And it's *easy* with her, is it?' I gave a bitter laugh. 'As opposed to really hard-going and boring with me because I went and got myself burned and I can't move from this bloody hospital?'

He frowned. 'Now you're just being melodramatic.'

I stared at him incredulously, wondering if he ever truly loved me. If he did, surely he'd want to be with me now, to help me through the worst time of my life?

Apparently, he didn't.

He wanted to fly off to Dubai with Natalie!

'Couldn't you have *told* me you were shagging

someone else?' I demanded. 'Instead of letting me carry on thinking things were totally fine between us?'

'I'm telling you now, Roxy,' he mumbled.

Tears started slipping down my face and I dashed them away angrily. 'But how can you *do* this to me? To *us*? After all we've been to each other? Don't you love me any more?'

He gazed down at the floor, raking a hand slowly through his hair.

Then it came to me in a flash.

'It's the burns, isn't it? I don't look the same as I used to, so you've gone off me. You don't fancy me any more. But you obviously fancy *Natalie*!' I grabbed his phone off the nearby table and it slipped from my shaking hand and skidded along the linoleum. 'Is that *her* on your screensaver?' I demanded, pointing as he went to pick it up. 'I suppose it should have occurred to me to wonder why you don't have a picture of *me* on there!'

I broke down completely then and Billy tried to put his arm around me, but it hurt. I shrieked with the pain and he flinched away from me. And then I was shouting at him to get out and that I never wanted to see him again.

He left without a word. And that's when my whole world crumbled around me.

I think I'd known all along that Billy wouldn't be

able to cope with the changed me; the damaged, scarred person I'd become after the fire.

In the lonely, anguish-filled weeks and months that followed, I told myself I was glad Billy had gone. The last thing I wanted was to be with a man who pitied me and was revolted by my scars . . .

Chapter 16

I'm really quite nervous serving up my apple crumble cake, but to my enormous relief, no one laughs – not even Sophie! In fact, everyone seems to be fairly impressed.

I pass around the jug of caramel sauce that I managed to make without a hitch, and the murmurs of pleasure are balm to my agitated soul.

The best part is when Alex gives me a big wink when no one is watching. Well, I say that, but after I've stopped smiling at him, I glance at Jackson and I catch him studying me with an odd look on his face. He doesn't look jealous exactly. If anything, he looks amused, as if he's calculating how to turn my head in his direction instead of Alex's . . .

I groan inwardly. This whole situation with Jackson is *way* too complicated.

After we've eaten dessert, which goes down surprisingly well, we all gather – with varying degrees of enthusiasm – in the living room for Sophie's health and beauty book presentation.

I'm quite interested to hear what she has to say. But unfortunately, she has a rather droning delivery that makes you listen more to the peculiar tone of her voice, rather than what she's saying. Consequently, I start to drift off on the end of the sofa, and Poppy has to jerk me awake with her elbow.

'So, a delicious juice of celery and broccoli makes the perfect start to everyone's day!' Sophie is saying. She holds up a pack of celery and a head of broccoli, as if she's introducing us heathens to the green stuff for the very first time. 'With perhaps a carrot for a touch of sweetness.' She puts down the other veg and holds up a carrot – pinky finger in the air – with the smug smile of someone who always practises what she preaches.

Poppy, who's squashed next to me on the sofa, with Ryan and Clemmy on her other side, leans fractionally sideways and murmurs, 'I know what I'd like to do with that carrot.'

I snort and quickly turn it into a cough.

Ruby, sitting cross-legged on the floor and hanging onto Sophie's every word, turns and glares at me.

'And if you must snack, try eating like a kid,' says Sophie. 'Think finger food such as carrot sticks and cherry tomatoes and melon cubes – all the stuff pre-schoolers have in their lunch boxes.'

Ruby holds up her hand and Sophie smiles. 'Yes, Ruby?'

'I was just wondering. When you say it's good to eat like a kid, do you mean it's okay to go to McDonald's for breakfast?'

Ryan lets out a guffaw of laughter and Jed joins in.

Sophie pointedly ignores the naughty boys at the back of the class and smiles patiently down at Ruby. 'Well, no, Ruby. McDonald's is mostly fast food. And fast food plays complete havoc with your digestive system. I really wouldn't recommend it.'

'Oh. Okay.' Ruby turns and glares at everyone. 'I was only asking.'

I glance at Alex to see his reaction. He's managing to keep a straight face. Jackson is studying his knees, trying not to smile, which would obviously annoy Sophie. He glances across at me and I look quickly away.

I keep catching him sneaking looks at me. It makes me feel bad because Sophie is sitting right there – but at the same time, my heart skips a beat every time. He was sitting opposite me at dinner, which made me feel really self-conscious and like my fingers had ballooned to the size of sausages so that I couldn't use my knife and fork properly.

After Sophie's presentation, I tell Poppy I'm feeling shattered and head for my room, hoping to escape

Jackson's attentions. But just as I reach the top of the stairs, I hear my name and, when I turn, he's taking the stairs two at a time to catch up with me.

'Have you thought about what I said?' he asks, laying his hand on my waist.

I nod, my heart beating fast.

'So what do you think? Have you missed me?' he asks softly.

'Of course.' I swallow. 'But this . . .' I fling my arm out vaguely. 'It's all a bit sudden. I mean, I was starting to get over you and now . . .'

He smiles. 'And now?'

We lock eyes and, suddenly, I'm finding breathing difficult. All the butterflies in the world have taken flight in my abdomen. Jackson could always make me feel like this. It feels so lovely and familiar and part of me longs to just throw myself into his arms.

'Jackson? Are you up there?' Sophie's voice travels up the stairs.

I'm expecting him to leave abruptly, but he just stands there, looking at me with this big wistful smile on his face. 'I'll be down in a minute,' he calls at last.

'Okay. Well, don't be too long.'

Her footsteps clack away down the hall and I breathe again.

'You're not free to be with me, Jackson,' I point out. 'What about Sophie?'

He sighs. 'I care about her, of course. But – well, you're different, Roxy.'

'Yes.' I joke. 'Three stone heavier with no dress sense whatsoever.'

'But you're so lovely. Everyone thinks so. And you're very beautiful, in your own way.'

'Right.' I try not to be needled by his complete failure to contradict my neat summing up of the differences between Sophie and me. And to appreciate my banter. But then, this is actually a very romantic moment. Perhaps it's not the time for jokes.

'Jed and Alex were going on last night about what a great person you are.'

'Really? What did Alex say about me?' I ask. 'And Jed?' I add, as a feeling of relief surges through me.

Alex doesn't think badly of me, after all! Despite the fact he must have seen me almost snogging Jackson on the ice rink!

'Oh, complimentary things,' he says vaguely.

'I don't know, Jackson. I was devastated by the way you moved on so quickly. To me, it proved you never loved me the way I utterly adored you.'

'Utterly adored? In the past tense?' He looks genuinely dismayed. 'Please tell me you still feel the same way, Roxy. I'll finish with Sophie, if that's what it'll take.'

I stare at him, perplexed.

I'm not Sophie's biggest fan but she definitely doesn't

deserve to have her Christmas destroyed in that way. And something else is niggling me about this statement, although my head is too muddled right now to think what it is.

But there's absolutely no denying the way just being close to him makes me feel.

'Jackson?' It's Sophie again, clacking along the hallway.

'Coming, my gorgeous one,' calls Jackson. Turning, he's down the stairs in a flash, leaving my head more confused than ever.

I go to bed and do some deep breathing to try and calm the thoughts going round and round in my head. But two hours later, I'm as wide awake as if I'd just drunk an entire pot of Alex's favourite super-strong Brazilian blend coffee.

In the end, I give up, slip into my snuggly robe and slippers and pad downstairs. It's after one and everyone is in bed. Creeping through the silent hall, I can see the welcoming embers of the log fire and, tempted by their cosy glow, I go into the living room and head for the comfiest sofa.

I'm just about to throw myself onto it when I realise someone has got there ahead of me.

Dressed in jeans but with bare feet, Alex is lying the full length of the sofa, linked hands supporting his head as he stares into the flames. He looks so deep in thought, I pause a moment before announcing myself.

He looks up in surprise and when he sees it's me, he smiles and shifts position so that there's a space for me to sit down. 'Hey, what are you doing still up? Couldn't sleep?'

I shake my head. 'More to the point, why are you still here? Shouldn't you be back at the hotel?'

He grins. 'Back to my lonely single bed, you mean? In the tiny box room that overlooks the bins?'

'Ah.' I nod, sitting down and curling into the other end of the sofa. 'And I bet you paid a single person's supplement for the privilege.'

'Got it in one.' He angles himself towards me, stretching out his arms and long legs, giving a long growl that turns into a yawn. 'No, I was just really comfortable here and couldn't bear to move.'

'Until I came along and ruined it for you.'

He studies me thoughtfully. 'I wouldn't say that.'

'You looked so far away. I'm afraid I interrupted some great thought process.'

He laughs shortly and reaches down for his whisky glass. 'Nothing you'd be interested in,' he says, with an odd little smile, before taking a long slug of his drink. 'Want to join me?' He holds up the glass.

'Um, yes, please.' A nightcap might help me sleep. 'Just a small one.'

Alex springs to his feet in a waft of some deliciously fragrant man-scent and I settle back against the sofa while he's gone, staring into the flames.

He comes back in and hands me a glass. Then he sits back down and reaches for his whisky and we both stare into the log fire.

'How are you and Jackson?' he asks after a while. 'Do you think you two might get back together?'

I glance at him, taken aback. 'What makes you think that?' *Is it that obvious there's still something between Jackson and me?*

Alex shrugs. 'I just get the impression there's unfinished business there, that's all.'

I avoid his eye, pretending I'm mesmerised by the flames. 'With supermodel Sophie on the scene? I don't think so.' I try – but fail – to keep my tone free of bitterness.

'Don't run yourself down. You have loads of qualities she doesn't have,' he murmurs. 'You're just very – um – *different.*'

'Yes, I'm three stone heavier with no dress sense whatsoever,' I say, wheeling out my joke of earlier that fell completely flat.

Alex laughs. It's a lovely rich sound that mingles with the crackling of the fire and calms my agitated heart. 'That's not what I meant. And you know it.' He wags a finger, pretending to be cross with me.

'Well, you deserve to be happy, too, especially after your – erm – broken engagement.'

He smiles wistfully and runs a hand through his dark blond hair. 'You mean Milly.'

'Lovely name.'

'Lovely girl,' he says wholeheartedly. 'Just not for me, as it turned out.'

'What happened? If you don't mind me asking.'

'No, I don't mind,' he says softly. 'You've got something on your cheek, by the way.' He indicates the spot on his own face.

'Probably mascara.' I lick my finger and attempt to rub it off. 'Gone?'

'Gone. But you've also got some here.' He points at a spot beside his ear and I'm starting to rub at it before realising he's having me on.

'Idiot,' I laugh. 'Did I really have mascara on my cheek?'

He grins. 'You did. The first time.'

'So what about Milly?'

'Ah, yes. Milly.' He does a languorous stretch and I notice the well-defined muscles in his upper arms.

'You weren't trying to avoid the subject by any chance, were you? With your mascara distraction tactics?'

He pushes out his lips thoughtfully. 'Maybe.'

'So what happened? Sorry, you don't have to tell me if you don't want to.'

'No, I'd like to.'

I smile. 'It's probably a bit ghoulish but ever since Jackson and I split up, I've been fascinated by other people's break-up stories.'

'Weirdo.'

'I know. It takes one to know one, though.'

He shifts position so his elbow is on the back of the sofa, supporting his head. 'Well, Roxy, to satisfy your ghoulish fascination . . . Milly was the love of my life. She wasn't conventionally beautiful and she certainly wasn't a supermodel, but she was my idea of complete perfection. She was quirky and interesting and a little bit unpredictable. And she liked to braid her hair and dye it a different colour practically every week. I'm sure lots of people thought *she* was a weirdo. Not that they'd tell me that. Obviously. But I loved her sharp wit and the way she never took life too seriously. And her uncompromising loyalty to the people and things she believed in. And the way she never sulked after we'd argued. She'd blow up and then it would all be over. She was lovely.' He smiles wistfully. 'Still is, I imagine.'

'She sounds amazing. You must really miss her.'

'I did. Horribly. For a long time. But I knew it would never work in the long run.'

'Why wouldn't it?'

He shrugs. 'We wanted different things. She was clear right from the start that she never wanted to have children and, at first, I was okay with that. Milly wanted us to travel the world, not be tied down in one place with kids. But I come from a big tribe, with two brothers and a sister and loads of nephews and nieces – and the idea of never being able to be a dad myself began to niggle at me. And, eventually, it became too big an issue to ignore.' He pauses. 'But fair play to her. She stuck to what she wanted deep down and I admire her for that.'

I nod sadly, thinking of Milly, who's clearly an extraordinary sort of person. There can't be many women who'd give up the love of a gorgeous man like Alex to follow their dreams and ideals.

'Such a shame. She must miss you terribly.'

Alex sighs. 'Maybe.' Then he grins. 'She won't be missing the way I have to take my socks off wherever I go.'

We look at his feet.

They're actually quite attractive feet. Well-shaped with neatly clipped toenails. Not like some men's feet, which are truly gnarled and ugly.

'I presume not *everywhere*,' I say. 'I mean, you wouldn't take your socks off on public transport?'

'Depends on the length of the journey.'

'Weirdo.'

Later, I lie in bed, lulled by the effects of the whisky, thinking what a truly nice man Alex Webster is. Milly must have been mad to let him go. It's such a shame he's returning to Australia after the Christmas break.

I could do with a male friend like him . . .

Chapter 17

Next morning, I'm up early.

When I go down to the kitchen, Poppy's nowhere in sight. But Alex is sitting at the breakfast bar in jeans and a T-shirt – with bare feet, of course – cradling a mug.

'Morning. Hope you slept eventually.' He grins at me then raises his hands above his head in a huge stretch. Admiring his muscle definition again, I wonder if he works out or maybe plays some kind of sport.

'I did, thank you. How was it on the sofa?'

He shrugs. 'Fine. Although to be honest, I could have slept on a tightrope, I was so knackered.'

'Oh, dear. I hope I didn't wear you out.'

He flashes me a look I can't quite interpret. Then he says, 'I enjoyed your company.'

'Me, too.' I smile, remembering our easy banter. 'You'd make someone a lovely boyfriend.'

He looks down into his mug but I can tell he's pleased.

I fill the kettle then I turn, leaning back against the worktop. 'Speaking of boyfriends, do you know what Jackson's doing today?'

He looks confused for a second. 'Erm, not sure. Did you want to talk to him?'

He's looking at me intently, and I suddenly realise what I said.

'I didn't mean Jackson was *my* boyfriend. I mean, quite clearly he's not.' I force a laugh. 'I just meant . . . oh, I don't know.'

Feeling unaccountably flustered, I turn back to make my tea, which I always have first thing.

Alex clears his throat. 'I'm heading back to the hotel after this. I can give him a message if you like.'

'No, no. It's fine.' Why on earth did I even *mention* Jackson? It must have sounded to Alex like I have ideas of getting him back. Which possibly I have. But I didn't want *Alex* to know that! I take a gulp of my tea, which mysteriously turns out to be coffee. I must have spooned in granules without realising.

'Right, I need to get back.' Alex slides off the stool and heads for the door. 'See you later, Roxy.' He smiles but there's a tension in his expression that wasn't there last night. Perhaps he's just tired after sleeping on the sofa.

I take my coffee-disguised-as-tea over to the seat he's just vacated and sit there, sipping my hot drink, staring out at the snowy scene beyond the big picture window. The story Alex told me about having to break up with the charismatic Milly is still haunting me. Their relationship has a kind of romantic 'star-crossed lovers' aura in my imagination. It's all so tragic. They probably would never have split up if Milly had wanted kids. How do you get over someone who was so special to you?

I'm not sure I ever felt a sense of 'epic love story' with Jackson and me.

Flo thought Jackson and I were meant for each other, though. She was quite upset when it ended. Although I think that was probably because she'd thought that, at long last, I'd finally found a man capable of breaking down the barriers I'd built up ever since the accident.

Later, I'm in the kitchen with Poppy when Clemmy comes in for a glass of water, dressed in her running gear, her eyes looking suspiciously red.

'Are you okay, hun?' asks Poppy.

Clemmy shakes her head and takes a long glug of water. Then she turns, her face full of despair. 'Ryan and I had our first argument. And, to be honest, I think it was my fault. I just feel so irritable all the time.'

'That's probably because you're hungry,' I point out.

She nods wearily. 'I'm actually *starving*. All the time. I must be suffering withdrawal symptoms.'

'So eat something, Clem,' urges Poppy.

'I really want to.' She stares longingly at the mince

pies cooling on racks nearby, looking as if she might cry. Then she folds her arms. 'I can't! I need to lose the weight.' The agony on her face reveals the full extent of the conflict that's raging in her head.

'You should do it slowly, though, and eat lots of healthy food,' I say, holding out the plate of mince pies. I frown at them. 'Sorry, I know they're not especially healthy, but a little of what you fancy definitely does you good . . .'

Clemmy stares at the plate.

I wiggle it a bit. And Poppy says, 'Go on. We won't tell. And anyway, crash diets *never* work.'

Just as Clemmy reaches out, the door opens and Sophie marches in.

'Clementine!' she barks, and Clemmy freezes in shock and pulls back her hand.

'Gosh, they're – um – so tempting, Roxy.' She looks flushed and guilty. 'But thank you, Sophie, for stopping me.'

'You're welcome,' says Sophie smoothly. 'You know, we did a survey at the magazine with incredibly revealing results. Apparently, if you're fat when you walk down the aisle, you're *fifty per cent more likely* to be cheated on by your husband in the first year of marriage.'

Clemmy's eyes open wide in horror. 'Really? God, that's terrible.'

'Doesn't say much for the men,' murmurs Poppy.

Sophie gives a superior shrug.

'I'm going for another run,' says Clemmy with new resolve.

'Clem, you did a three-mile run this morning already,' Poppy points out gently.

'Have you had any breakfast?' I ask.

'Oh, yes, I did, Roxy. I had a green smoothie.' She glances at Sophie. 'And I've lost five pounds already!'

She dives out of the door, already jogging.

'How many people did you survey to get those crushing statistics?' Poppy asks Sophie. 'I can't believe men are that shallow.'

Sophie is tip-tapping to the door in her skyscraper heels. She turns and gives a thin smile. 'They're not. I made it up.'

I stare at her in disbelief. 'But why? Poor Clemmy looked horrified.'

'Good. She needs to lose that blubber.' There's not a hint of shame in her expression. 'Think about it. There's no actual point in running a feature where the "after" pictures are the same as the "before".' She flicks back her hair and walks out of the kitchen.

Poppy and I stare after her, dumbstruck.

'What a piece of work,' murmurs Poppy at last.

'Nothing else matters but the magazine. Not even people's feelings.'

'*Especially* not people's feelings!'

'Clemmy hardly ate a thing at dinner last night. Did you notice?'

Poppy nods. 'I've *never* seen her refuse dessert. And it was your glorious apple crumble cake, too!'

My heart lifts at Poppy's praise for my dessert. It was a miracle I got away with it! Luckily, the cake was huge, so there's lots left over for tonight, which means I don't have the same pressure to be creative like I did yesterday.

'So what are you going to do about Jackson?' she asks suddenly.

I swallow hard. 'Not sure. He says he's missed me and wants me back.'

'It looked pretty intense between you when I saw you on the ice.' She grins. 'I thought you were going to melt the rink away.'

'He's with Sophie.' I shrug helplessly.

Poppy looks at me as if I'm a mince pie short of a full Tupperware. 'Roxy. You're not going to let *her* stand in your way of happiness, I hope. Do you love him?'

I think hard before I answer. Then, cautiously, I say, 'I've longed to hear him say he never stopped caring.'

'Well, then, go for it! What's stopping you, Roxy?'

I smile wistfully at her. It's not as simple as that. If Jackson were to break up with Sophie, then the way would be clear for us. But his comment, 'I'll finish with

Sophie, *if that's what it will take*', has been niggling away at me ever since he said it. If Jackson really has had a big 'light-bulb moment' when he's realised his future lies with me and not with Sophie, shouldn't he be honest with her, instead of pretending everything's normal – just in case I say no? It makes me uneasy.

I put Jackson on a pedestal when I first met him, thinking he was Mr Perfect, but now, I'm starting to notice little things about him that don't quite sit with that description. Not that anyone is 'perfect', of course . . .

But isn't that all perfectly normal? In the first flush of romance, you see this wonderful person who's added sparkle to your life through a slightly blurred lens. They can do no wrong because you're carried away by these delicious feelings of love and attraction.

And then reality kicks in and you have to work out if you have enough in common to go the distance . . .

Poppy's waiting for an answer.

I shrug. 'I don't want to cause an upset before Clemmy and Ryan's party. They should be the focus of people's attention right now – not me and Jackson.'

It all sounds a bit lame, even to me. But the truth is, I'm scared. My heart is still healing from the break-up. Can I really risk getting back with Jackson only for the same thing to happen all over again?

'And I need to work out how I feel,' I add.

Poppy nods. 'You and me both.' She stares away at the lake beyond the window.

'Are you still determined to keep the baby a secret from Jed?'

'I don't know what else I can do,' she says slowly. 'I don't want Jed feeling he has to make a commitment to me just because there's a baby on the way.'

She turns, her eyes full of torment. 'Oh God, I love him so much, Roxy, and it's *killing* me not being able to tell him he's going to be a dad. But I just *can't* . . .'

Chapter 18

'I want to be Cinderella,' says Clemmy, clasping her hands happily to her chest and doing a little twirl in an imaginary ball gown.

'Clemmy,' says Poppy, who's sitting with her laptop at the breakfast bar. 'You *shall* go to the ball.' She ticks a box on the screen and Clemmy does a funny little dance of delight. 'Right, I'm off to talk Ryan into ditching his Joker costume and going as Prince Charming instead.'

'Good luck with that, Clem,' grins Poppy as Cinders-to-be rushes out.

Ruby, Gloria and I remain, crowded around Poppy, looking at outfits available from the nearest shop hiring out fancy dress costumes.

Poppy decides she wants to go as a sexy Cruella de Vil.

'But what about Jed?' asks Ruby. 'Don't you want to go as Beauty and the Beast, or Romeo and Juliet, or something romantic like that?'

'No, thanks,' says Poppy rather too quickly. 'I want to be a strong woman who can survive perfectly well *without* a man!'

'And who terrorises puppies?' Ruby looks at her strangely.

Poppy laughs. 'I've always been the opposite of romantic.'

Ruby frowns, about to argue. So I step in quickly. 'I'm going to be Clemmy's fairy godmother.'

I've given it a lot of thought and this seems like the perfect solution. I need a costume that covers my top half completely, and the fairy godmothers I've seen in panto or on TV seem to come in one of two varieties: the glamorous diva in the sparkling, revealing dress or the quirky type with sharp one-liners and a penchant for motherly satin capes and hoods.

The latter will be perfect!

Ruby points at a glamorous version. 'You'd look fabulous in that, Roxy!'

'Er, no, I'm not keen on that one. I'll – um – have a look at the website later and choose.'

'I'll be picking them up tomorrow so can you decide soon?' says Ruby. 'Sophie's going to get her costume from the huge fashion store at *Dazzle*. Won't that be awesome?'

Some half-hearted murmurs follow in response. *Bloody typical*, I think to myself. *Sophie will look a million dollars and I'll look like somebody's weird, eccentric aunt.*

'Do they do camping equipment on that website?' groans Gloria. 'It's just I'll probably need to go to the party dressed as a tent if this abdominal bloating gets any worse!'

'A marquee would be far more sophisticated,' quips Sophie, entering the kitchen at that moment. 'You could get one in blush pink to match your hot flushes.' She gives one of her tinkly laughs. 'Although you're right, Gloria. A plain ridge tent is probably more your style.'

Gloria, who normally couldn't give two hoots what people say about her, looks a little crestfallen.

There's a beat of silence, then Ruby hoots with laughter. '*A plain ridge tent is probably more your style*! Good one, Sophie.'

Sophie smiles, basking in Ruby's open appreciation, while the rest of us look on in stunned silence.

It occurs to me that Sophie must have a whole host of *Dazzle*-reading fans who drool over the magazine and regard her as the high priestess of fashion. Like Miranda Priestly in *The Devil Wears Prada* movie. Come to think of it, Sophie probably styles herself on the Meryl Streep character. She's certainly ice-cold and ruthless enough.

Seeing her mum's face, Ruby has a change of heart. 'Mum, you'll look lovely whatever you wear.'

Gloria rallies a little at her daughter's words, and I find myself wishing Ruby would think before she spoke. Being a hormonal teenager is no excuse for bad behaviour.

'Oh my God!' Ruby is staring, wide-eyed, across the room. 'Who on earth did *that?*'

We all look over to where she's pointing, at the fridge door.

Everyone gasps in unison.

We were all too focused on choosing our costumes to have noticed before now. But the glamorous photo of Sophie has been 'enhanced' with a black felt tip pen. She's now reclining on her lounger, sporting a moustache reminiscent of an evil dictator's, plus several gaping holes where her teeth once were. Someone's drawn a big thought balloon coming out of her head that says, 'I'm editor-in-chief, you know. I love ME!'

Poppy and I look at each other with the exact same expression – a combination of shock, disbelief and a small measure of guilty glee.

'That is *so* disrespectful!' exclaims Ruby, speaking aloud what Sophie would probably say if she wasn't completely struck dumb. 'Did *you* do that, Poppy?'

'No, I bloody didn't.' She's trying not to smile as she denies it, and just for a second I wonder if Poppy *is* the culprit.

'Well, if you ask me, it's just plain sour grapes,' says

Ruby crossly. 'Whoever did it is obviously really jealous of you, Sophie, so I wouldn't waste a single second worrying about it.'

Sophie finds her voice. 'I don't intend to,' she says icily. 'Ruby, can you organise a courier for me? I need to get my costume biked over from *Dazzle*. I'll give you the phone number of the one we always use.' She whisks out of the room, her body language revealing her total displeasure.

'Some people are *so horrible*!' says Ruby, following her out of the kitchen.

Poppy sighs. 'I thought Ruby had more sense than to fawn over Sophie just because she's a magazine editor.'

'She's still just a kid, really,' murmurs Gloria, who's being a darned sight more forgiving of her daughter than *I* would be.

'Do you think one of the guys did it for a joke?' I ask, staring at the photo. Jackson is probably the only person who can be ruled out.

'I know Ryan's pretty pissed off at Sophie,' says Poppy. 'He'd be much happier with a small wedding and he hates that Clemmy's been talked into doing this fat-shaming magazine feature. All for the sake of a glamorous wedding venue.'

'Would Ryan have done that? It doesn't seem like his style. So who, then?' I wonder aloud.

I happen to glance at Gloria when I say it and she frowns and says quickly, 'It wasn't me.' Her cheeks are flushed bright red. But that could be just one of her 'glowing moments'. She certainly has more reason than any of us to deface a poster in protest. In fact, I really hope it *was* Gloria and that she's found some satisfaction in getting her own back on Sophie!

Chapter 19

Next day, the morning of the pairs skating contest, we wake to a surprise.

Snow has fallen thickly overnight, casting its fairytale spell on the trees and turning the entire landscape into a magical winter wonderland.

The snow lightens the atmosphere in the cabin, and Ruby, especially, seems completely entranced by it. She disappears soon after breakfast without telling Gloria where she's off to, and returns at lunchtime, announcing that she's been getting to know Sam, from the farm across the road.

'Who is this Sam?' Gloria wants to know. 'Would I like him? How old is he? What are his intentions towards you, Ruby? Because I know teenage lads and they're definitely a species apart.'

'Tom's all right,' points out Ruby.

'Your brother's got some sense, not like some of the youngsters I know,' concedes Gloria. 'Just don't go diving into anything, Ruby, that's all I'm saying. You're still far too young for boyfriends.'

Ruby, who's busy making a hot chocolate in the kitchen, gives a big sigh. 'Chill, Gloria. I'm *seventeen*! And anyway, Sam's just a friend. His dad owns the farm and we've been chatting, not smoking anything weird in case you were wondering.'

Gloria's eyes open wide in horror. 'Well, I *wasn't* wondering – until now! And don't call me Gloria!'

'Sorry, Mum.'

Poppy and I exchange a grin. We're busy making the extra mince pies that will be needed for the skating contest later. Thankfully, I don't have to think about making a dessert for tonight. The plan is we'll eat up leftovers when we return later from the ice rink – including the rest of my successful apple crumble cake.

The contest is due to start at six. By five-thirty, we're all gathered in the hall, suitably wrapped up in our scarves, gloves and thick winter coats against the gaspingly-cold December air, then we set off crunching through to the rink.

We're meeting Alex, Jackson and Sophie at the rink.

Ruby seems a bit distracted and keeps glancing over the fields to our right. Suddenly she stops and cheers, then starts waving. We all stare over the snow-blanketed fields and a loud mechanical noise fills the wintry air.

'It's Sam on his snowmobile. He said he'd give me a

lift!' yells Ruby. She opens a gate and starts marching across, converging with the figure on the snowmobile.

'Just be careful!' shouts Gloria, but her voice is drowned out by Sam revving the vehicle as Ruby clambers on behind him. They take off across the snowy field with an ear-splitting roar, Ruby clinging on perilously with one arm and turning to wave at us with her other.

'Hold on tight, Ruby!' yells Gloria, watching in dismay as her daughter disappears over the brow of a hill.

Bob puts his arm around Gloria. 'She'll be fine. Don't worry, love. Your daughter is more than capable of looking after herself.'

'You're absolutely right, Bob,' laughs Jed. 'Wish I'd thought of organising transport by snowmobile myself.' He moves closer to Poppy and takes her hand, but I can tell from their stiff body language that things aren't good between them.

Gloria snuggles into Bob and says, 'Thank God I have you to stop me tearing my hair out.'

When we get to the rink, Alex, Jackson, Ryan and Clemmy are standing with their skates on by the rink but there's no sign yet of Ruby.

'Where's Sophie?' asks Poppy.

Jackson glances at his watch. 'She's – erm – got a problem at work she's trying to sort out on the phone.

She said she'd be here for the start of the contest, though.'

Poppy frowns. 'Well, I hope she is. I'd hate to let Sylvia down after she's gone to so much trouble organising tonight.'

'Sophie will be here,' Jackson says grimly.

At six o'clock prompt, we all gather around the rink and Sylvia makes a little speech, welcoming everyone and saying how pleased she is to have representatives of so many fine local businesses here tonight. She invites those taking part to the café for wine and mince pies after the event, then says, 'And now, without further ado, let's give a big round of applause for the first daring couple onto the ice. It's Ronnie and Hazel Bickerstock, representing The Big Belly Deli.'

Ronnie and Hazel, who've really gone to town with the sparkle and are dressed as a pair of Christmas trees – with awkward-looking scaffolding under their bauble-covered green costumes – skate onto the ice, bow to the applause, then – to the soundtrack of 'I'm Dreaming of a White Christmas' – proceed to glide gracefully and competently around the rink. There's just a minor wobble as Ronnie loses the giant fairy from on top of his head and, in bending to rescue it, almost brings Hazel crashing down with him. But they manage to stay upright and fit in a fair few twirls and spins into the bargain. They get a huge round of applause when their routine ends.

The Big Belly Deli are followed by Doughnuts to Die For, Sugar-Coated News, Barney's All-American Burgers and Roy's Roast Chestnuts.

Sophie still hasn't appeared – and it's almost the turn of Truly Scrumptious to take to the ice.

Ruby has arrived with Sam, and Jackson is away trying to find Sophie. Poppy is looking more stressed by the second at the thought of having to tell Sylvia she doesn't have a pair to skate.

'There's Jackson,' she mutters and hurries over to meet him as he walks out of the hotel entrance.

Joining us, Jackson shrugs. 'No idea where she's got to.'

'Will we have to cancel?' asks Ruby, looking disappointed.

'Nope!' Jackson shakes his head. 'I'll just have to skate with someone else.' For some reason he turns to me and gives me a big smile.

Everyone else is now looking at me, too, and for a second I'm not quite sure what's happening.

Then Jackson holds out his hand. 'Roxy?'

My heart starts beating at a million miles an hour. I stare, aghast, at everyone. This has to be a joke.

Surely he can't mean he wants me to compete on the ice with him?

But apparently that's exactly what he's suggesting. More than suggesting, actually. His hand is at my waist, guiding me firmly towards the ice, and my feeble protests are being drowned out by everyone laughing and saying things like, 'Go, Roxy! You can do it. It's just a bit of fun.'

In my confusion, I catch Poppy's eye, swiftly followed by Alex's. They're the only ones who don't look enthusiastic about the idea of me skating with Jackson. But then, they're the only ones who know about my romantic history with him.

Sylvia is announcing us now and there's no going back if I don't want to let Poppy down . . .

Everyone is cheering and Jackson beams down at me and shouts, 'You've seen us perform it. Just do your best and follow my lead, okay?'

I'm sure he means this to be reassuring but tell that to my wobbly legs!

Jackson is skating off to the far side of the rink, so – my heart in my mouth and feeling about as likely to remain in an upright position as Bambi – I start making my way awkwardly over to the opposite side.

When I finally get there, remarkably in one piece, I see Ruby standing at the rail. She shouts, 'We're right behind you, Roxy!' and I realise the whole of the Truly Scrumptious team have moved round the rink to where I am. I'm not sure if I feel better, knowing they're supporting me. Or worse because I'm about to make a complete arse of myself in front of them.

Then I catch Alex's eye and he gives me a big smile and a double thumbs-up – and just the sight of him actually makes me relax a little. I give him a scared little smile then turn to face Jackson, ready to start skating towards him.

The space between us seems massive. How, I wonder, are we going to meet in the middle, since Jackson skates about five times as fast as me?

I turn to Ruby. 'Can you give me a push?' I hiss.

'A bush?' She looks puzzled.

'No, a *push*!' I mutter anxiously. 'Just to give me a bit of a head start on Jackson.'

Ruby's face clears. 'Oh, right. Gotcha! Right, here goes . . .'

'Not yet!'

But it's too late. I feel myself being shoved abruptly from behind and I'm off. Ruby must have some strength in her because, with a bit of effort on my part at keeping up the original momentum, I find myself flying along the ice with a speed I've never reached before.

Suddenly there's a shout from someone in the crowd. 'I'm here, darling!'

Jackson glances over and so do I. It's Sophie and she's climbing athletically over the barrier onto the rink, looking unbelievably cute in her crystal-encrusted skating dress. And, to my horror, Jackson stops in his tracks and starts skating towards her.

I'm travelling at a fair old speed but I was expecting to land in the safety of Jackson's arms and let him catch me and keep me on my feet. But now it's not going to happen and, although I've started to slow down, I've passed the middle point of the ice and the barrier on the other side is starting to loom horrendously close. I'm just going to whack straight into it if I can't stop on time.

Panic rears up inside me. Should I just deliberately sit down on the ice as a stopping tactic?

But a second later, I realise it's far too late to take evasive action. I'm going to crash into the barrier . . .

I close my eyes tightly, praying I'll survive the impact.

And then, suddenly, I'm grabbed by the waist by two strong hands and forcibly steered away from danger. Panting, I cling onto my rescuer as relief floods through me.

'You're okay. You're okay,' murmurs a soothing male voice.

Alex?

I collapse weakly into his arms, my whole body trembling, and allow him to lead me gently over to the rink entrance.

Chapter 20

We stand on the other side of the barrier to watch Jackson and Sophie skate their routine.

I'm still trembling quite violently but Alex keeps his arm firmly around me and I sink against him, so grateful to have the solid strength of his body supporting me. I feel as weak as a new-born chick and couldn't move away from him, even if I wanted to.

And I very definitely don't want to . . .

Jackson and Sophie are brilliant together and the audience applauds wildly when they finish. It's strange, but with Alex's arm around me, I feel so secure again that I don't even feel any anger towards Jackson for abandoning me on the ice the way he did. And I'm sure he didn't mean to desert me. He just reacted instinctively to Sophie's sudden shout, that was all. It could have happened to anyone . . .

'It looks as if Truly Scrumptious has the edge,' murmurs Alex into my ear, and a funny little shiver runs through me. Thinking it's the cold, I snuggle a little closer.

'I hope so, for Poppy's sake.' I nod at the TV cameramen who've set up in a special area at the rink side. 'Winning this would be great publicity for her business.'

'You were very brave to do what you did,' Alex says, and I laugh awkwardly and turn to say it was nothing. But my eyes collide with his and for the first time I notice how gorgeous and mesmerising they are – so the words on my lips just float away unsaid into the frosty air around us.

At last, I find my voice, although at first try, it comes out rather croakily. 'Thank you, Alex.' I clear my throat. 'Thank you from the bottom of my heart for saving me,' I tell him solemnly, meaning every single word. 'I don't know how you managed to get to me in time. You must have been literally flying across the ice. But I'm so grateful.'

He gazes down at me, his arm still tightly around me, and I can't help noticing the way his eyes crinkle attractively when he smiles. My heart gives a weird little lurch.

'You're very welcome, Roxy,' he says, in an even more solemn tone than me. Then we both start to laugh at the same time.

'Roxy, I'm *so sorry* you didn't get to have your

moment. It's just Sophie knows the routine so well and . . .'

The magic spell binding me to Alex is abruptly broken by the approach of Jackson and Sophie. Jackson is full of excuses. Sophie is anxiously checking her phone.

'These things happen,' I tell him.

'Right, who's up for a hot chocolate over there? While we wait to hear who wins?' He looks pointedly at me.

I shrug, and – thinking everyone will be going over to the café – I start following Jackson. As I do, Alex lets go of me, and I glance back at him, feeling suddenly cold and as if something is missing.

'No thanks, I'm heading back to the hotel for a drink,' says Alex, walking away. 'A stiff whisky, I think.'

I stare after him, feeling oddly panicky. To my surprise, I have a real urge to follow him. 'Is the whisky to combat the cold?' I call.

He turns back, still walking, and gives me a sad sort of smile that makes my heart lurch all over again. But instead of replying to my question, he just raises his hand and continues on his way, back to the hotel.

Jackson, who clearly hasn't picked up on the tension between Alex and me at all, says, 'Right. Hot chocolate, Roxy?'

At which point Sophie, who's off her phone now, takes Jackson's arm and purrs, 'Will you miss me when I'm away doing my modelling agency interview?'

He turns to her, looks deep into her eyes and murmurs, 'Sophie, just the thought of spending even one night without you is unbearable. What's the bee supposed to do without the honey?'

Sophie, looking overjoyed at the sentiment, dives on him and smothers him in kisses. 'Oh, what a lovely thing to say. You really are the most romantic man I've ever met, Jackson Cooper.'

He laps it all up, grinning at me. And I stare at him, stunned at the way the words just rolled off his tongue.

The very same words he said to me when we were together and I was madly in love with him!

A cold feeling slithers through my veins. Did Jackson mean those words when he said them to me? Does he mean them now, saying them to Sophie? It seems unlikely, given that he's offered to break up with her for me!

I feel as if I'm suddenly seeing him in a whole different light and it's not a very pretty picture . . .

Chapter 21

Over the next few days, I don't see much of Alex. He's apparently catching up with some friends who live on the other side of Guildford. According to Jed, it was a spur-of-the-moment decision to go and stay with them for a few nights.

It feels odd somehow not to have Alex popping into the kitchen for a coffee now and again and chatting to me while the kettle boils. Or seeing him when we all sit down to dinner in the evening.

I even miss my skating lessons.

But having said that, Poppy and I are so frantically busy baking for Sylvia that I don't actually have time to examine my feelings about the night of the skating contest very closely. Truly Scrumptious won the competition and there was a big photo of Jackson and Sophie in next day's local paper with the headline, 'Skating win is *Truly* delicious!'

As a consequence of the publicity, visitor numbers

at the rink have rocketed and Poppy's baking is even more in demand. To cope with Sylvia's increased order, I'm up very early every morning and, by the time I fall into bed, I'm so exhausted, I fall asleep as soon as my head touches the pillow.

After a day or two, when I've had time to think about things rationally, I realise that I only felt such a strong bond with Alex because he rescued me from potential disaster. Thinking I was going to crash into that barrier in front of the gathered crowd was terrifying, so it was no wonder I felt indebted to him after he saved me!

Jed says Alex will be returning in time for Clemmy and Ryan's engagement party on Saturday night, and I'm looking forward to that. It will be good to catch up with Alex, as a friend.

I've been so busy, I haven't even seen much of Jackson, which to be honest I'm quite relieved about. I'm vaguely aware that Sophie is down in the dumps about something but I'm not sure what because she hasn't confided in anyone, except Jackson. She seems to spend lots of time with her phone glued to her ear or shrieking hysterically at Jackson that 'they' are treating her scandalously (whoever 'they' are). When she's not doing that, she's ordering poor Clemmy on another exercise regime, which Poppy, Ryan and I don't really approve of. But Clemmy seems determined to lose the weight for the magazine feature, and nothing we say can dissuade her.

As for Poppy, she still hasn't told Jed about the baby and she seems to be growing paler and more unhappy every day.

She and I stay in the kitchen most of the time, with barely even time to talk as we pull trays in and out of the oven, mix yet more pastry, and check the pan of filling that seems to be constantly bubbling on the stove. Then there's the icing of the gingerbread Santas whose expressions, frankly, are becoming more shady-looking by the day as we try to ice so many in the time available. But there have been no complaints from Sylvia, so she's obviously happy with our work.

On Thursday, it snows again, turning everything into a winter wonderland. Ruby disappears for most of the day and, when questioned later, she grins and says her new friend, Sam – who lives at the nearby farm – has the use of a snowmobile and they've been testing it to see how fast it will go. At this revelation, poor Gloria turns almost as white as the snow itself.

By Friday, the day before Clemmy and Ryan's engagement party, I've attempted three different desserts, with varying success. The raspberry cream tarts tasted good, although the pastry was a little too crisp (verging on burnt), the lemon meringue pie was fiddly to do but turned into a triumph, if I do say so myself, and the chocolate mousse was nice and bubbly and rich, and seemed to go down a treat with everyone.

I still don't think Poppy has sussed that I'm actually learning on the job. But, to be honest, at the moment she's so distracted by her own problems that I doubt she'd even notice if I served up baked doormat with a topping of parsnip ice cream.

I keep thinking fondly of Alex and how he helped with the apple crumble cake. But I'm actually managing fine on my own, too, much to my surprise.

The day of the engagement party dawns bright and sunny.

Waiting for Poppy in the kitchen, I stare out at the dazzling expanse of snow leading down to the lake, thinking what a perfect day it is.

'Penny for them,' says Poppy coming into the kitchen.

She looks as bone-weary as I feel. There are dark patches below her eyes and it's fairly clear she's not sleeping properly.

'Oh, nothing exciting. How are you?' I ask.

Joining me at the window, she groans. 'Jed slept on the sofa bed in the study last night because I was tossing and turning so much. And to be honest, I was glad. I don't know if it's the hormones going wild in my system, but I can't stand him near me at the moment.' She turns watery eyes on me. 'How sad is that?'

I sigh heavily. 'No wonder things don't feel normal between you when you're keeping such a huge secret from him. You need to tell him about the baby, Poppy.'

She doesn't even reply. She just walks away and starts opening cupboards, getting out ingredients and slamming the doors shut.

I watch her for a moment. It's all very well me giving advice, but I'm not in Poppy's shoes. If I were, wouldn't I be feeling the same as she does? I know for a fact I'd never want a man to feel trapped into commitment because of a baby . . .

She turns and there are tears running down her face. 'Sorry, Roxy, I just feel powerless to know what to do. And until I can get my head clear on how I feel, I'm keeping the baby news to myself, okay? But I will tell Jed. Eventually. I promise.'

I nod and she attempts a smile. 'I'm so glad I bumped into you that day in the supermarket, Roxy. I'd be a complete wreck right now if I didn't have you to talk to!'

I grin. 'And bake with. Speaking of which, how many mince pies do we need to make today?'

She groans. 'Too many. Honestly, I had a nightmare last night where a giant gingerbread man was chasing me down a dark alley, brandishing a piping gun, and I couldn't escape because the exit was blocked with a mountain of mincers.'

We look at each other and burst out laughing.

Ruby walks in at that moment and demands to know what we're laughing at, so Poppy tells her about the dream.

'Ha! Brilliant!' she says. 'I used to have that dream where I'm falling from a high building and I was always terrified. But then I decided I wanted to be a stunt artist.'

'So do you land on something soft and bouncy these days?' I ask curiously.

'No, I just never have the dream now. Bloody typical! I'm all prepared and now it never happens!'

'That's life for you,' grins Poppy.

Ruby glances at her watch. 'Right, I'm taking Mum's car into Guildford to collect the fancy dress costumes.'

We both glance at her in alarm.

'Don't worry. She said I could. And the roads are clear now the snow plough has been along. There's no point passing my test if I'm not allowed to get behind the wheel, is there?'

'Well, drive carefully,' calls Poppy after her as she leaves, jingling the car keys with relish.

'I will.' She pops her head back round the door. 'Oh and a courier will be dropping off a parcel this morning. It's Sophie's costume from *Dazzle*. Don't open it until I get back!'

'Lucky Sophie, having the entire fashion world at her disposal!' Poppy says.

'Yes, she gave me the brief and I spoke to *such* a nice man in charge of the fashion store. We decided together what would suit Sophie perfectly. I can't wait for her to see it. She's going to be the belle of the ball. Well, after Clemmy, that is.' She beams and hurries out.

The mention of Sophie and the fabulous dress winging its way from *Dazzle* as we speak does nothing to improve my mood. And Ruby's obvious adoration of Sophie is just plain irritating!

'Why on earth she thinks that woman is so fabulous beats me,' says Poppy, echoing exactly what I was thinking.

'She's impressed with the packaging and not what's inside,' I murmur, and Poppy laughs and agrees.

An hour later, as the first batch of mince pies are filling the kitchen with a glorious Christmassy aroma and making me feel hungry, the doorbell rings.

Instantly, my heart starts hammering, thinking it might be Jackson. I've been successfully avoiding him for the past few days, but it's only a matter of time before he corners me and demands to know how I feel about him. I can tell from his expression recently that he's growing pretty fed up with Sophie's increasingly erratic moods.

But it's not Jackson. It's the courier Ruby ordered, with a package that presumably contains Sophie's fairy-tale 'Elsa' dress. Poppy doesn't even give it a second glance when I take it through, which just shows how down she is. Normally, she'd be wanting to take a peek at the contents.

I'm not keen on seeing the dress, either – but for a different reason. I don't especially want to see the outfit Sophie has chosen with Jackson in mind – especially since mine is a boringly conservative number with a matching cape that wouldn't look out of place on a woman three times my age.

I would have liked to feel glamorous or at least reasonably attractive at the party.

An image of Alex floats into my mind, as it's been doing oddly regularly of late. Ever since the night of the skating contest, to be exact. It would be nice to get dressed up and feel 'normal' for a change.

But the trouble is, it doesn't seem to matter how many times I tell myself that a person can still be attractive, even with burn scars like mine, it doesn't seem to register as true.

I should be used to my scars by now.

But even now, eleven years after it happened, if I accidentally catch sight of myself undressed in a mirror (which is rare), I want to break down and cry at the sight of the mottled bumps and ridges on my shoulder and part of the way down my arm, still visible even after two rounds of skin grafts.

I can't recall what it feels like to have smooth,

unblemished skin you can be proud of. And to be able to face a mirror without fear.

We're just starting on the icing of the gingerbread men when Ruby bursts in with a big box that she dumps breathlessly on the kitchen floor. Excitedly, she wastes no time in tearing off the brown tape and diving in amongst the cellophane-wrapped outfits.

'Mine!' She holds it up in triumph. It's a long, silky green dress.

I stare at it, puzzled. 'I thought you'd decided to go as Wonder Woman.'

She shakes her head. 'I changed my mind. I'm going to be Princess Fiona from the *Shrek* movie. I didn't fancy melting the night away as a superhero. And Fiona's a bit more glamorous.'

Poppy smiles. 'Perhaps you're growing up, Ruby.'

Ruby waggles her eyebrows. 'Maybe. Did Sophie's outfit arrive from *Dazzle*?'

'Yup.' Poppy points at the brown parcel on the worktop.

Ruby rubs her hands together. 'Brilliant. Can we have a grand try-on? Just the girls, I mean. The guys will probably look pretty boring. I really wouldn't want to be a boy. You'd have to pretend you hated getting dressed up!'

The 'grand try-on' takes place after lunch when everyone is here.

Ruby brings the box through to the living room and stands by the log fire doling out our outfits like Father Christmas.

Clemmy is thrilled with her Cinderella dress and rushes off to try it on immediately, dragging Ryan and his Batman outfit in her wake.

'Very sexy,' says Jed when Poppy holds up her beautiful Cruella de Vil dress. His face is full of love and affection but she quickly deflects his remark, saying she'll need to have her hair done specially to match the costume. Turning away from Jed, she asks if I'll do it for her.

'Of course I will.' My heart goes out to Jed, who's staring sadly into space. I should imagine the last thing he's interested in is his Woody cowboy outfit.

Ruby hands me my cellophane bag with a wink.

I glance at the folded-up costume and my heart skips a beat. This doesn't look like the outfit I ordered. It's far too sparkly!

Quickly I rip open the bag and shake it out.

'Ruby? I think you've ordered the wrong one. I wanted the fairy godmother costume with the cape and the hood, not the one with the "come hither and let me ravage you" cleavage.'

Jackson and Ryan glance over with interest.

Ruby casts me a sheepish look. 'I thought you'd look much better in the glam one. The other one looked like it was meant for a granny.'

I grin, pretending I'm not that bothered, but inside I'm panicking. Apart from a deep neckline, the dress has no sleeves. Far from being the cover-up I wanted, this dress will reveal everything I'm desperate to conceal.

I can't possibly wear it. Unless . . .

Thinking fast, I mentally sift through the clothes I brought. I'm sure I packed the little cream shrug that I always wear with dresses. It's not the perfect colour to slip over a pale pink satin dress, but it would definitely do the job.

I feel my heart rate slow with relief.

'Where's my dress?' asks Sophie. 'Can you bring it through, Ruby?'

Ruby scrambles to her feet immediately, which irritates me. Hero worship seems to have turned her into Sophie's unpaid assistant! I glance at Poppy and I can see she's thinking the same.

'I was saving yours for last,' says Ruby, presenting Sophie with her parcel.

Sophie waves it away. 'Open it, then!'

'Oh. Okay.' Ruby drops to the floor and starts wrestling with the tape. 'I was kinda hoping you would . . . okay, here goes. Drum roll everyone. Here comes the dress of the night!'

Sophie is sitting back in her chair, a smug look on her face, no doubt anticipating everyone's rapturous response to the *Dazzle* creation about to emerge.

'Ta-dah!' Ruby holds up the costume.

There's a shocked silence.

Sophie sits forward with an incredulous frown and barks, 'What the fuck is *that*?'

'Oh.' Ruby looks at the thing she's holding up and blanches. 'Christ, it's the Grinch. How did that happen?'

Ryan snorts. 'Good choice, Sophie. Very Christmassy.'

'You might have to re-think the diamond tiara, though,' says Jackson, grinning broadly.

Sophie has gone white with fury. She doesn't even bother responding to Jackson's droll comment. The atmosphere is electric.

'God, sorry, Sophie,' says Ruby, red-faced. 'I think the bloke I spoke to was a bit deaf. I definitely asked for *Breakfast at Tiffany's* but he must have thought I said *the Grinch*.'

Sophie stares coldly at Ruby. 'That makes no sense at all. And if you think I'm wearing *that* thing to the party tonight,' she announces, her voice tinged with hysteria, 'you are very much mistaken.'

Everyone is trying not to laugh. Out of the corner of my eye I see Poppy's shoulders shaking.

Sophie rises to her feet and sweeps across the carpet towards the door, but her foot catches the edge of the costume box and she staggers a little. Everyone holds their breath. She lands half in Gloria's lap and leaps away as if she's touched an electric fence, before making it out of the door.

At which point Ruby, whose complexion has been growing redder by the second, sinks to the floor and completely corpses.

'Ah-ha-ha-ha! Sorry. Ah-ha-ha-ha! Oh my God, that was the best laugh ever!' She's rolling around, clutching her stomach, tears rolling down her cheeks. '*If you think I'm wearing* that *thing*,' she says in a stern voice uncannily like Sophie's, '*you are very much mistaken!*'

'Did you order the wrong one deliberately?' asks Poppy, looking as if she can't believe it.

'No, of course not.' Ruby looks all wide-eyed innocence.

'Oh my God, you did, didn't you?' says Ryan. He laughs incredulously then reaches over and high-fives her. Then he glances apologetically at Jackson. 'Sorry, mate. But it *is* pretty funny.'

Jackson just smiles and shrugs. 'I'd better go and see how she is.' He gets up at a leisurely pace and saunters out.

'I can*not* believe you did that, Ruby!' gasps Gloria, who's been sitting with a stunned look on her face. 'I really can't take you anywhere!'

'It wasn't a nice thing to do, Ruby,' says Poppy, trying to look stern.

Something occurs to me. 'Oh my God, was it you who drew the moustache on Sophie's photo?'

Ruby turns sulky. 'What if it was?' Her chin comes up in defiance. 'No one tells my mum she's old, fat and unattractive. *I'm* allowed to because I'm her daughter and I love her – but not some rude woman who acts like she's a celebrity just because she's *editor-in-chief* of a stupid magazine!'

She scrambles to her feet and marches for the door. Gloria, who's looking dumbstruck, tries to catch her hand but Ruby shakes her off and disappears. When I pass the kitchen a moment later, on my way upstairs to try on the dress, Ruby is slouched at the breakfast bar, leaning her head on her hands, staring out at the snowy scene beyond the window.

'You okay?'

She sits up and stares glumly at me. 'She deserved it. She's been horrible to Mum. And she's got poor Clemmy paranoid about her weight, all for the sake of her stupid magazine.'

I smile. It's hard to argue with her. 'Would you like a gingerbread Santa?' I go into the kitchen and find the tin we keep in the cupboard, full of misshapes. Ruby shakes her head. 'Thanks, Roxy, but I'm not hungry. I think I'll FaceTime Chloe.'

'Okay. I'll leave you to it.' I press her shoulder to show I approve of her defending Gloria.

Upstairs, voices are coming from the main bathroom. It's Jackson and Sophie. I can't hear what Jackson's saying because he's speaking in a low, steady tone, but Sophie sounds as if she's verging on hysterical. As I pass, she wails, 'I can't believe this is happening. What the hell am I going to do?'

It seems a little over-the-top to get so emotional about an outfit for the party tonight, but then Sophie is editor of a fashion magazine. I suppose she has standards to uphold.

I disappear into my room and hold the fairy godmother dress up to myself in the mirror. With the shrug over the top, it will hopefully be fine to wear tonight.

I slip off my jeans and top, and – ignoring the mirror – step into the big, flouncy skirt. I'm pulling the bodice up when I hear footsteps outside. A man's voice shouts, 'Ruby?' then there's a tap on the door and someone bursts into the room.

I shove my arms in and hastily yank the dress up over my shoulders, turning at an angle so whoever it is can't see my scarred arm.

Ruby is standing in the doorway. And, with a shock, I see Alex just behind her.

Our eyes meet and a funny charge like a little electric shock runs through my entire body. He's here! I'm surprised at how pleased I am. I was starting to think he might not make it back for the party.

He seems as shocked as I am to suddenly see me. After a moment, he gives his head a little shake as if to get himself back on track. 'Hi, Roxy. Sorry, I didn't mean to . . .' He shrugs.

'Don't worry. It's fine.' I rush to reassure him but his face remains tense.

'Ruby, your mum's looking for you.' He gives me a fleeting smile and disappears.

'God, sorry, Roxy,' says Ruby. 'I shouldn't have just barged in like that. I just wanted to make sure you were okay with the dress I ordered for you.'

I lean down and pick up the shrug from the bed and slip into it without turning round. 'Yes, it's fine. You're probably right about the other one being a bit boring.'

She nods. 'That's good.'

Another desperate wail emanates from the bathroom.

'Right, I'll go and find Mum,' says Ruby quickly, and she disappears.

I breathe a sigh of relief and sink down onto the bed. At least I managed to cover up before the door opened.

At least, I hope I did . . .

Chapter 22

When it comes to deciding who's going in which car to the party, I somehow end up travelling in Jackson's car, with him and Sophie in the front and Alex next to me in the back seat.

I'd been looking forward to seeing Alex again, but he seems strangely silent. He barely says a word to me and stares out of the side window into the darkness the entire way to the venue.

Jackson makes an attempt at small talk but Sophie seems focused on her own woes. She's still acting as if she's stressed to the eyeballs for some reason and keeps up a stream of angry stage whispers to Jackson, who keeps shaking his head and giving her sympathetic looks. From what I can tell, she isn't cross with Jackson himself. But something is definitely going on.

She's obviously abandoned the Grinch costume – and the idea of fancy dress –and has chosen to wear a long, slinky, figure-hugging dress in kingfisher blue silk that she apparently brought with her.

I sit in the back, also staring out of the window, wishing I could be anywhere but here – however gorgeous the party venue sounds. My fairy godmother costume is slightly itchy around the plunging neckline with an incredibly tight bodice and drawn-in waist. When I breathe in and out, acres of pale upper boob flesh rises perkily above the fabric.

We round a bend and in front of us is the most amazing sight. A fairytale castle with turrets, all lit up with thousands of sparkling lights.

'There's a restaurant in there, and some function rooms where the party will be,' says Jackson. 'And over there is the entrance to the Enchanted Forest. We'll be able to wander through it later.'

Sophie's head is flung back against the headrest and she seems oblivious to the fact Jackson is speaking. But I glance over to our right, where he's pointing. Through the trees, a bridge is clearly visible, strung with fairy lights, and there seems to be some kind of laser light show going on with big flashes of rose pink, purple and midnight blue splitting the darkness.

The party venue in the castle is similarly magical. Two elaborately decorated Christmas trees adorn the entrance and the ceiling above us is like the night sky

– dark blue velvet, strung with tiny white lights like stars. A band is playing Christmas music and about twenty large circular tables and chairs are ranged around a dance floor. Clemmy is already up dancing with a group of girl friends, looking gorgeous in her dress.

There couldn't be a more romantic setting for an engagement party.

Heading over to Poppy, who's sitting by herself at a table, I pass the bar, where Jed, Alex and Ryan are standing chatting, and I hear Alex say, 'Yeah, in some ways I can't wait to get back home. I think I need a brand new start.'

For some reason, his words pierce my heart, making me feel even more melancholy than I did before. I like Alex so much and I want him to be happy with a new start and a new girl. I suppose I'm just sad because I thought we were becoming real friends and I wish he didn't have to go back to Australia after Christmas.

'Are you all right?' asks Poppy. 'Frankly, you look about as much in the mood for a party as I feel.'

'Not enjoying yourself?' I ask.

'It doesn't help that I can't drink,' grumbles Poppy. 'I've had to pretend my stomach is still playing up so people don't get suspicious.'

'If you told Jed about the baby, you wouldn't have to pretend any more,' I point out.

She glares at me. 'Any more bright ideas?' She shakes her head. 'To be honest, I'm thinking of ending the whole thing.'

'You can't do that! Jed adores you.'

'Does he? So why do I feel as if I come a poor second to his career?'

'Hormones?'

She shrugs gloomily. 'Why can't I just be a single mother? Wouldn't that be simpler? Rather than having to worry I'm with a man who's only there for the baby?'

I shake my head. 'Of course he wouldn't be.'

'You don't know that.'

She's got me there. Because of course I don't.

We sit there, Poppy sipping on a lime and soda and me nursing a glass of wine. I can't understand this feeling of despair that's suddenly descended. I wasn't exactly looking forward to a party that would include Jackson and Sophie as a couple, but I didn't feel this downhearted, even when I was sitting in the back of Jackson's car.

But now . . .

I decide I must just be feeling in sympathy with Poppy, who really is on a downer.

At least Clemmy and Ryan are enjoying themselves with all the friends they've invited tonight. That's the main thing. But the Log Fire Cabin crew seem in rather less of a party mood – apart from Gloria and Bob, who are currently whooping it up on the dance floor. I glance towards the bar, expecting to see Alex, but he's disappeared.

I've no idea where Ruby is but she invited Sam from the farm next door, so presumably she's with him somewhere.

Sophie is glued to her phone. She keeps sitting down at our table, but then within a minute or two her phone will ring and she'll spring up and walk to the door, presumably to escape the loud music so she can hear the person on the other end.

Jackson wanders over from the bar and sits next to me.

'She might be gorgeous but Christ! When she's stressed, she's impossible!' he says, frowning at the entrance where Sophie's taking yet another call. 'I wish she would calm down. It might not actually be the end of the world. *You* were never moody like this.'

'The end of the world how?' I ask, ignoring the backhanded compliment.

He frowns. 'Sophie's heard on the grapevine she might be moved sideways at work.'

'Really? That's awful.'

'Actually, I think it might be a demotion. They apparently want her to head up a new office in Malta.'

'In *Malta*? But what about her editorship of *Dazzle UK*?'

Jackson shrugs. 'They seem to be bringing in some young graduate type with loads of energy and an abundance of revolutionary new ideas.'

I frown. 'Poor Sophie.'

I really mean that, too. I don't much like the girl but she seems wedded to her job and I can see how a move away from the fashion buzz of London would absolutely devastate her.

'Anyway, what about you?' He gives me one of his smiles and my heart lurches. 'That dessert was pretty awesome the other night. Maybe you should open a bakery?'

'Why does it always have to be business with you?' I laugh, knowing him of old.

He shrugs, shuffling his chair a little closer. 'Just saying. You said you wanted to find a career you were passionate about. Maybe this is it.'

We exchange a smile. I forgot I said that to him when we were going out together. I can't help feeling flattered he actually remembered it.

'I'm just nipping out for some air,' says Poppy, getting up. Her face is very pale and I stare at her in alarm.

'Do you want me to come with you?'

'No, I'll be fine,' she says and hurries towards the main door.

I turn to Jackson, already rising to my feet. 'I think I'd better go after her.'

'Why?' He grabs my wrist and smiles up at me. 'She said she'd be okay.'

'Yes, but she might not be. She looked awful.'

'But I was enjoying talking to you. We haven't exactly had much chance, have we?'

He gazes up at me pleadingly, but for once, I feel unaffected by his puppy dog eyes on me. I'm remembering Poppy's white face.

'I'd better go,' I say, heading for the door.

I find Poppy leaning back against the wall, taking some deep breaths. 'I didn't feel too good for a moment but I think I'm okay now. Do you fancy a walk into the Enchanted Forest?'

I shrug. 'Yes, why not. I'll just grab our coats. It's freezing out here.'

We trudge across the car park through the snow to the Enchanted Forest entrance.

Breathing in the evocative Christmassy scent from the pine trees, we enter the forest and walk over the little bridge that's lit up with fairy lights strung along both sides.

'Isn't this gorgeous?' says Poppy, taking a lungful of air.

'Perfect,' I agree.

'Ooh, what's that on the other side of the bridge?'

We walk over and find ourselves in a small clearing among the trees. And, to my surprise, Alex is sitting there on a wooden bench at the side of the clearing, staring up into the branches. He seems lost in thought and doesn't see us at first.

'Alex,' says Poppy. 'God, this is amazing.'

He stands up. 'Yeah. It is. It feels really peaceful. Like you could solve the problems of the world just sitting here.'

'Any problems in particular?' she asks.

He laughs but it sounds a little forced. 'Nothing I can't handle. Better get back to the party.'

'Didn't you say an old school friend of yours developed this place?' says Poppy.

Alex nods. 'Yes. Graeme Swift. He's done an amazing job. He deserves to do well with it.'

We exchange a quick glance as he leaves.

'See you in there,' I say, curious to know why he looks so down. He smiles and raises a hand in response.

'Alex is right. If you sat here long enough, you could solve all your problems!' grins Poppy. She presses her abdomen with a frown and I glance at her worriedly.

'Are you sure you're okay?'

She nods and stares upwards. The branches form a kind of canopy overhead, which is strung with twinkling lights that look like stars. The aroma of pine forest is heavenly. We gaze up at the lights and suddenly the configuration changes and, instead of 'stars', there's a message written there: *Merry Christmas from the Enchanted Forest!*

'Ow!' Poppy gasps, holding her stomach.

'What is it? Are you in pain? Sit down.' We sink onto the bench.

'I suddenly feel really bad again.'

'Right, we're going to A&E. Shall I get Jed?'

'No!' Her frown deepens and she presses her stomach with a groan. 'I just want to go home. Will you come with me, Roxy?'

'Of course I will. Come on, let's get your coat. I'll tell Jackson we need a lift.'

She grabs my hand. 'Sorry to drag you away from the party when it's probably nothing.'

I shake my head firmly. 'Don't be silly. The baby is the important thing. Can you walk over the bridge? Hang onto me.'

I get Poppy a seat just inside the function room and find Jackson, and he says to go and look after Poppy and he'll be out at the car in just a minute. As I leave with Poppy's coat and bag, I glance across and see Jackson talking to Sophie in the entrance hall. She still has her phone pressed to her ear and waves him away, turning her back to him and blocking her other ear with her finger.

Jackson shepherds us into the car, gallantly holding the passenger door open for Poppy and making sure she's strapped in properly. And within fifteen minutes, we've done the reverse journey along the winding country lanes back to the Log Fire Cabin.

In the bright lights of the hallway, Poppy's complexion looks grey.

'Do you want me to call a doctor?' I ask anxiously.

She shakes her head. 'I just need to go to bed,' she mumbles and starts heading slowly up the stairs.

I glance worriedly at Jackson and he murmurs, 'Does she want anything? Aspirin? Tea?'

'I'll go and see.'

He nods. 'I'll put the kettle on.'

Upstairs, I help Poppy out of her Cruella de Vil dress. She smiles and strokes the fabric, then she crawls under the covers and lies on her side with her knees drawn up.

'Can I get you anything?'

She gives me a wan smile. 'I'll be fine if I can just go to sleep. Thanks, Roxy. Sorry if I ruined the party for you.'

'You didn't.'

She nods and closes her eyes.

I leave the room and close the door softly. Then I join Jackson in the kitchen.

'So tell me more about Sophie?' I ask him.

He groans. 'She's being asked to start up a new edition of *Dazzle* for ex-pats in Europe. So she'll be shipped out of London to Malta straight after Christmas.'

'What if she says she doesn't want to?'

He shrugs. 'There's no other option. It's either that

or nothing. Readership of *Dazzle* in the UK has fallen dramatically over the past five years, so they're promoting a relative newcomer in Sophie's place. I think this new girl is the grand-daughter of someone important. Sophie's livid.'

'I'm not surprised.'

'She heard the rumours just before she went off on her Christmas break, so she's been like a cat on a hot tin roof since we got here. Anyway, now it seems they weren't just rumours.'

'Oh, God. Poor Sophie.'

'She's hoping to do some modelling if the worst comes to the worst.'

I nod. 'She did mention she was having some photos done for her portfolio. Surely she'll be snapped up by some modelling agency?'

He shrugs. 'It's a competitive business and they tend to want a particular sort of look. The uncertainty is making her even more jumpy.'

'Where did you meet Sophie?' I ask. I've been curious to know ever since I arrived here and saw them together. I presumed it was at some business function.

'Actually, it was at the Winter Ball. She came as the plus-one of my head of communications, and we just clicked.'

I stare at him as he talks on. *The Winter Ball*? But surely that was the event I was going to as *his* plus-one?

The one I had my dress all picked out for. The very same Winter Ball that was a mere *six days* after our disastrous night at the TV dating show!

I miss most of what he's saying because my head is spinning at this revelation. I could almost excuse his dalliance with the French woman who answered his phone in such a flirty manner. *Almost*. But the fact that he found a brand new girlfriend less than a week after we stopped seeing each other feels like a huge slap in the face.

We hear someone come in and, a moment later, Jed pops his head round the door. 'Hi, folks. Is Poppy in bed?'

'Yes, I think she just needed to sleep.'

'She's working much too hard. I've never seen her look so exhausted but she point-blank refuses to talk about it.' He gives a heavy sigh. 'I know she's desperate for the business to be a success but I just wish it wasn't at the expense of everything else.'

He looks so defeated, I want to go over and give him a hug. If only he knew what was *really* going on with Poppy. It seems so cruel that he's being kept in the dark. But I do understand Poppy's dilemma. And I'm not about to break her confidence by revealing that she's pregnant.

'You okay?' asks Jackson when Jed has gone. 'You've got that look you get when you're mulling something over.'

'Yes, I'm fine. Just a bit worried about Poppy, that's all.'

He smiles and smooths back a lock of my hair. My heart stalls. 'You're a natural carer, Roxy. No wonder everyone comes to you with their problems.'

I laugh. 'You think so?'

'I do.' He tries to put his arms around me but I pull away.

He looks exasperated. 'What is it? Is there something wrong? Is it me?'

'What do you mean?'

'You pull away from me. You always did. Even when we were together. I mean, you obviously fancy me, so why . . .?'

I swallow hard. I've kept it from him for far too long. It's time he heard the truth.

Chapter 23

Jackson listens attentively as I tell him all about being trapped in the fire on my nineteenth birthday. He looks horrified when I start talking about the scars I've been left with, although I prefer to think he's aghast because of the struggles I went through, not because he's revolted at the thought of my damaged skin.

When I've finished, he gives a long whistle and says, 'Why didn't you tell me all this before?'

I shrug. 'I was frightened you wouldn't like me any more if you knew I was scarred.'

He nods thoughtfully.

'You know, that you might find my scars repulsive?'

He smiles sadly at me and folds his arms.

'Silly of me, I know. Because of *course* you'd like me just the same . . .' I say, trying to prompt a positive response from him. When he still doesn't reply, I can't help adding: 'Wouldn't you?'

He looks puzzled. 'Sorry?'

'I'm saying I'm sure you'd like me just the same, with scars or without.'

His face clears. 'Of course, of course. So, have you had proper plastic surgery? They can really work wonders these days apparently.'

I'm saved from having to give him a run-down of my procedures by the sound of a key in the lock. Everyone else piles into the hallway, all sounding very merry, except for Alex who'd offered to do the driving.

Sophie barges into the kitchen. 'Jackson? What the hell happened to you?' she demands.

He shrugs. 'I did explain but you were busy on the phone. Poppy wasn't well. I brought her and Roxy back.'

Sophie's eyes narrow fractionally as she casts an icy glance in my direction.

Hastily, I say, 'Speaking of Poppy, I'm just going to check on her.' The last thing I need is to be caught in the middle of a Jackson/Sophie row.

Hurrying out of the kitchen, I can hear the others in the living room chatting around the log fire, but I head for the stairs. And not a minute too soon, apparently, because Poppy is standing at the top, peering down at me, an anguished look on her face.

'Oh, Roxy, I'm really scared.' Her voice is a whisper. I guess she doesn't want to disturb Jed.

'Why?' I look up at her in alarm and start climbing the stairs.

'I'm bleeding.' She looks so small and vulnerable, standing there barefoot in just her cotton T-shirt-style nightie, clutching a towel in front of her.

My heart dives into my jewelled shoes. Impatiently, I kick them off so I can get to her faster, then I guide her down the stairs.

'We need to get you to hospital,' I murmur. 'You *have* to let me tell Jed now.' I'm pleading with her but even in her frightened, weakened state, she's still resolute that he mustn't know.

'He's asleep,' she whispers. 'Don't wake him up.'

I'm about to bellow for Jackson to come but, instead, I tell her to sit down on the stairs while I run into the kitchen.

He's now alone and can see immediately that some-thing's wrong.

'It's Poppy. She's pregnant. But don't tell Jed; he doesn't know. She's bleeding.'

'Oh. Right.' He frowns. 'Should I call an ambulance?'

I rush back through to Poppy, telling her not to worry. We'll get her the help she needs. 'Jackson's going to phone for an ambulance.'

When I turn, Jackson is standing in the doorway, looking shell-shocked.

'Did you phone?' I prompt him.

'No. Right. I'll just get my mobile.'

He disappears into the kitchen and I sit down next

to Poppy, who's looking white as a sheet. She gets up gingerly. 'I just need to . . .' She points at the downstairs loo and I jump up and follow her.

While she's in there, Alex and Clemmy come out of the living room, wondering what's going on. Quickly, I explain. 'Jackson's phoning for an ambulance. At least, I think he is. *Jackson?*' I call for him, feeling panic starting to rise up. If we don't get Poppy to hospital soon, I dread to think what will be the result . . .

The door opens and a white-faced Poppy appears. 'It won't stop.'

I glance worriedly at Alex.

'Right, come on.' He moves swiftly into action. 'We'll take my car. Roxy, can you get Poppy's coat? Get her into some warm clothes and I'll just grab my keys.' He sprints down the hall, while I run upstairs and creep into Poppy's room, desperately scared I'll awaken Jed, who's in bed fast asleep. I grab Poppy's tracksuit from a nearby chair then run into my own room for some socks.

Alex helps me to dress a bewildered Poppy, then he gently guides her to sit down on the bottom step while he quickly but carefully puts on her socks and boots, all the time talking in a brisk but gentle tone. I'm so grateful for him taking charge, I feel like hugging him.

Finally, he gives me his keys. 'Can you unlock my car, Roxy?' He smiles at Poppy. 'Ready for a lift? We don't want you slipping on the ice.'

She gives him a wan smile.

As I pull on some loafers lying by the door and run out to Alex's car, he scoops Poppy up and carries her out.

'What about Jed?' he asks, as I hold the passenger door open.

Quickly, I shake my head and he seems to get the message. 'Are you coming?' he asks me.

When I nod, he says, 'Probably best if you're both in the back.'

I open the back car door then dive into the house for my coat. When I return to the car, Poppy has been belted up and Alex is in the driving seat, the engine humming.

When we're on our way, I take Poppy's hand. 'I can phone Jed now, if you like?'

She turns, her face full of anguish, and I think she might change her mind at last. But she shakes her head. 'There might be nothing to tell now,' she croaks, and my heart plummets at her meaning. She thinks she's losing her baby.

I squeeze her hand, desperately hoping she's wrong . . .

Chapter 24

We make the ten-minute drive to the hospital in tense silence, Poppy gripping my hand the whole way.

When we arrive outside A&E, Alex hands me the keys to park the car, then he supports Poppy in through the main entrance, practically carrying her again as she's so weak with fear. I watch them disappear into the hospital. Then I fumble for my phone and make a call.

When I finally go into the building myself, I see Poppy lying on a gurney with Alex standing by, waiting to be seen by a doctor. He's actually managing to make her smile, which is quite a feat in itself, and my heart swells with affection for him. Alex has been so great in all of this. He's exactly the sort of guy you want on your side when the going gets tough . . .

He sees me and smiles. 'I was just telling Poppy I once heard a joke about amnesia but I forgot how it goes.'

I groan at Poppy and she shakes her head. 'Your jokes should come with a warning,' she grins.

It's a relief to see Poppy looking more relaxed, although goodness knows how she's feeling beneath the smile.

My insides shift uneasily thinking of the phone call I made out in the car park. She might not be smiling for long and it will be all my fault . . .

The nurse comes to check on Poppy, and Alex and I stand back.

'So no one else knows she's pregnant?' he murmurs.

I frown. 'It's complicated. She asked me to keep it to myself.'

'Jed doesn't know?'

I turn at the sound of voices along the corridor. A nurse is pointing someone our way, and my heart sinks. 'He's not in the dark any more.'

Jed is striding towards us, his face wreathed in concern. 'Poppy?'

Poppy and the nurse look up at him.

He stands by the gurney staring down at his girlfriend, running his hands through his hair. 'I came as soon as I got Roxy's phone call. Why on earth didn't you tell me?'

The nurse stands back to let him take her place and he hunkers down so his face is level with hers. He takes her hand as if it's something very precious, and when she tries to sit up and explain, he shushes her gently and makes her lie back down again, murmuring that what's important now is that she's okay.

'How did you know I was here?' she asks.

'Roxy.' Jed smiles back at me and she just nods.

Alex and I say our goodbyes, thinking it best to leave Poppy in Jed's care, and as we walk away, I glance back.

Poppy is being wheeled away, still holding Jed's hand. But the look she gives me makes my heart go cold.

Will I actually have a job tomorrow?

More importantly, will Poppy ever be able to forgive me for telling Jed about the baby?

On the journey back, Alex breaks the silence. 'I take it you let Jed know about the baby?'

I nod miserably and he says, 'Good call, Roxy. He needed to know. Especially now.'

'Do you think?'

'I do think. So stop worrying.' He smiles across at me – it's a really warm smile this time – and I feel my whole body relax a little.

Perhaps Alex is right. Maybe when Poppy's had time to think about it, she'll be glad I told Jed. I can only hope so. I've known Poppy for just a few short weeks but already I think of her as a good friend. I only hope I haven't destroyed our fledgling friendship.

We draw up outside the Log Fire Cabin and Alex switches off the engine.

Neither of us moves. We both just sit there, listening to the clicks of the engine cooling down, watching the occasional snowflake float gently past the windscreen.

'Why didn't she want Jed to know?' asks Alex. 'Isn't she serious about their relationship?'

I turn to face him. In the semi-dark, I can see reflected in his eyes the white fairy lights strung in a nearby tree. They look like stars.

'Quite the opposite, actually. Poppy's crazy about him, but she doesn't think he feels the same.'

He nods and stares pensively ahead, his big shoulders hunched against the cold that's creeping into the car. 'I have a feeling he's crazy about her, too.'

'I hope so.'

'Yeah, me too. They seem good together.'

I stare at Alex, thinking what a lovely, warm person he is. He's the sort of man you could literally trust with your life.

'And what about you, Roxy?' he asks.

He turns his gaze on me and, in the silence of the frosty night, it suddenly feels incredibly intimate to be sitting there in the car with him. He's quite tall – his head almost brushes the car roof. Not as tall as Jackson, who has the build of a runner. But Alex's shoulders are attractively broad, as if he'd be more at home on a rugby pitch than a running track. He's regarding me intently and I'm vaguely aware he just asked me a question but my muddled brain can't seem to remember what it was. I find myself unable to tear my eyes away from his, which is strange because, normally, I find it quite hard to hold a man's gaze. Especially a man I find attractive. I suppose I'm always afraid they might see past the superficial to my imperfections beneath.

My heart does a little flip of surprise as I acknowledge that Alex is a really attractive guy. Why have I never noticed it before? I suppose I've always just thought of him as Jed and Jackson's friend.

His eyes look very dark but what colour are they actually, in daylight?

'Are you still crazy about Jackson?' he asks.

I know he's got long lashes – I notice that every time we speak. I think his eyes are green . . .

Alex's question filters through.

Am I still crazy about Jackson?

I swallow hard. 'He says he's going to end things with Sophie and then . . . who knows?'

Alex nods and gives a funny little wistful smile.

He takes a big breath and says, 'Come on, then. Let's go in. I suppose we keep Poppy's pregnancy to ourselves for now?'

'Yes. I guess so. It's up to her and Jed now to break

the news to everyone.' I shiver, wondering what the news will be. 'God, I hope it's a happy ending.'

I stare miserably at Alex.

He sighs. 'You and me both, Roxy.' He reaches over and pulls me into a big bear hug and I relax into his arms. 'Hopefully, it's just a scare,' he murmurs into my hair, 'and she'll have to be careful. That's what happened to my sister and it all worked out fine in the end.'

'You've got a nephew? A niece?' My face is pressed into the warmth of his chest and my voice sounds muffled.

'Nephew. He's five now and a right little rat-bag.'

I sit up. 'Why? What does he do?'

Alex laughs. 'Oh, nothing. He's mischievous but charming with it. In Australia, "rat-bag" is used as a term of endearment.'

'Oh, right.'

I sink back against his chest. Then I suddenly realise what I'm doing and pull away. 'God, sorry.' *Thank goodness he can't see my blushes in the semi-dark!*

'Hey, no worries!' he says, mimicking the Australian accent perfectly.

He lets us into the house, holding the door for me.

'Alex, thank you. You've been brilliant, seeing to Poppy and everything.'

'It's fine. I was glad to do it.'

'You're definitely one of the good guys.' I grin at him

but he doesn't acknowledge my compliment. He just walks on through to the kitchen and my throat tightens. Perhaps he's just exhausted. I know I am.

I take off my coat and the oversized loafers in the hallway, suddenly struck by the strange wailing sound that's coming from the kitchen.

What on earth . . .?

It sounds like a cat in pain.

Hurrying in, an odd scene greets me.

Sophie is slumped at the breakfast bar, lying across the counter, the skirt of her lovely dress ballooning out. 'I can't believe that *bitch* is taking my place,' she wails to Clemmy, who's sitting next to her in her Cinderella dress, patting Sophie's back and looking completely out of her depth.

'What's happened?' I mouth to Clemmy.

She heaves a sigh and shakes her head. '*Dazzle* magazine have told Sophie they're moving her from London to head up a brand new office and she's really not happy about it.'

So it's true what Jackson was saying.

'Oh, dear.' My exclamation is drowned out by another wail from Sophie.

'My staff have apparently been hearing rumours about this for weeks but did anyone bother to tell me?' she demands. 'No, of course they fucking didn't!'

'That's terrible,' says Clemmy.

I nod. 'And what an awful time to break news like that. Just before Christmas.'

Sophie raises her head and glares at me. 'Plus the bastards are moving me to Malta! I mean, where the bloody hell is *that* on the world map?'

'Um, it's a little island in the Mediterranean just below Italy,' says Clemmy. 'I went to Gozo once, which is right next door, and it was lovely!'

'I know where bloody Malta *is*!' screeches Sophie. 'I'm talking about where it sits in the rankings of fashion capitals of the frigging world! Right at the bottom just above Western Siberia, I should imagine!'

Clemmy and I watch in horror as she starts wailing and banging her fists on the counter, working herself up into an even greater frenzy of despair.

Clemmy glances anxiously at me and indicates the kettle.

I nod. 'A nice strong black coffee would be lovely,' I say calmly.

Sophie has apparently drunk enough alcohol tonight, following her terrible news, to sink a small fleet of ships.

Clemmy gets up and tiptoes over to the kettle, as if any sound from her and Sophie might blow her top altogether, like a lid flying off a pressure cooker.

'How could they *do* this to me?' agonises Sophie. 'When I've been at the helm of *Dazzle* for so long!'

'How long have you been there?' I ask gently.

'Eighteen months. But that's not the point. I've done a great job. A bloody *brilliant* job and they know it!'

'Isn't it a compliment that they want you to head up a brand new office?' I point out. 'That's a big responsibility.'

She rears up and stares at me as if I've suddenly sprouted another two heads. 'If it was *Paris*. Or *New York*. Or *Rome*. Then I might be cheering. But frigging *Malta*?'

I'm at a loss to know what to say, but she's staring at me with such despair, as if she expects me to say something that will make it all better.

I open my mouth. 'I – well, I haven't been there, but Malta's meant to be *gorgeous*. So maybe it'll turn out to be a great move.' I swallow hard. 'And Jackson can come out and visit you. How romantic will that be?'

Her eyes turn steely. 'Jackson can fuck off as well.'

'Sorry?'

'I said, Jackson can take a running jump. He's as big a bastard as those bloody financial executives who've decided readership has slumped since I took over!'

I swallow hard. 'Why exactly is Jackson an – erm – bastard?' Oh God, maybe he's done what he said he would, then. Broken up with Sophie so he can be with me.

A torrent of emotion rushes through me.

267

'I think he might have dumped her,' murmurs Clemmy in my ear, placing a big mug of black coffee in front of us – just as Sophie's wailing starts up again, reaching a crescendo that almost rattles the windows.

I stare at Clemmy, aghast, and Sophie blows her nose noisily on a piece of kitchen towel Clemmy provides.

I feel shocked to the core. I guess I never expected this to happen. For all Jackson's protestations about wanting to get back with me, deep down I never thought he'd actually do the deed and break it off with Sophie.

Maybe we always *were* right for each other, Jackson and I, and my hasty proposal only derailed us temporarily. I've always wondered where we'd be now if I hadn't been so stupidly drunk that night and ruined everything. Perhaps we'd be right here, with Jackson in love with me. Wanting to be with only me . . .

'Oh, Christ, bloody *Malta*!' Sophie flings her arms in the air and sends a vase of flowers crashing to the floor. She briefly registers the sound of something crashing, turning her head vaguely in that direction, but doesn't seem to realise she caused it, and flumps back on the counter.

I gaze at her now less-than-perfect hair, with strands escaping all over, and can't help feeling sorry for her. It makes me feel slightly less guilty that she's clearly more bothered about the job crisis than Jackson telling her they're over.

Clemmy scrambles off the stool and starts picking up pieces of pottery and I rush to help her.

'Careful. You'll spoil your dress,' I tell her.

'And I'm so hungry!' wails Sophie. 'I could eat a whole loaf of bread made into toast and spread so thickly with butter it would give me a muffin top just looking at it on the plate.'

'Shall I make some toast?' Clemmy looks at me and I nod.

Clemmy sees to the toast. Then Alex comes into the kitchen to ask if everything's all right. He helps me clear the broken pottery into the bin. At one point, our hands touch and we both leap away as if we've had an electric shock. I glance up at him and the intense look in his eyes makes my heart race.

'And apart from everything else shit that's happened,' shrieks Sophie, 'I'm a lonely bloody singleton again because all men are bastards!'

'It would probably be best if Sophie crashed out here tonight,' murmurs Alex.

I nod, feeling instantly better now that he's taking charge. 'She can have the room I've been sleeping in. I'll be okay on the sofa once everyone's gone back to the hotel.' I nod in the direction of the living room, wondering how Jackson is feeling, hearing Sophie so upset and knowing he's the cause of it.

I feel bad enough, knowing I'm the reason he's

dumped her. So he must feel a thousand times worse.

I think longingly of Flo and the flat. Suddenly, I have an urge to run for the hills and escape all of the drama. Except Flo is in New York, of course. The strength of this feeling of wanting to get away puzzles me because now I know that Jackson is free to be with me, why wouldn't I want to stay?

I guess my head is too muddled to think logically right now. I could really do with some space to be on my own and work out what I really want. But, however much I might want to flee, I have to stay.

Poppy needs me now, more than ever. I feel so guilty for having told Jed about the baby, even though I only did it because I knew deep down that it was absolutely right that he should know. But with Poppy in hospital, I owe it to her to make sure the contract with Sylvia is fulfilled. Even if I have to work day and night to do it.

One thing's for certain; Jackson might be free now, but there's no way we'll be getting back together straight away. We'll need to take some breathing space and make sure we don't rush things. Perhaps after everything has gone back to normal after Christmas, we'll arrange to meet and decide if it's what we want. There's absolutely no hurry . . .

But, deep down, I know I'm only stalling for time. There's a cold feeling deep down inside that I'm trying to ignore. I've been trying to ignore it ever since the night of the skating contest. But I know I have to face up to it.

The big question that's taunting me is: Jackson may be free to be with me. But do I really want to be with him?

'Roxy?'

I turn and Jackson is standing in the doorway, beckoning me. I glance anxiously at Sophie, who's quietened down and is sipping her coffee with Clemmy's encouragement.

If Sophie sees Jackson, I have a feeling the other vase on the breakfast bar might meet a similar fate to its twin – except it wouldn't be an accident this time. So I quickly slip out before she realises he's there.

'How is she?' he asks, looking worried.

'Not great. It doesn't help that she's so drunk, but I think she's completely devastated that your relationship is over. We think she should stay here tonight. Sleep in my room.'

His face lights up. 'Really? Oh well, you can come and sleep in the hotel. In my room.'

I stare at him. 'No, of course I can't.'

'Why not?'

'Because . . . it wouldn't be right. You've just broken up with Sophie and she's in there crying her eyes out. Could you really, in all conscience, have me spend the

271

night with you, knowing how that would make Sophie feel when she finds out? Because obviously, she *would* find out.'

He sighs again. 'Okay. So where are *you* sleeping tonight?'

I shrug, feeling bemused. 'The sofa? Or on cushions in the study? Anywhere. It doesn't really matter.'

'Right. Well, I think I'll head back to the hotel now with Ryan and Clemmy.'

'Oh. Okay.'

'Sophie's mum lives near here. I think she's coming to collect her.'

'What, *now*?'

'Well, no, I presume in the morning.' He shrugs. 'I'm not sure.'

I stare at him, unable to fathom his cool attitude to poor Sophie's emotional trauma. He doesn't seem to be feeling much guilt over dumping her just a few days before Christmas.

Perhaps he's just putting on a manly front, not wanting to show his feelings?

Sophie gives a loud wail.

'I expect you feel really bad that Sophie's feeling so wretched,' I say. 'Especially since it's only three days till Christmas.'

He shrugs. 'These things happen. Relationships end and you move on. That's life. She'll be fine in a day or two.' He smiles at me. 'You worry too much about people.'

'Do I?'

'Yes. You're a real softie, which is one of the things I love about you.' He moves closer and pulls me towards him and I realise he's actually going to kiss me. I can't believe the callousness of the man. *He's happy to kiss me with Sophie breaking her heart on the other side of that door?*

Somewhere in the distance, I'm aware of a noise. But it's only when someone clears their throat that I realise it was the kitchen door opening.

I squirm away from Jackson and turn around guiltily.

It's not Sophie.

But even if it was, I couldn't feel any worse than I do now.

It's Alex standing there. And the disgust on his face is clear for all to see.

He shakes his head and walks out of the cabin.

Chapter 25

I wake up next morning on the living room sofa and my first thought is Alex's face when he saw Jackson and I in what he must have thought was a romantic embrace.

Then my mind flashes to Poppy.

Oh God, I hope she's all right.

I didn't hear them come back from the hospital last night. But maybe I slept through it. Alex seems to think I did the right thing, calling Jed from the hospital.

I wish I could be so sure.

'Morning, Roxy!' Ruby bursts in. 'Jed just called to say that Poppy's bleeding has stopped. Isn't that great?'

I breathe a sigh of relief. 'It certainly is. So are they coming back?'

Ruby shakes her head. 'The doctors want to keep her in hospital for another night just to make sure she's okay.' Her face lights up. 'Ooh, it's Christmas Eve tomorrow!'

'It is, indeed.'

'I can't believe we've got all this snow, just in time for the Big Day. There's a lot more arriving apparently.'

'We might get snowed in.' I grin at her. 'Have you been waiting outside for me to wake up?'

'No. Just good timing, I suppose.' She gives a huge yawn and collapses back onto the end of the sofa, narrowly missing my feet. 'I had a horrible nightmare last night. I was being chased through a field by lots of savage-looking women with war paint on their faces. Then a bull was chasing them and they all ran away.'

'Wow. What do you think it means?' I grin at her.

She turns and says gloomily, 'I think it means I'm a bull in a bloody china shop, barging in without thinking and getting myself into loads of trouble in the process.'

'Really? Gosh, you've given the dream a lot of thought. Usually I forget mine three seconds after I wake up.'

She turns in her seat to face me, with her arm on the back of the sofa. 'I feel really bad now about that stunt I pulled on Sophie, pretending they sent the Grinch instead of Holly Hepburn.'

'*Audrey* Hepburn.'

'I thought she was called Holly?'

'Holly Golightly was the character she played in the movie.'

'So was Holly Golightly a really famous actress?'

'No, she . . .' I laugh. 'Never mind. What do you plan on doing about Sophie?'

'I've apologised to her.'

'That was nice of you. Poor Sophie's already feeling crap because Jackson dumped her.'

Ruby stares at me. 'No, he didn't.'

'What do you mean?'

'He didn't dump her. She dumped him because he refused to go and live in Malta with her when she takes up this new job.'

'Oh.' I frown, thinking back to the previous night. I could have sworn Jackson didn't contradict me when I accused him of ending it with Sophie. Why on earth didn't he tell me what really happened? 'Ruby, are you sure about this?'

'Absolutely. Jackson told me he wasn't bothered because he's gone off Sophie anyway.'

I laugh incredulously. It obviously suited Jackson's purpose to have me believe he'd finished with Sophie just so he could be with me! When, actually, it was Sophie who had given *him* his marching orders!

Just what sort of a snake *is* my ex? I really thought the sun shone out of him but I'm beginning to think I never really knew the real Jackson at all. It was all just a sham. And he's probably ladled the same superficially charming half-truths on Sophie that he did on me!

'Why are you laughing?' asks Ruby.

I shake my head. 'I'm laughing at how stupid I've been.'

But actually, I feel like crying.

All this time I've been feeling cut up over Jackson, it's now becoming horribly clear to me that I was just one of his many playthings. And if Sophie hadn't pipped him to the post, I feel sure she would have been next in line to be ditched from his life in favour of the next pretty girl that turned up.

'Sophie's just gone,' says Ruby. 'Her mum picked her up and they left.'

'Sophie's gone?'

Ruby nods. 'The mother was horrible. She was ordering poor Sophie about like she was twelve years old. Sophie told me she used to make her get on the scales every day from when she was five years old to make sure she never went over her ideal weight.'

We look at each other in horror.

'Isn't that sad?' says Ruby.

'It certainly is.' I gaze at Ruby in dismay. After all the horrible things I've said about Sophie, all I can feel right now is sympathy for her. 'Imagine having a mother who'd do that . . .'

'Are you okay? You look weird,' says Ruby.

'I was just thinking about Jackson. It seems leaving one relationship behind and moving on immediately with someone else is something he's rather good at . . .'

'Really? Who's he moving on with, then?'

'Oh, no one,' I say hurriedly. 'I was just thinking aloud.'

Ruby frowns. 'Yeah, I do that all the time. Thinking aloud. Mum's always saying I should think before I speak.'

'Mums are usually right.'

She nods grudgingly. 'I'm going to turn down the volume from now on. Be more considerate to my fellow men. And women. I mean, you never know what stuff they've gone through, do you? Like Sophie.'

'That's very true, Ruby.'

'I'm going to be much more tolerant of people from now on.'

I grin at her. 'Good luck with that.'

'By the way, you shouldn't be ashamed of them.'

'Ashamed of what?'

'Your scars. I saw you trying to hide them when I came into your room the other day.' She groans. 'Without waiting to be asked to come in, of course.' She raises her eyes to the ceiling at her own rudeness. 'Sorry!'

'That's all right.' My heart has started to race. And my mouth is so dry, I can barely get the words out.

'Actually, I've got some imperfections of my own. Look.' She whips up her pyjama top and shows me a large strawberry birthmark that covers the left side of her abdomen.

She grins. 'I call it my safari stamp because, if you look, it's sort of shaped like Africa. And I've always wanted to go on safari. The kids at school thought it was hilarious, especially in the changing rooms, but I realised early on that if I laughed first, it took away their pleasure. So I made a point of showing everyone, as if I was proud of it, and then they sort of forgot all about it. It's part of me. And if people don't like it, they can lump it.' She turns and says matter-of-factly, 'Did you get burned? Is that what your scars are from?'

I swallow. 'I did get burned, yes.'

'How? Do you mind me asking?'

I shake my head, although I do mind. I mind very much.

It's just that hearing Ruby talk so matter-of-factly about something that could easily have made her shy and self-conscious makes me think that with her, at least, I can be honest. So I tell her about the night of the accident and how I ran back into the fire to find Gus and she listens with her mouth slightly open, not saying a word until I've finished.

'Wow. You were so brave.' She frowns. 'But was Gus all right?'

I smile. 'Yes, he was. The little tinker lived a good long life after that, thank goodness.'

'That's a relief.' Her brow clears. 'Right, breakfast time. I'm starving,' she says, before dashing out.

'See you later, Ruby.'

I don't get straight up. Instead, I lie back on the sofa for a moment, thinking how wonderful it is that Poppy and the baby are likely to be fine after all, and about my conversation with Ruby. She has a very wise head on her shoulders, that girl. I feel quite emotional imagining her being laughed at in the changing rooms but being brave enough to show everyone the birthmark. Kids can be so cruel but Ruby triumphed!

I feel quite immature by comparison. The very opposite of brave.

It's part of me, she said. *And if people don't like it, they can lump it!*

I've never thought of it that way, which is quite unbelievable, really. I suppose I've never had that innate confidence in myself that Ruby seems to have. Even at such a young age, she never apologises for being who she is. Well, except when she's deciding not to be a bull in a china shop any more.

I should *own* my scars. Like Ruby owns her birthmark. Instead of trying always to pretend they're not there and the accident never happened. It strikes me that if I adopted Ruby's attitude, I'd have the confidence to reveal my scars to absolutely anyone.

And if certain people don't like them – they can lump it . . .

Chapter 26

I walk purposefully along the road to the hotel with my head held high.

I feel strong and sort of triumphant, although at the same time, my heart is in my mouth. I'm going to do this, though. I'm determined to push through my fears.

Entering the hotel, I walk straight up to reception and ask the girl behind the desk if she can call Jackson's room and let him know I'm here. My heart is beating like crazy. Oh God, *please* let Jackson be in his room! Please, please, *please* . . .

The receptionist smiles and says, 'Certainly, Madam.' Then she checks on her system, which seems to take forever. Not that I'm anxious or anything. Then she very calmly picks up the phone and presses some buttons, smiling serenely at me, with no idea of the psyching-up session that's currently going on within me.

I feel like I'm at the foot of Ben Nevis, raring to go,

and desperate to get to the top before the weather turns and I chicken out!

'How do you like the Christmas tree?' she asks me, as she waits for Jackson to answer. 'It went up this morning.'

'Christmas tree?' I didn't even notice a tree when I came in.

She points behind me and, when I turn, standing just a couple of feet away is the biggest, most sparkly, in-your-face Christmas tree I've ever seen in my life. It actually fills almost the entire reception area. How I could have walked past such a gigantic display of festive celebration without seeing it, I have literally no idea.

I guess I must have been preoccupied . . .

'He says could you just go up to his room,' the receptionist says. 'Number thirteen. Second floor.'

'Thank you.' I start towards the stairs.

'There's a lift over there,' calls the receptionist.

'It's fine. I'm in a bit of a hurry.' *A lift would take forever!*

I take the stairs at a run, arriving at the second floor gasping for breath and all my nerve endings zinging with exhilaration, as if I've just stepped off a particularly hairy roller-coaster.

I race along the corridor but manage to overshoot, arriving at door numbers in the twenties.

Stopping, I force myself to take a breath. Then another

and another, telling myself to calm down. Jackson's not going anywhere. There's absolutely no rush . . .

I gallop off again, searching frantically for number thirteen, all logic forgotten. I've no idea what I'll do when Jackson opens the door. I suppose I'm just assuming instinct will tell me.

I find number thirteen and knock urgently on the door, my heart in my mouth.

Can I do this? Yes, of course I can!

The door opens and Jackson is standing on the threshold, smiling at me. 'Well, this is a surprise,' he says and stands back to let me in.

I march straight past him and go over to the window, pretending to look out at the view. But I know I'm just stalling for time – and I've been doing that for what seems like forever. *The time has come for action!*

I take a big deep breath, and my reflection in the window stands tall. 'Jackson, I used to assume all men would find me repulsive. But I don't believe that any more. I know now that I'm me and I should never feel ashamed of that.' My voice is shaking slightly, this is so momentous for me. 'You've been saying for ages that you want to see me naked. Well, I'm ready now!'

I swing round, a confident smile on my face. Ready to kick ass – or bare it, at any rate!

The toilet flushes and Jackson wanders out of the

bathroom, a quizzical look on his face. 'Sorry, Roxy, were you saying something?'

My spirits sink a little on finding I've just delivered the rousing speech of my life – to a completely empty room. But I grasp my courage in both hands and walk over to Jackson.

'I was saying that I'm ready for you to see me naked!'

A bemused look crosses his handsome features. 'But are you sure . . .? I mean, what about your scars?'

'That's precisely what I'm saying. It's high time I forgot about trying to hide my scars and let people see the real me.'

He grimaces, clearly horrified at the very idea of viewing my scarred skin. As deep down I knew he would be.

Undeterred, I start stripping off. I'm on a mission and every cell in my body is determined to teach Jackson Cooper a lesson. To show him just how bloody self-centred and superficial he actually is!

I fling off every stitch of clothing and stand there in the raw, facing him. Jackson gapes at me, completely lost for words for a moment. Then he gulps and starts gathering up my clothing.

'You really don't need to do this, Roxy. It's not necessary. Come on, put them back on.'

I fold my arms. 'Absolutely not. You wanted to see me naked. Well, this is it!'

I pause for just a moment. Then, remembering Ruby's words, I swallow hard and turn around so he can see the livid marks on my shoulder and upper back, and down the back of my arm.

My heart is beating crazily but I tell myself it's fine. I need to start as I mean to go on, accepting myself exactly the way I am and not being ashamed for people to see the real me. Jackson knows about the scars. It's not as if they'll be a shock to him. It's going to be okay.

I hear Jackson's intake of breath and my heart plummets painfully. The sudden tension in the room is like a physical thing.

I sit there, waiting, picturing in my mind's eye what he must be seeing. The reddened rough patches on the left side of my upper body, particularly bad above my shoulder blade. The way the flesh is puckered in places. The uneven skin tone.

All I've wanted since the fire was to feel normal, whatever that is. I don't want a man who's repulsed by what he sees. I want a man who loves me in spite of my scars. Or even *because* of them!

The truth is, I want Jackson to touch me. Even though I know we don't belong together, I'd like him to prove that he's not the shallow person I now think he is.

I want to be thrown on the bed and manhandled to within an inch of my life!

My mouth curves in a sad smile.

That was never going to happen with Jackson. He's far too obsessed with physical beauty to be able to love the person beneath the scars. I even wonder if he knows what love actually is.

I know now that in loving Jackson I was never going to win in the happiness stakes. Because he would never have been able to accept me as I truly am.

I turn round and catch the pity in his eyes before he hitches his mouth up in a smile. But I feel fine. I really do. It wasn't really for his benefit anyway, showing him my scars. It was something I had to do for me. And I feel stronger now that it's done . . .

I smile at him. 'Got to get back to work. Clemmy will be wondering where I am.'

'Clemmy?'

'Yes, she's offered to help while Poppy's . . .' I trail off. 'And there's so much to do.'

'Ah.' He nods. 'Yes. Nearly Christmas Day. We'll soon be back to our normal routines.' This thought seems to cheer him. I get dressed and he holds the door open for me.

'Goodbye, Jackson,' I say to him as I leave.

He looks surprised. 'Well, I will see you later, Roxy. By the way, I know a brilliant plastic surgeon in Switzerland. I'll dig out his number and give him a call.'

'Oh. Right. Thanks.'

'If anyone can get that skin of yours nice and smooth, it's this guy.'

I want to say that, actually, the NHS have done a great job and that I doubt his surgeon could get much better results, but he looks so pleased with himself, I just smile sadly.

I leave his room and walk down the corridor feeling as if a weight that's been bogging me down for years has just rolled off my shoulders.

'Lazy,' says a voice as I press the lift button. 'What's wrong with the stairs?'

I swing round and Alex is standing there.

Chapter 27

'Oh, hi!'

'Here to sample the delights of this wonderful hotel?' he asks. He says it in a perfectly amiable way but his face seems tense.

I laugh awkwardly. 'Er, yes. Is your room on this floor?' I ask, trying to look innocent.

He nods. 'It's next door to Jackson's.'

'Ah.' *Shit! He must have followed a split second behind me and spotted me coming out of Jackson's room, which will have given him entirely the wrong impression.*

I feel a devastation that seems way out of proportion to Alex jumping to the wrong conclusion. But I can't exactly come out and say, 'Hey, I was in Jackson's room but it was totally innocent!' Because that would just seem as if I was protesting far too much . . .

And so, I say nothing, and we stand slightly apart, waiting for the lift in silence.

The lift pings, the door opens and I step inside with relief, eager to get away from Alex's censure.

Having emerged from Jackson's room feeling so triumphant, I've been hurled into the depths of despair in a matter of seconds! All because Alex now thinks Jackson and I are an item.

We travel to the ground floor in silence.

Then I have to say it because it's practically bursting out of me. Even if he doesn't believe me, I need to tell him.

'We're not together, you know. Jackson and I.'

Alex shrugs. 'It's none of my business.'

I'm about to say that it *is* his business, but that would be silly. Because of course it isn't. I've no reason to think Alex sees me as anything other than a friend. A friend who has disappointed him.

But I really wish it was his business!

The thought comes to me like a light bulb flashing above my head. I want Alex to care about me enough to *mind* that I might be seeing Jackson.

I'm hoping he'll offer me a lift along to the cabin. And I decide that, if he does, I'll talk to him and tell him all about what's been going on with Jackson. I'll tell him that I've finished with Jackson for good and that we were never right for each other in the first place. Then if there's even a tiny chance that Alex might like me, at least he'll know . . .

Getting out of the lift, my heart is hammering at the thought of baring my soul to him . . .

But as it turns out, he's just collecting a book from his car.

'Want a lift along?' he asks humourlessly.

'No, thanks,' I reply stiffly. 'I fancy a walk.'

'Okay.' He turns and walks off without another word, and I feel like sitting down in the snow and crying my eyes out.

Because when I saw his stern face in the corridor just then, clearly so disappointed and so annoyed at me, the full force of my feelings for him hit me so hard I couldn't even look at him, never mind speak to him.

I know Clemmy is waiting for me to get started on the mince pies, but I need to think so I go over to the rink and stand by the rail, watching the skaters having fun on the ice. I think wistfully of Alex trying to teach me. His patience. His chat. His jokes. The easy way we are with each other. Well, *were* – until Jackson got in the way big time.

I've fallen for Alex hook, line and sinker.

My feelings for him have been growing from the first time we met, but I didn't even realise it because my judgement was clouded by my feelings for Jackson.

But it can never happen for Alex and me.

Because even if I *did* manage to convince him that Jackson and I are over . . . and even if it turns out he *does* actually have feelings for me . . . it would be no use anyway because he'll be flying back to Australia on Boxing Day.

So really, it's all over even before it's started!

I can't believe how devastated I feel at the thought of Alex so far away, living on a different continent. I'll probably never see him again. Unless he returns next year for Christmas – but by that time, I'm sure he'll have met someone better . . .

A girl standing nearby peers at me as if she's going to ask if I'm all right, so I attempt a smile and hurry away, in the direction of the cabin.

When I get back, Clemmy is sitting at the breakfast bar, munching on a croissant.

With a super-human effort, I paste on a smile. 'Glad to see you're off the super-extreme eating plan!'

She gives a little guilty grimace. 'I feel bad about poor Sophie but I can't say I'm missing the green food.'

'Moderation in all things,' I say. 'Sorry, that's so clichéd!'

'Well, it is – but it's absolutely right. I just think it's sad Sophie felt she had to present a certain image in order to hang onto her job.'

'Parents can have a lot to answer for as well,' I say, remembering what Ruby told me about Sophie's mum weighing her every day as a little girl.

'I think we probably saw Sophie at her worst.

Apparently she was really stressed the whole time at the thought of losing her job, but she never told anyone. Except Jackson.'

'Yes. Relationships, huh?' My throat tightens up again but I smile and say, 'Thank goodness you and Ryan are happy! You need to tell me all about your wedding plans while we bake!'

Clemmy's already so excited about her Big Day, she needs little encouragement to chat about it.

Sylvia needs this batch by four o'clock today, so we bake solidly without even taking a lunch break and Clemmy tells me that now she's no longer taking part in Sophie's wedding feature (which she seems quite relieved about), they've decided to go for the smaller wedding that Ryan always wanted. Our in-depth discussion about flowers and cakes and cars helps take my mind off Alex and the hopelessness of my feelings for him.

There's also something really calming about being in the cosy warmth of a kitchen, listening to music on the radio while conjuring mouth-watering results from just a few ingredients. It strikes me as amazing that, even though Poppy isn't here, we're still managing to get the job done.

Could I ever have imagined, even a fortnight ago, that I could be directing proceedings here with Clem as my assistant, and successfully turning out hundreds of mince pies and gingerbread Santas that I know Sylvia will be pleased with?

My romantic life might be well and truly on the skids. But I've discovered a real passion here at the Log Fire Cabin. Baking is something I never imagined in a million years I could actually do – but apparently I can. And, more than that, I seem to be quite good at it, too.

Sadly, though, Poppy's contract with Sylvia draws to a close tomorrow, which is Christmas Eve. And that will also be the end of my job here, working with Poppy.

I feel so sad thinking about this. I'll miss working with Poppy so much. And now that I've foolishly stuck my oar in over her baby secret, we probably won't even part as friends . . .

Jed calls from the hospital in the afternoon to say that Poppy's doing well. He sounds elated about the fact that he's going to be a dad. I'm desperate to know how Poppy feels about him knowing – and if she's forgiven me for telling him. But of course it's not the right time to ask. So I congratulate Jed instead and tell him to send Poppy all our love.

Clemmy and I finish the final order and run it over in my car to Sylvia. Then we get back and make dinner together, deciding on a simple pasta dish followed by Eton Mess, made with shop-bought meringues, which makes it really easy to do.

I'm nervous, thinking about seeing Alex again at dinner. But in the end, he doesn't even make it over. He calls Clemmy to say he's got a headache and will just have an early night at the hotel.

So we are a very small party at the dinner table, with Poppy, Jed, Sophie and Alex all missing. It's just as well we have the wedding to talk about – and Ruby's plans to take up paragliding (much to Gloria's horror) – otherwise the evening would be completely flat.

I fall asleep with tear-stained cheeks, wishing I'd never met Jackson Cooper and thinking miserably about Alex in his hotel room.

Only one more day and I'll never have to see him again . . .

Chapter 28

The following day is Christmas Eve, and Bob somehow manages to get a last-minute booking for dinner at the Enchanted Forest. He's agreed that Ruby can invite Sam along.

Clemmy and I spend another day baking up a storm – the final day of Poppy's contract. Later, delivering the mince pies and gingerbread Santas to Sylvia for a final time feels so sad, I even get a lump in my throat. I suppose I'm thinking of Poppy and wondering if she'll even want to talk to me when she gets back tomorrow.

Alex stays away from the cabin all day and I get the distinct feeling he's avoiding me. But I'm on my way downstairs, all ready to go out for dinner, when I bump into him in the hall.

He's just arrived and is taking off his coat and hanging it on a peg. 'Had a good day?' he asks.

My heart sinks at his cool tone. He obviously hasn't forgiven Jackson and me for supposedly going behind

Sophie's back. I wish he'd realise I'm not the bad person he thinks I am.

'Not bad.' Despite my best efforts, a sigh escapes.

He frowns. 'Are you okay? Has something happened?'

I stare at him helplessly.

You could say that! I think I've fallen for you and I really want to kiss you but I don't know if you'd like that, so I can't!

'Is it Jackson?' He's looking into my eyes as if he really cares. 'Because I'm sure he really likes you. You'll get back together if it's right for you.'

'But I don't *want* to get back with Jackson.'

He frowns at me. 'You don't?'

'No. I told you that yesterday but you obviously didn't believe me.' My voice is raised because I'm so eager to make him understand.

He shrugs. 'Sometimes people don't actually know what they want until it's far too late.' The rough way he says it, his eyes boring into mine, knocks me off track for a moment. I'm used to the friendly, easy-going Alex who I can banter with and who can always make me laugh. I hate this sudden friction between us.

'What the hell does *that* mean?' I demand in frustration.

'*Do you* want to be with Jackson or *don't you*? If you'll pardon me saying so, you seem to change your mind with the wind direction!'

The harsh tone of his voice is a shock. He's looking at me as if I'm a prize idiot, not knowing my own mind.

'No, I do *not* want to be with Jackson!'

'Really?' The look on his face is close to a sneer.

I fold my arms and glare at him. 'Yes, *really*. Why don't you believe me?'

'Everything okay, folks?' Bob saunters down the hall, followed by Gloria and Ruby.

'Yes, fine,' we both mutter.

Everyone gathers at the door, putting on boots and coats and gloves. It's clear the conversation between Alex and I will have to wait. But after my clash with him, I feel as if I'm on the brink of tears all night.

The meal at the Enchanted Forest is lovely but I can barely eat a thing. The whole day has bruised and battered me emotionally and I can't understand why Alex is still angry with me. The only reason I can think of is that he might be worried about Jackson and how my uncertainty about our relationship might affect his friend.

But even that doesn't really ring true. I get the feeling that, while Alex and Jackson may have been mates years ago at university, the passage of time has made them into totally different people and they don't have much in common any more.

I don't know what the hell is going on with Alex,

but one thing I definitely do know: his behaviour is really unsettling me.

Every time he cracks a joke, I keep wanting him to look over at me, like he used to. But it's as if he's deliberately ignoring me – even though he knows I'm usually the first one to crack up at his daft remarks.

I can't believe how devastated I feel.

After the meal, we all head outside into a winter wonderland. The snow, which has been falling gently all day, has started to come down thickly now. We all make for the cars but I'm in such a daze, I completely forget my coat until I feel the frigid air outside, and I have to run back in for it. When I come out again, there's only Alex lingering outside the entrance, hunched into his own coat, waiting for me. Everyone else seems to have gone.

'My car's over there,' he says. Digging his hands deeper in his pockets, he strides off, and I slide and stumble my way after him, wishing I'd worn something more practical than these high-heeled boots.

I get into the passenger seat, feeling grateful the journey back to the cabin is a short one. Alex is definitely not in the mood for small talk.

But I try anyway. 'So, are you heading back to Australia on Boxing Day?' I ask cheerfully.

He nods, fumbling for the wiper controls. 'All good things come to an end,' he says shortly, and I glance across at him. His jaw is rigid, his expression uncompromisingly grim. I sigh and give up on the small talk. But his moodiness continues to rattle me, so eventually, when we're almost back at the cabin, I break the silence.

'Are you okay? You seem annoyed at me.'

He looks across at me. 'Annoyed? Not really. I suppose it's more a feeling of disappointment.'

My stomach lurches uncomfortably. '*Disappointment*? How have I disappointed you, Alex?'

He shrugs and pulls into the side of the road by the Log Fire Cabin, keeping the engine running. 'I suppose I thought I was getting to know you. I thought we were on the same wavelength and that doesn't happen very often, not for me anyway. But now I'm not so sure.'

I stare across at him, 'Why? What's changed?'

He gives me an odd look as if I should know what he's talking about. But I really don't!

At last he murmurs, 'It's like you always hold something of yourself back.' He shakes his head. 'I've given up trying to work you out.'

I sit there, shocked at his summing up of me. He knows me too well. Ever since Billy left me, I've made sure to keep a distance from people, never wanting to risk being rejected like that again. But I never realised it was so obvious – to Alex, at any rate.

He very deliberately leans across me and opens my door for me to get out.

Angry and tearful, I take the hint. Once I'm out in the snow, I turn and slam the door shut with all the force I can muster. The snow muffles the sound but it's still pretty loud.

Alex hits the accelerator a second later and attempts to roar off. But his tyres spin in the snow for a few seconds before gaining traction, which gives me a certain spiteful pleasure.

I slide my way along the path to the front door, snow blowing into my face, stinging my eyes and mingling with the angry tears and the hurt Alex's careless remarks have stirred up.

How dare he accuse me of 'holding something back' when he hasn't even bothered to find out if there's a *reason* I feel the need to do that! Maybe, when Alex has worked through his grumpy mood, he'll realise how unfair he's been . . .

But maybe he won't. So he'll return to Australia with a bad impression of me, instead of remembering the fun we had when he tried to teach me to skate.

I freeze, my key in the lock.

The thought of Alex thinking badly of me is such a distressing thought, I know I can't let him leave the day after tomorrow without setting the record straight.

But it will be no use trying to talk to him tomorrow,

Christmas Day, when everyone else is around celebrating and enjoying the festivities, with Poppy back
from hospital.

I need to talk to him *now*!

I glance over at my car. It's already buried under a
few inches of snow and it's likely to get a lot worse
before morning. If Alex's tyres made hard work of the
severe weather, mine will be even worse.

Entering the cabin, I quickly change into my trainers,
which are by the door in the shoe rack. Then, before
anyone can come out into the hall and tell me not to
be so silly, I slip back out into the snowy night and
close the door softly behind me.

I take a big breath, bury my nose in my scarf to keep
out the worst of the weather, and set off after Alex . . .

Chapter 29

It's a good twenty-minute walk along the lakeside road to the hotel under normal weather conditions – but, tonight, with heavy snow falling constantly, it takes me longer. My feet are already sinking in it up to my ankles when I set off.

It's after eleven when I arrive at the hotel. Soaked through, I shake snow off my coat and stamp my feet in the entrance before going inside to reception. There's no one there. So, after waiting for a minute or two, I glance around and head for the stairs.

I know the room Alex is in.

My trudge through the snow has calmed me down but as I walk along the same gloomy corridor for the second time in as many days, I'm starting to wonder what I'll say to him.

Then when I knock and Alex comes to the door, he takes one look at me and swears under his breath with such ferocity that I immediately remember exactly why I'm there.

I glare at him and he glares right back.

'I walked all the way here to try and explain to you why I might seem a bit . . . detached sometimes,' I murmur in an urgent tone, aware that Jackson is in the room next door. 'But seriously, Alex, if this is the reception I get, I've changed my mind. I'm not going to waste my time.'

I turn to go but he grabs my arm to stop me.

'You *walked* here? Jesus, are you mad?' he demands.

'No, I'm not mad,' I blurt out, trying but failing to reclaim my arm from his iron grip. 'At least, not in the sense *you* mean. But I *am* mad that you feel you can judge me so harshly without even bothering to find out why I might be this way. Reluctant to show my true self to people.'

He frowns and his expression softens slightly. 'So will you come in,' he says slowly, 'instead of charging back out into the snow and getting pneumonia?'

He releases my arm and holds the door wide.

I shrug and walk on in.

I'm shaking at the confrontation. And the thought that I'm going to have to start talking to Alex about the night of the accident, something I normally avoid like the plague.

'Won't Jackson wonder why you're here?'

'I'm *not with Jackson*.' I practically shout it in utter frustration.

But he still stares at me as if he doesn't believe me.

'It's true, so don't look at me like that! I might have hang-ups the size of a small continent but I'm not a liar!'

He studies me with a hint of a smile on his face.

'Except when you told Poppy you could bake, perhaps?'

I feel myself flush. 'That was a *small white lie*, mainly because she was so utterly desperate for help, bless her. I have a feeling she suspected I'd probably be clueless.'

'You don't seem clueless to me. You've produced some pretty spectacular desserts over the past few weeks.'

His expression has softened a little.

I smile triumphantly. 'Yes, I think I might just have a talent for baking I never knew about.'

He grins. 'I'm sure that's not your only talent.'

'What do you mean by that?'

He shrugs. 'There's your skating?'

'Funny.' I glower at him.

'I'm glad I make you laugh.'

'You haven't today. Not one bit, actually. You've been a right royal pain in the arse!'

'Well, if you *will* go around spending time in other men's rooms, you can't really blame me for feeling jealous, can you?'

I laugh incredulously. '*You? Jealous?* Come off it!'

He just looks at me then. This long intense stare, his green eyes burning into mine.

My heart starts beating frantically.

'What's happening here, Alex?' I walk towards him, curiously. 'You're not telling me that you—' I raise my hands in query and, quick as a flash, he grabs one of them and pulls me towards him.

Shocked to find myself suddenly rammed up against him, I stare at him wordlessly, knowing I should probably be objecting but finding, weirdly, that the words I'm looking for just won't come out.

And when his mouth comes down on mine, all the words in the world fly out of my head anyway. So, instead, I just give in to the urgency of the moment, which seems to be stretching into many, many moments as I reach up to tangle my hands in his hair and he pulls me against him so hard, there's not a hair's breadth between us.

We make it to the bed and then he's on top of me and the feelings of utter bliss are making my head spin. I arch my back, wanting more of him. His hands are under my top, travelling upwards and over my back and, for a second, I flinch. But he draws me to a kneeling position and pulls off my top, then he turns me around and grasps me round my midriff, and starts kissing my back. It's bliss and agony all at once, because my need for him feels so overwhelming. My skin is so unbearably sensitive to his kisses, I want him to never stop but just carry on doing what he's doing – and he does, brushing his lips all the way up to my neck and my shoulders.

Then I twist round and find his mouth with mine and stars start exploding in my head.

A fog of passion is rendering all thought obsolete. But in the faraway recesses of my mind, a little voice is whispering. At first, it's too distant to pay attention to. But gradually it grows louder and more insistent, until finally a single thought arrives in my head.

He's seen my scars – kissed my roughened skin – and yet he's still here.

I pull slightly away from him, wanting to look into his eyes. Because then I might be able to believe it's true.

And that's when the bedside phone rings, bringing us back to cold reality.

We break apart, stunned by the sudden piercing noise. Alex sits back, looking slightly bemused, and runs a hand through his hair. He looks at me. Then he glances at the phone.

'Maybe you should answer it,' I say shyly, looking around for my top.

He gives a big drawn-out groan and reaches for the phone.

I pull on my top and go to the mirror to smooth my

own hair, trying not to listen to his phone conversation. When he hangs up, I turn and he says, 'It's just reception. They were checking to see if my flight will be leaving the day after tomorrow as scheduled.'

My heart plummets at the mention of his flight and I realise what a stupid, hopeless idiot I've been, allowing myself to get carried away like this. He'll be leaving on Boxing Day, the day after tomorrow. All we've done is make things worse. Because now it will be even harder for me to say goodbye to him.

'I'd better go,' I mutter, jumping off the bed and heading for the door.

'Roxy, no, please don't go!' he shouts. 'Let me give you a lift back at least.'

'No, Alex, it's no use.'

I duck out and run along the corridor and down the stairs towards the exit.

It's stopped snowing when I get outside but it's freezing. I stand in the entrance, doing up my coat and putting on my scarf. Then Alex is there, trying to stop me from leaving.

'I'll be fine,' I tell Alex firmly. 'I don't need a lift. Please don't follow me.'

And then, to make sure he doesn't, I look him straight in the eye and say the one thing that just might stop him.

'This was all just a big mistake.'

Chapter 30

I walk back through the snow to the cabin in a daze, my brain struggling to process what just happened with Alex.

All I can think is that it must have been some primitive instinct taking over in the wake of my over-whelmingly emotional day.

I feel utterly exhausted and just want to fall into bed and sleep.

But strangely, when I finally make it back to my bedroom, change into my cosy pyjamas and slide between the covers, sleep evades me completely. I toss and turn, trying desperately to drift off, but my mind just won't relax. It's like a naughty toddler resisting sleep by jumping up and down on the bed and yelling at the top of its voice.

My thoughts are all jumbled, like in a strange dream, and eventually I get out of bed and creep downstairs to make myself a hot drink, hoping that might do the trick. With Poppy still in hospital (although she's coming back tomorrow – well, today, actually; it's long after midnight now) I will be in charge of the Christmas lunch so I could do with some shuteye to prepare myself.

I'm actually dreading Poppy's return because I've no idea if she's even going to be speaking to me after I dropped her in it with Jed about the pregnancy. My stomach flutters with panic every time I think of what she'll say.

But there's no point worrying. What will be will be. I just need to throw all my energy into serving up a good Christmas lunch.

Standing there waiting for the milk to boil, it strikes me as amazing that I'm not at all fazed by the prospect of cooking a turkey – even though I've only ever watched Mum do it. It's as if these few weeks, baking and cooking with Poppy, have lit a fire inside me and revealed a natural ability I didn't know existed . . .

I sit in bed drinking my hot chocolate, trying to focus on the lunch, but snatches from my steamy encounter with Alex keep intruding on my thoughts, making me flush hotly and think about opening a window.

The drink helps but the dreams that follow are the exhausting kind where I'm racing to get somewhere but find myself thwarted at every turn.

At one point during the night, I wake up and have a moment of absolute clarity.

It hits me with the force of a ten-ton truck.

I've fallen for Alex harder than I've ever fallen for a man before. Even Billy.

But now, I'm going to have to start the impossible process of trying to forget him . . .

I wake to the sound of Christmas classics blaring from Ruby's room.

Instantly, my thoughts turn to the night before and Alex.

I slip out of bed, cross to the window and stare out at the perfect festive scene before me. The winter sun sparkles on the lake and the branches of the fir trees hang heavy with the fresh falls of snow that arrived the night before.

I can see the hotel in the distance, where Alex will be waking up. Will he be thinking about me?

My throat aches, remembering how we parted the night before. I should never have gone over there . . .

Ruby's Christmas music intrudes on my thoughts, and with a shock, I suddenly remember something.

It's Christmas Day!

I need to get busy with the big celebration lunch.

I shower, dress in jeans and my favourite comfortable T-shirt, and run down to the kitchen to take the turkey out of the fridge.

The huge bird arrived yesterday with a delivery of other Christmas goodies from a local supermarket. I eye it uncertainly. Grappling with this is going to be interesting. But I'm not daunted!

To be honest, I'll be more than happy to remain in the kitchen all day, cooking from now until midnight. If I'm hidden away in here, I won't have to see Alex . . .

I keep thinking of his face when I said what we did last night was just a big mistake. My heart lurches painfully every time I remember. But there would be no use taking it back.

As the morning wears on and I try to focus on preparing sprouts and peeling what seems like a million chestnuts for the stuffing – thankfully with some help from Clemmy – anxiety is building inside me.

I'm dreading Poppy's return.

Soon after ten, Jed popped his head round the door to let us know he was off to pick her up. Last night, when he got back from the hospital, he parked his car in a spot near the main road, just in case more snow-fall overnight made it difficult to get it out in the morning.

He seemed his usual chirpy self and was clearly still buzzing at the news of becoming a dad, now that it was clear Poppy and the baby were both fine.

'I can't thank you enough, Roxy, for letting me know about the baby,' he added before he left.

I smiled in reply, but beneath it all, I was really worried. I'd upset Poppy's plans and had no idea how she'd be feeling. I supposed at least Jed would plead my cause to her if the worst happened and she couldn't forgive me.

I hear Jackson arriving a little while later, and as I expect, he comes into the kitchen and we have a slightly awkward hug.

'Is Alex coming over for lunch?' I ask him. I've been longing to know – and also dreading it – since I got up this morning.

'Yes, he's coming over soon.'

I'm also a bag of nerves at the prospect of Poppy's return from the hospital. As I mix aromatic sausage meat, bought from a nearby farm shop, with the chestnuts and liberal sprinklings of fresh herbs, I calculate how long it's likely to take Jed to get there and back, bearing in mind the tricky weather conditions.

By my reckoning, he and Poppy could be here as early as one o'clock.

My insides start up a protest at the very idea, so I turn up the radio and soon Clemmy and I are singing along to some classic Christmas songs, which makes me feel a little less stressy.

At last everything is prepared for the three o'clock lunch, timed to fit in with Poppy's return. The turkey and my herby homemade stuffing are in the oven, filling the whole house with the most mouth-watering savoury smells, and the vegetables are all peeled and chopped and sitting in pans on the hob.

'Coffee?' asks Clemmy, holding up the kettle. 'Or something stronger?'

I grin. 'Tempting. But I think Jed's planning on popping the champagne when they get back. I'll wait till then. Coffee would be lovely, though.'

A shot of vodka would hit the spot so much better!

Ryan comes in and beckons Clemmy through to look at something to do with weddings on the TV. So I finish making the coffee myself. And instead of going through to join the others in the living room, I shrug on my coat and gloves, click open the French windows and walk out into the snow with my coffee cup, closing the doors softly behind me.

It's a brilliant day of blue skies and sunshine, with not a hint of the tumultuous snow clouds of yesterday, but more snow is forecast for later. My car is pretty stuck, not having snow tyres, but no doubt a snow plough will eventually make its way along, so I'm not too worried. If I needed to, I could always walk to the main road, which is apparently perfectly clear of snow, and get a bus home from there.

I hear voices in the kitchen and turn to see who it is.

Jed is peering in the oven at the turkey and Poppy, looking pale but smiling at least, is walking over to join him. I swallow hard. Hopefully she'll be pleased with what I've done in her absence . . .

She glances outside and sees me. Then she walks over to the window and stares right at me and my stomach plummets.

It's clear she's furious. Her eyes are cold and as hard as steel. My heart is pounding miserably as she yanks open the door.

'Roxy, I just don't believe what you did!'

'Oh God, I'm so sorry, Poppy!' I begin, feeling utterly wretched. 'I know I shouldn't have told Jed but I just did what I thought was right. It was a spur-of-the-moment thing and I've honestly regretted it so many times.'

'No, I meant the amazing work you did in my absence,' she says.

I stare at her, tears springing to my eyes.

She looks horrified. 'Oh Roxy, what's wrong? I was only kidding. I'm not angry at all.' She puts her arm round my shoulders and grins. 'At least, I was. But I've had a chance to think about it and you did absolutely the right thing!'

She passes me a hanky and I snuffle into it, feeling the teeniest bit pathetic. 'You think?'

She nods. 'I do think! Now, come in out of the cold and I'll get a tea for myself. There'll be no champagne for me today, sadly,' she adds, patting her tummy and not looking the slightest bit bothered.

Jed has apparently gone out to the front to help Ryan and Jackson to shovel snow and get the cars free. And Clemmy, who's still determined to get fit, has decided to help. So Poppy and I settle ourselves at the breakfast bar to catch up on what's been happening.

'So how are you? What did the doctors say?' I ask.

She touches wood and smiles. 'Everything seems fine now, thank goodness. Apparently, the likelihood is that I'll go on to have a perfectly normal pregnancy.'

'That's great. You must be so relieved.'

'I am, actually.' She lays a protective hand on her small bump. 'I . . . never realised how much I wanted this baby until I thought I might be losing it.'

'And you really don't mind that I told Jed?' I ask anxiously.

She smiles. 'Stop worrying about that. You did the right thing. I should have told him ages ago but my twisted logic said . . .' She shrugs. 'Well, you know what I thought – and *still* think, if I'm honest.'

'But Jed's clearly so delighted.'

She sighs. 'Yes, but with a baby on the way, I'll never know now whether he's with me because I'm genuinely the woman he'd have chosen to be with, above all others. Or whether we'd have had a good time but gone on to be with other people.' She shrugs. 'I just find that lack of certainty quite sad.'

I nod. 'I know what you mean. But life is full of

uncertainties. None of us know what the future will bring. Even if Jed *had* made a commitment to you, before the baby was on the way, it doesn't mean you would have stayed together forever.'

'That's true.'

'And actually, all that really matters is that you and Jed are together right now and you make each other happy. Isn't it? That's all any of us can hope for.'

Thoughts of Alex swim into my head but I push them away.

Poppy smiles wistfully, but I can tell she's still bogged down with doubts.

'Anyway, how are you, you brilliant baker?' She grins. 'You saved the day by getting the order in, no doubt about that. Sylvia's already signed me up to supply her with Christmas goodies next year!'

'Oh, that's fab!' I feel my cheeks flush with delight, so glad Poppy's pleased with my work.

'And I've been thinking.'

I grin. 'Steady.'

'Well, I've had a lot of time to think being stuck with bed rest for the past few days – and, well, I've decided the time has come to find myself a partner.'

I stare at her stupidly. 'You're not going to finish with Jed. Not now?'

She laughs. 'No, I mean a *business* partner!'

'Oh.'

'So are you up for it?'

My eyes open wide. '*Me?* You want *me* to be your partner in the *business?*'

My face must be an absolute picture of shock because Poppy starts laughing. 'Don't look so surprised, Roxy. Erin could only ever help out occasionally. I need a full-time person, especially with motherhood on the horizon.' She pats her bump with a smile. 'You and I get on really well – and that's absolutely vital if we're going to be working together every day. Plus you've got a flair for baking. I could see that almost immediately and you've learned so much in such a short space of time – largely due to the fact that you were shoved in at the deep end by yours truly and left to sink or swim!' She shrugs. 'Well, you certainly didn't drown – quite the opposite – so I'd be an idiot to start looking around for a business partner when I've got the best candidate of all sitting right opposite me now.'

'Wow, that's amazing,' I begin. 'I never expected that. But are you sure?'

My old uncertainties kick in like clockwork. I've always felt at a disadvantage in the world of work because, while most of my school friends were starting their careers, I was stuck in a hospital and then in recovery during those important years. As a consequence, I suppose I've always felt I lagged behind everyone else.

'Of course I'm sure. Roxy, you need to start believing in yourself. You're brilliant and I just don't know why you're so negative about yourself sometimes.'

I swallow. And then I say it. 'There's something I haven't told you.'

And then I tell her the story of my accident and it feels so freeing to be able to talk about it without worrying, as I always used to, that the person I'm telling will view me differently afterwards.

After I've finished talking about it and Poppy has nodded sympathetically and told me she understands, we go on to talk about something else altogether. And nothing bad happens, which is such a huge relief it's quite a heady feeling.

Poppy hasn't changed her opinion of me, just because I'm not 'perfect'.

Because why would she?

Half way through talking Poppy through the meals Clemmy and I made in her absence, I hear Alex's voice in the hall and my heart starts to pound. I swallow hard and try to carry on the conversation as normal, but Poppy's too perceptive.

'Is something wrong?' She peers at me. 'You seem nervous. You're not going to say no to my offer, are you?'

I gaze at her in alarm. 'No, of course not. I'd love to be your business partner.'

'So what is it? Because you don't look like a woman on the threshold of a brand new career!'

I shake my head and stare at the floor.

'It's Jackson, isn't it?' she guesses. 'Oh God, I was sort of hoping when Jed told me about Sophie leaving that you two would get together again. But hasn't it worked out that way?'

I shake my head again. 'It's not Jackson.'

'Oh. So what . . .?'

I swallow hard. 'It's Alex. I'm in love with Alex.'

Chapter 31

'Alex? Really?' Poppy smiles delightedly. 'So what's wrong?' Her face falls. 'Oh, doesn't he feel the same way about you?'

I stare at her miserably. 'I don't know. I think he might. But it makes no difference anyway because he's going back to Australia.'

She sighs. 'The course of true love never runs smooth.'

'Smoothly.'

'Sorry?'

I stare at her glumly. 'It should be smooth-*ly*. Shouldn't it? Grammatically speaking?'

'I think you might be right there. See, I knew it was wise offering you a partnership. Intelligence as well as creativity!'

Smiling, I rise to my feet. 'Right, I'll get the vegetables on but you have to stay put and have another cuppa.'

'No way,' she says, leaping up. 'I'm absolutely fine. Let's get this show on the road! And Roxy?'

'Don't give up on Alex. If it's meant to be . . .'

I smile and shake my head at her optimism.

Lunch is finally served soon after three.

It's a lively affair with lots of cracker-pulling and reading the bad jokes aloud. To my horror, Poppy has seated Alex right opposite me, which is making me feel horribly self-conscious. Every time he cracks a joke, I hardly dare look at him or laugh in case it's painfully obvious to everyone round the table that I'm crazy in love with him! And my appetite is non-existent, although I do at least have an excuse, considering I made the food myself.

It's all really awkward.

'Did you forget the champagne?' Poppy says suddenly, looking at Jed. 'At least, *I'm* not going to be having any, obviously, but—'

Jed shakes his head. 'The wine goes better with the turkey. Why don't we have the champagne later?'

Poppy nods. 'And we can raise a glass to Roxy!' She clears her throat to draw everyone's attention. 'Because Roxy is going to be my new business partner!'

There's an outpouring of congratulations, which is lovely but I could really do without all the focus being on me.

I'm highly relieved when Clemmy starts talking about her own idea for a business, and the spotlight turns on her instead.

'I just adore glamping! And I keep thinking the lakeside here would make the perfect setting.' She beams at Ryan. 'We went glamping in the summer and it was fabulous, wasn't it?'

Ryan nods. 'Yeah, it was just like staying in a hotel with all the home comforts. No traipsing across to the communal toilet block if you got caught short in the middle of the night.'

I escape into the kitchen, leaving them all talking about log burners and the romance of eating by candle-light, on the pretext of checking the Christmas pudding. Leaning back against the worktop, I run my hands through my hair with a sigh. How did I get myself into such a predicament? I must have been falling for Alex all the time without realising it – and now, it's just agony sitting next to him, knowing that, after today, he'll be gone from my life.

I hear footsteps along the corridor and I relax slightly, thinking it's Poppy. I'll be able to offload a little about her placing Alex opposite me at the table!

But when the door opens, it's Alex.

He quickly crosses the room to where I'm standing, his eyes locked onto mine. 'Roxy, I'm so sorry about last night,' he murmurs urgently.

'Oh. It's fine,' I say stiffly. 'As I said, it was a big mistake.'

As if he hasn't even heard me, he murmurs, 'Last

night was incredible, Roxy,' his eyes burning into mine.

I sniff. 'Yes, it was. But you're leaving tomorrow to go back to Australia. So what's your point, Alex?'

My heart is thudding so hard, I think it might explode out of my chest. I have to get out of here, otherwise I'll end up flinging myself at him and never wanting to let him go.

I flee from the room before he has a chance to see the tears flowing freely down my face.

Chapter 32

I run up to my room and stand by the big picture window, staring out across the lake. Across the far side, I can see the lights and festive decorations of the hotel. A surprising number of people have taken to the ice for the final day.

Sylvia's Christmas break will begin tomorrow, Boxing Day.

But Alex's holiday will be coming to an end.

My throat tightens. If only I hadn't gone to his room last night, I'd be waving him off quite happily, still ignorant of the huge chemistry between us. Then I could have moved on with my life, relishing the thought of my brand new career as Poppy's partner in the catering business.

If only I hadn't been so caught up with Jackson, I would have realised a lot sooner that Alex was special – that he made me laugh and feel more alive than any man ever has. It's so ironic that all the time I've been at the cabin, still half-hoping for a life with Jackson, after all, I've been wasting time I could have spent getting to know Alex better.

Thinking about it now, there were signs that Alex liked me, too. But because of the Jackson-shaped block that was fogging up my brain, I failed to see them.

There's a knock on the door and I quickly wipe my wet face with both hands. Pasting on a smile, I turn and, thankfully, it's just Poppy.

She looks alarmed. 'Oh God, are you all right?'

I shake my head, my face crumpling.

'Is it Alex?'

Her sympathetic expression makes me want to break down completely and pour out my heart to her. But I can't. They're waiting for pudding. I've got to tidy myself up and go downstairs and put on a happy face. Make sure that Alex doesn't see I've been crying . . .

Poppy sighs. 'Oh, Roxy, this must be torture for you. I didn't have time after you told me about Alex to re-jig the table plan!'

She plops down on the bed beside me and we stare at each other gloomily.

'How are you and Jed?' I ask.

'We're okay.' But her expression is tinged with sadness and I can see that she's not okay at all. 'I just wish I could get it out of my head – the thought that Jed might feel trapped because of the baby. I really couldn't bear to think I got him by foul means.'

Incredulous laughter bursts from me. 'Now you're being *really* daft! It wasn't as if you set out to deliberately ensnare the man by getting yourself pregnant!'

She gives a wan smile. 'I know. Obvs. I could never be that scheming. But—' She shrugs. 'Life, eh? It's only ever predictable when you don't want it to be.'

I nod. 'There's a pair of us!'

She gets up. 'Right, you get yourself sorted while I go and dish up the pud. Ten minutes do you?'

I nod. 'Thanks, Poppy. For everything.'

When I stand, she pulls me into a tight hug. 'And thank you, Roxy. For helping me through a bad time – in more ways than one.'

'I promise I won't blabber any more of your secrets to Jed.' I give her a rueful grin.

She turns at the door. 'Oh, blabber away! You talk a lot of common sense and I have a feeling that's going to be a big boon to our business.'

Somehow I make it through the rest of the afternoon, although, by teatime, my cheeks are aching with trying to smile all the time.

When Gloria suggests a game of charades, Jackson comes over and asks if he can talk to me. It would be good to clear the air, I decide, so I suggest we go up to my room where we'll have some privacy. As we're walking down the hall, Alex emerges from the kitchen. We exchange a glance and my heart leaps in my chest. He looks like I feel – full of longing and regret.

'Coming, Roxy?' murmurs Jackson, and Alex's face clouds over, the connection between us broken.

I stare after Alex for a second as he heads back to the living room with his beer, suddenly weak with lust at the sight of his gorgeous bum in those dark, fitted jeans. Memories of the night before come flooding back in full technicolour. The feel of his body next to me, his mouth on mine, the way we kissed with such desperate passion, as though making up for the time we'd wasted.

'Roxy?' Jed is half way up the stairs.

'Yes. Sorry.' I walk up after him with a heavy heart. *What the hell will Alex think now?*

In my room, Jackson sits down and pats the place on the bed beside him, and I sit down at a slight angle, facing him.

'Are we okay, Roxy?' he asks with a slightly strained smile.

I pause. Does he mean are we okay as a couple? Or was that just a general how's-it-going sort of remark?

'Er, I'm fine, thanks,' I say, plumping for the latter. 'But you're right. We probably need to talk. There hasn't really been much chance, what with everything that's been going on.'

And the fact that we've been avoiding each other . . .

He nods. 'Absolutely. Why don't you say what's on your mind? Ladies first!'

I groan inwardly. Why does 'ladies first' sometimes seem like you're being pushed ahead to suss out unfamiliar terrain?

I take a big breath. 'Right, well, can I first of all say sorry again for embarrassing you like that on live TV, by proposing and everything?'

He waves away my apology. 'You'd had a lot to drink, Roxy. And to be honest, after I'd recovered from the shock, I didn't take it seriously anyway. I mean, we'd only been together five minutes, right?'

'Right.' I nod, thinking sadly of how differently we'd been viewing the relationship. I'd hoped it would blossom into something lasting, while for Jackson, he probably hadn't even been thinking beyond the next date. 'Well, anyway, I was quite surprised at how quickly you seemed to move on and I was hurt at first. But then I came here, to the Log Fire Cabin, and that's when I began to see our relationship in a whole new light. I hope you'll forgive me when I tell you this, Jackson,' I say, staring down at my hands. 'But . . . I think I've fallen properly in love for the very first time.'

I glance up at him and see the alarm spring to his face. It takes a few seconds for me to realise that I obviously haven't made myself clear. He thinks I'm talking about *him* and he looks downright horrified!

I open my mouth to reassure him but before I can say a word, he grasps my hands, looks into my eyes and says earnestly, 'But don't you think you should see a counsellor, Roxy? Before you even *think* of having a relationship? Then you could talk about your – erm – disfigurement and the effect it's had on you. I really think that would be best.' There's a pause, then he adds quickly, 'For you.'

I stare back at him. 'Maybe you're right,' I say slowly.

'Oh, I'm sure I am. I mean, there are plastic surgeons who can work absolute miracles and I'm sure that one day, with all the advances in technology, they'll be able to make your back look – well, almost brand new.' He pats my hands and smiles, like he's the doctor and I'm one of his patients. 'But until that day, you'll need help accepting your scars – and sadly, I just don't think I'm the man to help you do that.'

He gives a big sigh of regret and shrugs as if to say, *It's unfortunate but what can I do?*

'You're right, Jackson. I had a big hang-up about being scarred because I thought no one would ever find me attractive again.' I glance at him, giving him the chance to contradict me. But he just nods sadly. So I plough on. 'But I've recently realised that's not the case at all. There are men out there who will happily accept me just the way I am.' *Well, one in particular . . .*

He continues his empathetic nodding for a while, before suddenly catching on. 'Er, no! I mean, yes! Absolutely! Because of *course* you're attractive, Roxy!'

'Thank you, Jackson,' I reply calmly, with only a small amount of irony.

'You're very welcome, Roxy. So what I'm trying to say is that, before you can even think about being in a relationship, you really need to do the work, accepting your scars. Right? And that could take a long time.'

I nod solemnly. Has he listened to a single word I've been saying?

'Obviously, I'm saying all this because I'm thinking of what's best for you.'

'Of course you are. And that's so – um – *wise* of you. And very considerate, too.'

He smiles as if to say, 'Aw shucks, it's nothing.'

'So . . . friends?' I glance at him hopefully.

'Friends!' he replies heartily, pumping my hand up and down, as if a great weight has just rolled off his shoulders.

After he's gone, promising to keep in touch and take me out for 'a beer' some time, I sit back on the propped-up pillows and reflect on what is, finally, the end for me and Jackson Cooper.

Did he ever really love me? Perhaps he did, in his own way. But I'm beginning to think that the reason he started pursuing me again when I arrived at the cabin was because he'd already grown disenchanted with Sophie and her stressed-out behaviour. So I was a better prospect for a while – until he saw my 'disfigurement' and realised he couldn't cope with my imperfections. At which point it was 'game over'.

I'm not worried about Jackson finding love again. He'll probably have another girlfriend by next Tuesday – possibly sooner.

Whereas me?

I'll be living with my regrets over Alex far beyond next week . . .

Chapter 33

When I walk back with Jackson into the living room, where everyone's gathered watching TV, I feel Alex's eyes on us and my heart feels like a lead weight in my chest. I want him to know we weren't up to anything romantic – quite the reverse, in fact – but I'm not about to announce that to everyone.

I plonk myself down and try to concentrate on the film but, with Alex on the other end of the sofa, it's impossible.

I have a sudden mad idea that maybe I could try digging my car out so I could head home. I told Poppy I'd stay tonight so that we could talk about the business in the morning, but she wouldn't mind if I left now. She knows how I feel about Alex. And I could come back tomorrow, once Alex has gone.

I wait for a tense bit in the movie when everyone is glued, then I slip out to the hall and pull on wellies and my coat. There's a couple of big shovels outside by the door that the guys were using earlier, but when I glance over at my car, I see that they've already beaten me to it. The snow around my vehicle has been shovelled away. Digging the keys out of my pocket, I get into the driver's seat and start the car, just to see how far I can move it.

If I can just get it up onto the road from the little parking area, I might just be able to make it. The wheels slipping and sliding on the ice, I manage to turn the car around but getting it up the slope onto the road proves to be much trickier. But my desperation to escape the increasingly impossible situation I find myself in drives me on. Revving the engine, I try again and again, sweating yet determined not to be defeated. But each time, I almost make it to the top – then slide back down again.

After the fourth attempt, I grit my teeth, groan with frustration and thump the steering wheel. Then, exhausted emotionally and physically, I close my eyes and throw myself back against the headrest.

Seconds later, someone taps on the window.

It's Alex, frowning in at me.

I stare at him, wishing he would just go away and leave me alone. But he motions for me to wind down the window, so with a great deal of reluctance, I do.

'What are you doing?' he demands roughly. 'You can't possibly be thinking of driving in this! You'll have to wait for the snow plough to shift it.'

'What if I don't *want* to wait?' I say truculently, knowing I'm not being logical but unable to throw off the urgency of feeling I need to escape. I rev the engine and try one more time to get it up the slope. But it rolls right back down again.

A painful lump is wedged in my throat and I'm fighting back the tears. I want to thump the steering wheel again but I manage to resist.

Instead, when Alex opens the car door, I get out calmly.

He waits, presumably to make sure I'm not going to try anything stupid again. Then he follows me inside and watches while I shed my coat. One of the wellies proves impossible to remove and I dance around a bit trying to get it off.

'Sit down,' he orders, pointing at the stairs.

'I'm fine,' I say obstinately, a second before I over-balance and cannon into the wall.

Alex sighs. 'Will you sit down please?'

Pursing my lips and feeling like a naughty child, I sink onto the second step from the bottom and he takes a firm hold of my foot and pulls off my stubborn footwear.

'Thank you,' I say pertly, my heart racing so fast at the nearness of him that my head swims. I turn away and hide my face in the process of lining up the wellies beside the others.

'You can't drive off on such treacherous roads,' he murmurs.

I slip my feet into my ballet pumps and smooth down my hair. Then I take a deep breath and say in a small, tremulous voice: 'There's something I need to tell you, Alex.' I'm going to tell him the truth. That our encounter last night was far from a mistake . . .

I wait a second but he doesn't respond. And when I turn round, I realise why. He's already gone back to join the rest. He didn't even hear me . . .

Jed comes slowly down the stairs just as I'm psyching myself up to go back in. Deep in thought, he looks surprised when he sees me.

'Are you coming in?' He nods towards the living room.

'Er, yes. Yes, I was just getting something from the car.'

'Snow plough should be along tomorrow morning. Hopefully before Alex needs to drive to the airport. I'd hate him to be stranded and miss his flight.'

I force a smile. 'Yes. That would be awful!'

He follows me along the corridor but when I sit back down on the sofa, Jed remains standing in the middle of the room.

'Sorry, do you mind if I just pause this?' he says, and Ruby leaps up to grab the remote. 'I need to ask Poppy something.'

Everyone looks at Poppy and she says, 'Oh yes, the Christmas cake! I cut it into slices and it's in a box in the cupboard.'

Jed doesn't move. A smile spreads slowly across his face. 'Actually, I wasn't thinking about cake.'

'Oh.' Poppy looks confused. 'So what . . .?'

He grins. Then, reaching into his pocket, he draws out a small box. Clemmy, beside me, lets out a huge gasp.

Then, in front of everyone, Jed goes down on one knee, smiles at Poppy and murmurs, 'Poppy, will you marry me?' He draws the ring out of its box.

Poppy's face is a picture of stunned bemusement changing into sheer delight as she stares from his face to the ring and back again. Through her blushes, she somehow manages to stammer 'Yes, of course I will.' Her fingers are trembling so much, they fumble over the ring, but once it's on, she admires it, flashes it around in wonder for everyone to see, then throws her arms around Jed's neck. He rises to his feet and lifts her off the ground and she loops her legs around his waist and squeals with excitement.

Everyone is laughing and cheering, and Ruby's shouting, 'Can I be bridesmaid? *Please* can I be bridesmaid?'

Gloria shushes her, looking embarrassed. 'You can't *ask* to be a bridesmaid, love.'

Ruby looks bemused. 'Why on earth not? I won't be offended if they say no.'

336

'When did you buy the ring?' Poppy asks. 'Was it while I was in hospital?'

Jed shakes his head. 'I bought it months ago but I was waiting for the right time.' He grins ruefully. 'Actually, who am I kidding? I was terrified of proposing in case you said no.'

With a gulp, I glance across at Jackson, who has the grace to look slightly awkward.

'Why would you think I might say no?' shrieks Poppy in amazement.

Jed shrugs. 'I thought my workaholic tendencies might have turned you off the idea of spending the rest of your life with me. But, with a baby on the way, I was pretty sure you'd say yes.'

Poppy's smile is so wide and dazzling, it could light up a room.

She shoots a quick glance in my direction and I know exactly what she's thinking. Far from feeling trapped, Jed had clearly been planning the proposal for ages, and he'd even had doubts she'd say yes!

'Right, champagne for everyone?' She leaps up but Jed gently pushes her back down on the sofa and says he'll do it.

'Got to look after you now, wife- and mother-to-be,' he says with a broad grin. Ruby pretends to throw up, which makes everyone laugh.

I'm so delighted for Poppy, I feel myself being swept

along on the tide of happiness. Then I catch Alex's eye. He's smiling, but he's looking directly at me and my heart lurches in my chest.

All of a sudden, I can't bear it. I need to be somewhere else, where people aren't being so bloody unbearably joyous!

When Jed pours the champagne, I take a few sips from the glass he hands me and toast the happy couple.

Then quietly, I slip out of the room, leaving them all to it.

Up in my room, I glance at the bedside clock. It's nearly ten. A perfectly legitimate time to retire for the night. I'm sure it will be fine if I don't go down to say goodnight. They're all having such a lovely time, I'm sure no one will even notice I'm gone.

Except maybe Alex.

I've sensed his eyes on me many times today but it's just added to the misery I feel, remembering the other night but knowing there's no future for us.

I undress slowly and take a long shower, the water flowing with my tears and washing my face clean. Then I get into my night things and slip into bed.

I'll never sleep. Not with the level of chatter and laughter rising up to distract me. But maybe I'll just sink my head into the pillow and relax.

Within seconds, exhausted from the last few days' tumultuous happenings, I fall off the cliff into a deep sleep . . .

Chapter 34

I wake with a start. It's still dark in the room but my door is being pushed open, making a shushing noise across the thick cream carpet.

'Are you awake?' whispers a voice.

I struggle to a sitting position, as a shaft of light from the corridor beyond illuminates my visitor.

'Ruby? What time is it?'

'Nearly eight. Everyone else is still conked out. A *lot* of champagne was drunk last night – except by poor Poppy, who was on the non-alcoholic wine.'

'I don't suppose she minded too much. Not after Jed's lovely proposal.' I rub my bleary eyes, amazed I slept so long. 'Did . . . everyone walk back to the hotel?'

She nods. 'It was really late and they were pretty drunk.' She snaps on the bedside light, snatching away the comforting half-darkness and leaving me feeling horribly exposed. 'What's wrong with you, then?' She peers at me. 'You can't have a hangover. You only had half a glass of champagne before you snuck away.'

I laugh. 'I didn't *sneak*.'

'Well, it looked like that.'

'Have you been keeping tabs on me, then?'

'No, I just notice what's going on, that's all.'

'You do, don't you? You're very sharp and extremely observant.' I grin at her. 'You could be a detective. The next Miss Marple.'

She shakes her head firmly. 'No, I'm still keen on being a stunt woman. But failing that, I'll settle for becoming an actor.'

I laugh. 'Wow, and you're only seventeen. I wish I'd known so clearly at that age what I wanted to be when I grew up!'

She frowns. 'When you were my age, you were only two years away from having your accident, so things probably wouldn't have worked out how you wanted them to, anyway.'

'That's true.'

'I know you asked Jackson to marry you on that dating programme,' she says suddenly.

'Oh, do you, now?' I laugh, amazed to find that mention of that horrible night no longer has the power to hurt or make me cringe. 'Who told you?'

'No one. I saw the programme and I recognised you both as soon as I got here.'

'But you didn't say anything to anyone?'

She shakes her head. 'Well, I told my friend, Chloe. But it was obvious no one else was talking about it here, so I assumed you and Jackson wanted to keep it quiet. So I didn't say anything.'

'Wow, Ruby, that's very mature and considerate of you.'

'Did you think he was The One?'

I nod. 'I did but I was wrong.'

'So is there someone else?'

I gulp and look away with a shake of the head.

'Ooh, Roxy, there is, isn't there! You've gone bright red. You can tell me if you like. I won't tell anyone else.'

I grin at her. 'No point telling you because it's completely hopeless.'

'But you don't know that. Have you told him you like him?'

'No, because it couldn't go anywhere. This is not the Cinderella film set, you know. Not all potential romances have happy endings!'

I'm trying to make a joke of it but it's hard to keep my tone light, as if I'm really not that bothered one way or the other.

'Why couldn't it work?' she wants to know.

I sigh. 'Well, geography.'

'What do you mean by geography?'

'We – er – don't live in the same place so it would be impossible to see each other.'

She frowns. 'Long-distance relationships can work, though. My Auntie Paula married a man from Oregano in America and she'd only visited him twice. What are you laughing at? It's true.'

'I'm sure it is and congratulations to Auntie Paula. But I think you mean the state of *Oregon*?'

'That's what I said, didn't I?' She stares at me, puzzled. 'So where does your man live? He can't be further away than America.'

'He can, actually.'

She gapes at me. 'Really? Fuck, that *is* hopeless! Oops, sorry.' She grimaces at the swear word. 'You don't mean he's from somewhere like Australia, do you?'

I shrug, trying to keep my face as bland as possible, but Ruby is too sharp.

'*Australia?*' She stares into the distance. Then, to my dismay, I see the light bulb go on above her head. 'Oh my God, it's Alex! Of course! Why didn't I guess? You're always joking with each other. You've got great banter.'

'Do we?' I stare at her in confusion.

'Yes, you know, in a cute way.'

I smile. 'He does make me laugh.'

'And you fancy him, right? I mean, he's definitely fit. For an oldie.'

I ignore her question by laughing at Alex, aged thirty, being described by Ruby as an oldie.

'So?'

'So what?'

'Are you really into him? In which case, what the hell are you doing here, talking to me, when you could be over at the hotel banging on his door?'

'Banging on his door? I'd never do that!' I gasp, colouring slightly as I recall doing exactly that just two nights ago – and the mind-blowing passion that followed.

'Why not?' She folds her arms and gives me an old-fashioned look. 'You never told him you liked him, did you?!' It's more an accusation than a question.

'Well, no, not exactly.' *But sometimes actions can speak louder than words!*

'And I bet he still thinks you're into Jackson.'

I shrug. 'I don't think he does. But I might have given him the impression I wasn't interested in him.'

'But why? This is your life – your future – we're talking about here. What if he's *The One* and you let him fly back to Australia without ever trying to find out exactly how he feels about you?'

I raise my eyebrows slightly, thinking about this.

'How sad would it be if you missed your opportunity? I mean, there's a chance he doesn't feel as strongly as you do but I think you need to find out, don't you?' She shrugs. 'You might make a massive tit of yourself, but at least you'd *know*.'

'Gee thanks, Ruby, that's very reassuring.'

'So get going!'

'Where?'

'To the hotel! Honestly, for an intelligent human being, you can be a bit thick at times, Roxy.'

I burst out laughing, which is more from the butterflies within that have just started frantically partying than anything else. Ruby's right. I should stop being such a coward and tell Alex exactly how I feel. Because, actually, I've been using Australia as an excuse to say nothing – out of the usual terror of being rejected.

But something deep inside is telling me that Alex wouldn't reject me and I should just go for it, like Ruby says. Alex has seen my imperfect skin and run his hands all over my body.

He wasn't revolted, like Billy.

He didn't start talking about plastic surgeons, like Jackson did . . .

'I can't go now. He'll still be in bed.'

'Still making excuses?'

I grin at her, my heart beating wildly. 'Fine. No more excuses.'

'Yes!' Ruby springs off the bed and crossing to the wardrobe. 'Right, outfit for seduction,' she murmurs. Her eyes light on my favourite, fairly low-cut top. Pulling it out with a pair of skinny jeans, she plonks the clothes on my bed. 'I'll get you a cuppa while you get ready.'

'Er no, it's fine, thanks.' I've experienced Ruby's tea.

You could stand a spoon in it. And to be honest, my stomach is in such an uproar, I doubt I could get anything at all past my lips.

Ruby gives me a thumbs-up and wanders out.

I collapse back onto the propped-up pillows, thinking. Alex's flight is at three this afternoon, so he'll have to be at the airport for around noon, I guess – assuming that the flight isn't cancelled because of the weather. So I've got plenty of time if I want to catch him before he goes.

Less than an hour later, I'm in the hall getting into my coat, scarf and boots, ready to walk along to the hotel through the snow. Ruby, still in her pyjamas, is there with her arms folded, making sure I actually go.

When I open the door, a blast of freezing air rushes in, cooling my flushed cheeks. The intense cold brings me to my senses. *What am I doing?*

'Good luck,' says Ruby, practically pushing me out into the snow. 'I'll have everything crossed for you.'

I love walking through untrampled snow, making those very first footprints. We've had a new covering overnight, so my trudge along to the hotel turns out to be quite satisfying and takes my mind off what's coming up.

In fact, I have no clear idea at all of what I'm going to do when I get to the hotel. I tell myself I'll let instinct decide.

The trouble is, the closer I get to the hotel, the more

I'm starting to suspect that my instinct must have buggered off on its annual Christmas break. Because I still have no idea what I'm going to say to Alex.

If he's still there.

In the car park, a couple of staff are working to clear the snow, and thankfully, Alex's car is still there. With five days of snow piled up around it, he won't be going anywhere very soon. I approach the hotel entrance, my heart thumping wildly, thinking that I could always just go in and order a coffee in the bar area, and wait to see if he appears.

But then I get cold feet all over again and find myself walking round to the ice rink instead. Perhaps I'll just hide out here for a bit, out of sight of the main entrance, then head back to the cabin.

Because what the hell am I doing here anyway? If it wasn't for Ruby psyching me up with her crazy ideas . . .

I lean on the cushioned barrier, recalling the times over the last two weeks that I've stood in this exact spot, watching the skaters, chatting with Poppy. And remembering Alex trying to teach me to skate. Mostly, I remember the fun. The falling down, the being helped up and all the laughter.

Ruby's right, I think sadly. We had great banter . . .

Tears prick my eyes. If we'd left it at that, I'd have had some lovely memories. But I'd have been spared the deep ache inside that's been plaguing me for the past few days at the thought I might never see Alex again after today . . .

Because it's impossible not to keep thinking about the great chemistry we have – a connection that I may never have with anyone else ever again.

Swallowing hard, I make my decision. I'm going to speak to him. Tell him how I feel. Stop chickening out like I always have in the past . . .

Feeling determined now, I walk round to the hotel entrance and over to reception. And I ask to be put through to Alex's room.

The receptionist checks, frowning. Then she looks up. 'I'm so sorry. But Mr Webster checked out half an hour ago. He couldn't get the car out, so he decided to walk across the fields with his backpack to his friend's place – the one who owns the restaurant?' She smiles. 'I guess he's fit enough to do it but I still don't envy him hiking across all that deep snow!'

Panic flutters in my chest. 'You mean the restaurant at the Enchanted Forest?'

She nods. 'That's the one. Apparently it's right on a main road, so his friend's going to give him a lift to the airport.'

'Right, thank you very much.' I attempt a smile but I'm dying inside.

That's that, then. I'm too late.

Alex has already gone . . .

Chapter 35

When I arrive back at the Log Fire Cabin, I realise that – thanks to the daze I was in when I left – I forgot to take my key.

But when I ring the bell, Ruby comes straight to the door, which makes me think she's been hanging around waiting for me, wanting to know exactly what happened with Alex.

My face tells her everything. But she still asks a dozen questions.

Was Alex still there? Am I just going to give up? Or am I planning to go after him?

I answer her with as much patience as I can muster, but all I really want to do is run upstairs to my room, pack my belongings and escape back to the flat and Flo. She gets back from New York today and it will be so good to talk to her about the ups and downs of the past few weeks.

If I tell Flo that Alex was just a silly crush, I might

be able to convince myself it's true. Then I can forget about him and move on . . .

'You're not really just going to give up, are you, Roxy?' Ruby's face is contorted with amazement.

I sigh and say, 'Ruby, you might have the energy to trudge through about five fields that are knee-deep in snow, but I'm afraid I don't. I know when I'm beaten.'

I trail wearily up the stairs and, finding Poppy reclining on her bed, go in to chat. I tell her all about my abortive trip to the hotel and I can tell she's really disappointed for me.

'Never mind. Don't give up.' She smiles encouragingly. 'You never know, Alex might come back again *next* Christmas.'

But we both know she's just trying to cheer me up.

'Where's Ruby?' she asks.

'No idea. She was here a moment ago.'

Poppy nods. 'She was supposed to be making hot chocolate. Never mind, shall we have a chat about the business?' she suggests, I guess to take my mind off things.

So we go down to the kitchen and Poppy starts making hot chocolate while I arrange some leftover mince pies on a plate. I'm not sure I'll ever be able to thoroughly enjoy one again after the hundreds I've made these past few weeks – but it gives me something to do.

'I normally cook and bake from home,' Poppy says, 'but I'm wondering if we should find ourselves some small premises somewhere. Make it into a real business, if you like.'

I laugh. 'Great idea. But it's a real business already, isn't it?'

'Yes, I suppose it is.' She grins. 'But it still felt a bit like a hobby when I was doing it myself, even though I was earning good money. I just think that with you coming on board, it will be proper and official, and we'll be able to—'

The end of her sentence is drowned out by a loud noise outside.

'What on earth . . .?' She crosses to the window and looks out over the lake. 'There's nothing there,' she shouts as the noise continues. 'It must be at the front.'

We go through to the hall and open the front door.

And then we find out what Ruby has been up to.

'The snowmobile?' I gasp in amazement.

We watch open-mouthed as she manoeuvres very niftily between the cars and comes to an abrupt stand-still by the door. She switches off the engine and blessed silence reigns once more.

'Well? Are you going to hop on board, Roxy? There's room for two!'

I turn to Poppy and laugh incredulously. Then I frown at Ruby. 'You're honestly thinking of transporting me over to the Enchanted Forest on the back of *that thing*? Do you think I've got a death wish or something?'

'Not a death wish – but definitely a *wish*,' says Poppy. I turn and she grins. 'To see Alex again before he leaves?'

'You think I should *go*?' I squawk in astonishment. 'On *that*?'

Poppy shrugs. 'Depends how much you want to see him,' she says with a sly smile.

'Oh, come on!' says daredevil Ruby, a glint in her eye. 'It's fantastic fun. You'll love it. And I know a super-fast way to get across country to the restaurant. I've already done the route with Sam.'

A bubble of excitement is expanding inside me. 'I'll just get my coat!'

'And your scarf and gloves and boots because, when we're flying along, it's *freezing*!'

'God, I hope he's worth it,' grins Poppy, helping me into my armour against the arctic wind.

I smile happily. 'He is. Do you think we'll get there in time?'

Oh, please let me get there in time!

'With Ruby at the wheel, do you really need to ask that?' laughs Poppy.

With a grimace of apprehension, mixed with excitement, I climb on the back and before I can say, *Don't go too fast*, Ruby guns the engine and we're off with such a jolt, I'd be tumbling off the back if I hadn't already realised it might be wise to hang onto Ruby as tightly as I can.

The exhilaration as we roar across fields and along country lanes, previously untouched by man or beast, is so incredible, I'm squealing and giggling all the way. Luckily, I doubt I can be heard above the whirring of the snowmobile's motor.

Still holding on tightly and peering round Ruby at the way ahead, I can see the restaurant coming into view as the icy wind whips at my hair and cheeks. Ruby was right. This way really is fast – almost as the crow flies! We're going to be there in no time and, desperate as I am to catch Alex, I almost wish this journey could go on for longer!

But, almost before I know it, we're there.

Ruby steers the machine into the huge Enchanted Forest car park and comes to a standstill near the entrance to the restaurant, parking the snowmobile on what would be the grass verge if we could actually see it under the carpet of snow.

'Go find him!' she orders with a big grin.

I stagger off, my legs as wobbly as jelly, and make a half-hearted attempt to smooth down my hair. After the wildest ride of my life, I must truly resemble a scarecrow the morning after a heavy drinking session.

Then I think: if Alex is *really fond of me*, will he care what my hair looks like?

'I'll wait for you in case he's not here,' says Ruby.

'Great!' I wave and start trudging through the snow towards the restaurant. It's hard-going because it's so deep, and I can't believe Alex has walked the entire distance from the hotel. I was watching out for him all the way, but either he was taking a different route or he arrived ahead of us.

The restaurant is deserted but Alex's old friend, Graeme – who I recognise from the night we came here for dinner – pops his head round the swing doors to the kitchen when he hears me come in.

'Hi, Graeme. Is Alex here?' I ask.

He gives me a friendly smile but shakes his head and my heart sinks into my flat-heeled boots. Surely I haven't missed him?

'I'm giving him a lift to the airport,' Graeme explains, 'but I've got a job in the kitchen to do first, so he said he'd have a wander outside.' He grins. 'Sorry I can't be more precise. But he won't have gone far. Try the forest.'

'The forest?' *Oh God, do I need the snowmobile again?*

'The Enchanted Forest next door,' he clarifies, pointing.

'Ah! Okay. Thanks, Graeme.'

Breathing deeply to steady my frantic heartbeat, I head out of the restaurant, bumping into Ruby coming in.

'Is he here?' she asks.

'Graeme thinks he's in the Enchanted Forest.'

She nods. 'Well, off you go!' She shoos me away like a mother hen.

Grinning, I walk across the car park, turning back to see where Ruby is. The restaurant door has been left open and I can see her in conversation with Graeme. Probably hoping to charm him into letting her have a hot chocolate on the house!

I take the snow-logged path that leads to the fabulously festive Enchanted Forest winter wonderland. The scent from the pine trees is so uplifting, and as I walk over the little bridge, I'm already guessing where I'll find Alex. The little clearing in the forest, strung with twinkling lights. It's like a magical hideaway inhabited by cosy woodland creatures from a child's book of fairytales.

I quicken my pace, almost slipping on the slope at the other side of the bridge. I can see the beautiful clearing and the breathlessness I'm feeling isn't simply because I'm hurrying. Pausing outside, I take a deep breath and walk in.

Alex isn't there.

My insides lurch with disappointment.

I stare up at the thousands of starry lights in the trees above me and breathe in the aromatic scent of the forest.

'Roxy?'

I spin round.

Alex is standing there at the entrance, staring at me as if he can't believe his eyes.

'Hi, Alex.' My heart is thumping so fast, it feels as if my ears are vibrating. 'I . . . um . . . was hoping to catch you before you flew back to Australia. I didn't get a chance to say goodbye.'

He glances behind him. 'Is Jackson here?'

I sigh in frustration. 'Will you please *shut up about Jackson*? I honestly don't care if I never see him again. I apologise for talking that way about a friend of yours but it's the truth.'

Alex laughs. 'You're not with Jackson. Message received, loud and clear.'

I shrug. 'We weren't right for each other . . . in the end. It took a while for me to realise it, though.'

He nods slowly as if he's processing this, his eyes never leaving mine. 'So the other night? You said it was a big mistake. I have to say, that killed me.'

I shake my head, emboldened by his confession. '*We* weren't the mistake. The biggest mistake was me *telling you* we were a mistake when I actually didn't mean it at all.' I frown, confusing myself, never mind him. 'If you get my meaning?'

He smiles in that lazy, heart-stopping way of his. 'Amazingly, I do, Roxy.'

'That's good, then.' I smile shyly at him, shuffling

slightly forward so the gap between us grows smaller.

'It is.'

'So when's your flight?'

'What flight?'

'What do you mean, what flight?'

'It's an open ticket. I might decide to stay for New Year.'

I swallow hard. 'So . . . what might make you change your plans?'

His beautiful green eyes lock onto mine, sending a visible shiver through my whole body. He's so close now that if I reached out, I could touch him.

'Are you cold?' he asks at last.

I laugh uncertainly. 'Er, are fir trees green?'

He grins. 'I'm guessing you might need a hug. Just to warm you up, of course.'

'You guessed right. So . . . what you're saying is, you're willing to change your travel plans in order to keep me warm today?'

He shrugs. 'Beyond the call of duty, I realise, but it's in a good cause. Would you agree?'

'The best cause ever.'

'I was hoping you'd say that.' He steps forward and slips his arms around me, pulling me towards him. Then he envelops me in the biggest, closest bear hug ever, and we stay like that for a while, revelling in the closeness. Little fireworks are going off in my head and

I've never in my life felt this level of blissful happiness.

'You're the most amazing, gorgeous, cute girl I've ever met,' he murmurs into my hair. 'And you're funny as well. Killer combination.'

My heart soars at his words. 'I'm very glad you think so. I feel the same about you.'

'Yeah?' He pulls away to look into my eyes and my whole body melts. 'I think I fell for you that very first time I saw you at the ice rink.'

I laugh softly. 'I think it was *me* doing the falling. On my butt.'

'See? Funny.' He pulls me closer with a big sigh, snuggling me inside his coat so I can hear the thud of his heartbeat and feel the lovely warmth of his body.

Then his mouth finds mine and our embrace becomes more frantic and intense. We sink down onto the wooden bench at one point, misjudging it slightly because we're so wrapped up in each other.

I cling onto him, laughing, as he only just manages to stop me falling off. Then we sit there, close together, his arm firmly around me, my head resting on his shoulder, just breathing in the wonderful Christmassy scent and staring up at the fairy light stars.

And then something amazing happens.

The pattern of stars suddenly changes and delivers a message.

Roxy and Alex. Together forever.

'Oh my God!' I gasp in amazement, unable to believe my eyes. 'Did you do that?'

He laughs softly. 'I'd love to say I did. But no, it wasn't me.'

'Hang on.' I smile, remembering Ruby chatting to Graeme in the restaurant. 'I have a feeling I know who's responsible. She may be only seventeen, but she's very wise for her age. She's forever surprising me.'

'Ruby?'

I nod.

'So did she get it right?'

His warm breath brushes my ear and I give a little shiver of pleasure. 'Together forever?' I turn to him with a shy smile. 'I think she got it spot on.'

And then we kiss and the message fades back to stars, and I know that, wherever Alex decides he's going to live, from now on, I'm going to be right there beside him . . .

**Loved *Second Chances at the Log Fire Cabin*?
Then why not head back to very beginning with
Poppy and Jed . . .**

Cosy up this winter with the perfect Christmas read
from the ebook bestseller.

Can love flourish amongst the treetops?

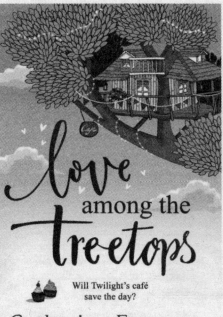

A funny, feel-good read from ebook bestseller,
Catherine Ferguson.